Desire
& Devour

ALSO BY JEFF MANN

POETRY

Bones Washed with Wine
On the Tongue
Loving Mountains, Loving Men
Ash: Poems from Norse Mythology

ESSAYS

Edge: Travels of an Appalachian Leather Bear
Binding the God: Ursine Essays from the Mountain South

SHORT FICTION

A History of Barbed Wire

NOVELS

Fog: A Novel of Desire and Reprisal
Purgatory: A Novel of the Civil War

DESIRE

& DEVOUR

STORIES OF BLOOD AND SWEAT

JEFF MANN

Published in 2012 by Bear Bones Books,
an imprint of Lethe Press, Inc.
118 Heritage Avenue • Maple Shade, NJ 08052-3018
www.lethepressbooks.com • lethepress@aol.com
www.BearBonesBooks.com • bearsoup@gmail.com
ISBN: 978-1-59021-393-3 / 1-59021-393-9
e-ISBN: 978-1-59021-430-5 / 1-59021-430-7

Set in Hoefler Text, LTC Metropolitan, Still Time, and Willow.
Interior & cover design: Alex Jeffers.
Cover image: "Licked," Ronaldo Donizeti.

LIBRARY OF CONGRESS CATALOGING-IN-PUBLICATION DATA
available on request

For John Ross, who's tolerated my penchant for vampires and horror films for fifteen years.

For Steve Berman, Ron Suresha, Tiffany Trent, Kathleen Bradean, and 'Nathan Burgoine. Thanks for your friendship and support!

In memory of Dan Curtis, the creator of Dark Shadows, and Jonathan Frid, who played the vampire Barnabas Collins in the original version of DS.

Acknowledgments

Thanks to the editors of the following collections in which five of these stories were previously published.

"Hemlock Lake" appeared in *Blood Lust: Erotic Vampire Tales*, edited by M. Christian and Todd Gregory.

"Saving Tobias" appeared in *Icarus: The Magazine of Gay Speculative Fiction* 2 and was reprinted in *Best Gay Erotica 2011*, edited by Richard Labonté, and in *Tales from the Den: Wild & Weird Stories for Bears*, edited by R. Jackson.

"Whitby" appeared in *Men at Noon, Monsters at Midnight*, edited by Christopher Pierce.

"Wolf Moon/Hunger Moon" appeared in *Erotica Exotica: Tales of Sex, Magic, and the Supernatural*, edited by Richard Labonté.

"Black Sambuca" appeared in *Blood Sacraments*, edited by Todd Gregory.

Many thanks to the folks at Saints and Sinners Literary Festival, in particular Paul J. Willis, Greg Herren, and Amie Evans. Bless y'all for fine times in the French Quarter!

Thanks to Andrew Beierle, who lent me the opportunity to create Derek Maclaine back in 2002.

Thanks to Alex Jeffers, whose considerable talents have made this a beautifully produced book.

Contents

Derek & Angus

Red in its setting, the summer sun is devoured by storm. Another chilly squall sweeps over the Isle of Mull, the drizzle swiftly becoming a downpour. In a high pasture above the loch, two bushy-bearded young men clad only in short boots and great kilts race through gray curtains of rain toward the barn. Lightning splits the sky over the mountain; the dark-haired lad yelps and runs faster. His companion overtakes him, giving his wet back a brotherly slap. Before the building's threshold the two lads pause. For laughing seconds, they're grappling and panting, full of challenge, feet slippery and uncertain in the mud. Then together they tumble into the barn's musty shadows and onto a pile of hay.

For a few minutes they lie there side by side, catching their breaths and listening to the violent cascades of rain on the roof, the thunder rolling over the island. Both boys are teenagers; both are good-looking and strongly built, both a little over six feet in height, tall for their time. The more powerfully built of the two, Angus, is a thickly muscled lad with blue-green eyes, a wide, tanned face, a strong jaw, long red-gold hair bound back in a ponytail, and a full beard of the same hue. The boy of more moderate musculature, Derek, has keen brown eyes, shaggy black hair and beard, high cheekbones, a pale, oval face and full lips.

Angus stands, reaches down, takes his companion's hand, and tugs him to his feet. "So much for our attempt at a midsummer bonfire, eh?" he says. "Smells like spiders and cow-shite down here. Let's up to the loft."

Grinning, Derek nods. "Lead the way, Angus, m'man. Might as well get cozy. I'm thinking this tempest will be taking its time. We may well have to spend the night here."

He wipes his muddy boots in straw, shakes wet from his hair, then follows his handsome friend, ascending a rickety ladder into the loft, a hay-heaped space above empty stalls. There, they unbuckle their sporrans and dirks before stretching out. Angus shrugs the fold of great kilt off his shoulder, pillows it behind his head, then lies, bare-chested now, on his back, eyes closed. "Tired. Up before the sun to work on that new wall. Mind if I tak me a wee nap?"

Derek rolls onto his side. Before he can open his mouth to reply, Angus is snoring. Derek lies there, smiling, yearning, eyes ranging over his friend's broad bare chest. With a forefinger, he strokes, ever so lightly, the mat of honey-hued hair plastering the bigger man's belly and filling the shallow ravine between his work-hardened pectorals. Then Derek sighs, rolls onto his back, makes a pillow of his own great kilt's fabric, and falls asleep.

A clap of thunder wakes Derek with a jolt. The sun's set, but the rain continues, even harder now, a steady roaring that fills the barn, pounding on the roof mere inches above their heads. The long gloaming of the Highland summer lingers, making of the loft a dim gray cave. Angus is cross-legged, only a foot away, fumbling through his sporran. Folds of tartan sag around his lean waist. Derek stares at his friend's naked torso, rubs his eyes, yawns, and licks his lips.

"Awake, eh?" says Angus. "Spending the night, ye were right. It's tearing down. Here, though, let's have some supper." Angus pulls out a flask. "Whisky? Chilly it's getting, and I could do with some warming."

Angus takes a pull on the flask before handing it to Derek, who receives it with a wide grin and follows suit. "Here's some crowdie cheese with oatcakes," Angus mutters, pulling food from the pouch, "and here's some berries, a mite mushed...and here's some bannock."

"Maister McCormick, ye're prepared!" Derek smacks his lips.

"Always, Maister Maclaine. Can't let the laird's son starve, now can we?" Angus doles out the food. The two lads fall silent, eating slowly. Done, they take turns pissing out the loft's window. Outside, a fog's gathering over the loch far below. In the twilit pasture beyond the muddy barnyard, cattle, delighting in the cool, crop the summer-high grasses.

"Wet and cold," Angus grouses. "Wish we were back in yer family's keep before a fine fire." He tugs his long hair free from the leather cord binding it, then pulls off his kilt and kicks off his dirty boots. He stands naked, shivering, arms wrapped around himself, looking out over the mountainside. Behind him, Derek gazes at the youth's broad back, the curves of his pale buttocks, and shakes his head. Beneath his tartans, his cock hardens. He strokes it twice, then, with slow deliberation, arranges his kilt to conceal his erection.

"Well." Angus turns, grinning, his limp sex swinging in a slow, subsiding arc that Derek studies from the corner of an eye. "Nothing to do now but drink, get warm, and tell tales. Give us a story, laird's son. Something with pixies and kelpies and other such surly fey." Angus makes a nest of the yards of tartan, a layer beneath him, folds atop him. Derek hesitates, then does the same, stripping off his own kilt, making a makeshift bed of moist wool beside his comrade. Across the inches of chilly air and straw, the two naked youths pass the flask, smiling at one another in the dim light.

"Ye keep calling me 'laird's son,' Angus, like it's some kind of nobility I am. Why do ye do that?"

Angus balls up his fist and gives Derek the slightest cuff on the chin. "Ah, envy, I guess. Of that fine castle of yers. Yer faither's the chief of the clan, ye know. Mine's merely a crofter."

"A crofter who grows finer crops than anyone else on the Ross of Mull. And Moy Castle is little more than a square tower, friend. Draftier than yer croft-house and not half as cozy. Exposed to the winds off the loch. Ye know that." Derek takes a swig of liquor, passes the flask, and gives Angus a light punch on the shoulder.

"Ah, sure. Easy for ye to say, boy." Angus smirks.

"Boy?" Derek rolls his eyes. "I'm only a year younger than ye, and ye know it."

"And a guid bit smaller. Boy." Angus grins, tossing a long strand of hair from his blue-green eyes.

"Big enough to beat yer bum."

Cocking a defiant eyebrow, Angus corks the flask. "Ah, that song again." Angus pats Derek's bare shoulder, then punches it softly. "I've heard that boast before. And saying it doesn't make it true, laird's son."

Derek returns the gesture, his blow a little harder. Angus pats Derek's bearded cheek, then gives it a gentle slap. Derek tugs Angus's beard, softly, then harder.

"Tweak not my whiskers, ye landed bruit!" Angus tosses off the tartans and springs, wrapping his arms around Derek's torso, pinning his arms to his sides.

Cursing and giggling, the two naked youths roll and flop and thrash. Derek wriggles loose, wrenches Angus's arms behind him, is tossed off and thrown onto his back. Angus leaps atop him, grabbing Derek's wrists and forcing them above him. Derek fights back, trying to flip his moist opponent off, trying to hook a leg around his calf. They roll and roll, sweat-wet hands scrabbling at sweat-wet limbs, slipping and bucking, cursing and gasping, and come to a stop only a couple of feet from the loft's edge. Angus is on top now, one hand gripping Derek's right wrist, one hand gripping Derek's throat. Derek, in turn, has one arm wrapped around Angus's shoulders, another hand digging into Angus's considerable biceps.

"Yield, boy!" Angus growls, grinning. He tightens his grip around Derek's throat. Derek rolls his eyes, shakes his head, and thrashes. Between the two men, their hairy bellies and groins slam together; their erections joust, rub, and throb, just as they do every time the youths wrestle.

Angus blushes. "Sorry," he mutters. Releasing his hands' grip on Derek, he slides off him. "Can't control that wee beastie."

"Nothing wee there. And I have no control over my own monster, as ye know." Derek, face as flushed as his friend's, rolls onto his belly, hiding his own erection.

Angus, in contrast, stretches out on his back. To Derek's amazement, Angus strokes his still-hard cock for a long moment before releasing it and folding his arms behind his head. Both boys watch Angus's member bob and gradually decline.

"What does it mean, do ye think?" Angus clears his throat. "What does it mean? Our cocks are like cur-dogs who rise and sniff each other every time they meet. As if they're greeting a friend."

Derek's throat is dry; his heart speeds up. He rolls over, back to his friend, looking out over the barn to the door below, where rain drips from the lintel and, beyond, veils the misty pasture. "I don't know, my friend. The Christians would say...."

Angus snorts. "I know what the Christians would say. Just as I know what they would say about our families' faith. The faith we keep secret. Our faith in the Old Ways. To hell with the Christians. Why should we not do what we please? Why should we care what they think?"

Rolling over, Derek rests on his side, facing Angus. "Because they surround us. Because they're too many and we're too few. Because they'd hate us and hunt us if they knew. Ye know why we should care, Angus."

"Ah, fuck 'em and all their talk of sin." Angus flexes his right arm and spits. "I'd slaughter them if they interfered with us. If they tried to hurt ye, laird's son."

"Spoken like a true clansman." Derek chuckles. "I feel the same. Ye're like a brither to me, the only brither I've ever had. No one's harming ye while I'm around. Even if my arm isn't half as thick as yers." Derek reaches over to give his friend's biceps a shy squeeze. "And are ye still courting Mary? Ye know it pleases yer family."

"We see each other every so often." Angus sighs. "And are ye going to wed that little lassie in Craignure? Nessa? Give yer parents an heir to the Maclaine estate? Host a grand party for the island to celebrate the bairn's birth?" His voice is husky and sad. He takes a long draught from the flask and curses. "Empty."

"I'm not wedding any one. Here." Derek removes his own flask from his sporran. "I came prepared too. Here's some of that malt they brew in Tobermory."

Both boys drink. "Ah, guid!" Angus says. "Chilly as I am, tonight's hinnie-sweet. Just ye and me and the hay and mist and rain and a few fine drams. Here." He spreads out his kilt. "Climb on here and put yers on top. 'Twill be warmer, I think."

Derek pauses briefly, then nods, obeying. Many have been the nights they've chastely shared a bed; why should this evening be any different? They settle in again, saying nothing till the second flask is drained.

"My mither verra much wants me to marry Nessa. But I can't seem to feel for the lass what everyone thinks I should. So, nay, no new heir to Moy Castle will be birthed any time soon. But speaking of births...." Derek reaches over, pulling something from his sporran. "Here."

"What's this?" Angus takes the gleaming piece of metal.

"A pin for yer kilt, man. Today's the day, isn't it? Ye turn eighteen today."

"Aye." Angus fondles the brooch. "Thank ye, friend. Verra kind. Fine it is. A bonny bauble. Nothing I could afford. I can't requite ye, ye know. When yer birthday comes in August."

"God, Angus. Last year for my birthday ye gave me a bottle of yer faither's best home-brewed heather ale, and a bucket of the sweetest bramble berries...and the week after that ye helped me fend off that thieving band of cattle raiders. I might have been carved up like a roast ox without yer brawn beside me. Hush now. Every gift ye've given me has been grand."

Angus slips the brooch into his sporran and gives Derek's hand a quick squeeze. "That was quite a fight. That one bastard with the dirk...agh, that hurt. Took me weeks to heal up."

"Aye. I recollect. A bad cut across yer flank."

"Here. Beneath my ribs. Feel." Angus takes Derek's hand and places it against his side. Derek, trembling all over, fingers the ridged scar.

"And here, across the right thigh." Angus presses his friend's hand against a second scar. "I got that one the same day."

"So hairy." Derek shakes his head, delighting in this god-sent excuse to touch his friend. Tugging at the fine tendrils of fur on Angus's thigh, he's silently marveling at the hard muscle beneath the skin. "Ye're like one of those bear-men berserkers they tell of in the Orkneys."

Angus chuckles. "And ye're much the same," he says, rubbing a fingertip along Derek's fuzzy forearm. "Ye're shaking, friend. Cold?"

"Aye. I-I well remember that fight and the wounds ye received. I blamed myself. For a while, ye had the fever. Yer mither swore ye were dying. I was addled with terror."

"Afraid ye'd have to find someone else to beat yer arse in wrestling matches, eh?"

"Aye." Derek chuckles. "I can't really imagine a life without ye, ye arrogant prick. When did we first meet? I was six, I think."

"And I was seven. Many years indeed. Plowing and hunting and harvesting side by side. And fighting. We make quite the team, laird's son. That troll of a raider who cut me, ye surely made him pay with that claymore of yers. Though, speaking of wounds, ye got this." Angus turns to Derek and pulls the tartan blanketing him down to his waist. He runs a forefinger through Derek's dark chest-pelt till he finds the hard runnel of a scar bisecting his breast.

Derek closes his eyes, trying to slow the pounding of his heart.

"And this, I think." The finger moves to Derek's hip, circling a pocked scar there.

"Nay." Derek takes a shaky breath. "That was when we got in that street fight in Oban. Yer fault. Ye started the brawl."

"True, and I'm sorry. I was rairin drunk. He was a frigging Mac-Donald. He called my cousin a fat-arsed quim and my faither a lying bastard. Derek?" Angus's hand brushes Derek's beard, then rests on his breast.

"Aye?" Beneath Angus's touch, Derek's body tenses. His sex is stiffening again. He lies very still, afraid to open his eyes.

"I know what it means," Angus murmurs, his breath a hot waft across Derek's ear.

"What?"

"Our cocks. Why they rise. Does yer cock ever grow hard around Nessa?"

Derek's eyes fly open. The two lads stare at one another. "Angus, what a question! I—"

"Tell me." Angus grips Derek's arm.

Derek gives his head a slow shake and emits a grim laugh. "Nay. It doesn't get hard. Stays as limp as a gutted salmon."

"Other girls?"

"Nay."

"Mine the same. And have ye been with a woman?"

"Ye know the answer to that. Nay. Never."

"I neither. We're the same, brither. We're the same. And we're wasting time." Angus reaches over, giving Derek's cheek a shy stroke. "Get over here, laird's son. I'm cold. Lend me some of that hot-bluided warmth of yers." He arches an eyebrow and grins, that broad, cocky grin that has always made Derek's heart throb and his palms sweat.

"What are ye intending, man?"

"I'm intending to warm us both. I-I'm intending to do what I please for the first time in my life, Christians or no. I'm thinking it's high time that our time together was not wasted but used to the full. Surely ye've considered it too? For I-I...." Suddenly hesitant, Angus drops his eyes.

"Say it, Angus. I always feel safe with ye by my side. Ye should feel the same. Ye're safe with me. Just say it. I know what ye're meaning already."

"I want ye, Derek," Angus whispers, raising his gaze to his friend's face. "Like a man does a woman. But I don't want any woman. I want ye."

For a long moment, Derek doesn't reply; the barn's silent save for the steady drumming of rain. Then Derek reaches over and takes Angus's hand.

"I feel the same, Angus. Gods preserve us, I do. But...."

"But what? It's a longing that needs to become a deed! If ye feel the same, then why are we talking instead of—of luving?"

A jerky trembling courses through Derek's limbs. "I'm afeart."

"What are ye afraid of? Shame? Sin? Faugh! Our bodies luve each other. That's what our pricks are trying to tell us. I know ye're clever, but ye're not as clever as yer cock. See?" Angus grips his friend's erection. "See? Hard as pink granite." Angus commences a slow stroking. "I think it's wiser than us both. I think we should follow its advice."

Derek shudders and groans. He seizes Angus's hand, meaning to remove his eager grip, but, awash with pleasure, thinks better of it.

"I'm afraid of what might happen if anyone found out. It's sodomy, what ye're suggesting. It's a crime. It's a death sentence if we're caught. I could be disinherited. Our families' names could be ruined. And why are ye saying all these things tonight of all nights? We've been wrestling nakit and sleeping in the same bed and getting stiff around each other for years now."

"Because." Angus rubs his thumb over his comrade's cockhead and kisses him on the brow. "Because ye were right, as much as I've made a joke of it: the fever from that dirk-wound almost carried me off. Because my kinsman Aidan died last week in that shipwreck off the coast of Skye only weeks before he was to be married. Because ye're leaving next month with yer faither for that trip to Inverness and then Edinburgh, and who knows when ye'll return? Because the world is hard and fearsome, and because ye're a splendor in my eyes. Because I could leave the light of the world without warning, gathered in to join my forefaithers beneath the sod, and...." Angus pauses to wipe wet from his eyes. "I want to know ye, Derek. I've got to lay with ye before I come to my end. Whatever the risks. I tell ye, we've wasted time enough."

With that, Angus leans forward, giving Derek a soft kiss upon the mouth. "Touch me, brither Maclaine. Please. Don't be afeart. I'll make sure no harm comes to us."

Derek runs his trembling hand through Angus's long hair, then through the thick red-gold fur coating Angus's belly, then through his wild beard and over the strength-dense muscles of his shoulders. Angus wraps his arms around Derek and pulls him closer. Derek grasps Angus's thick cock. Their lips meet again, wetly, roughly. This time their tongues slide together, each exploring the other's mouth. Both lads' bodies are trembling violently, their hearts pounding, cocks pulsing in the tight grip of fists.

Derek pulls back, brown eyes wide. "By the gods, ye're magnificent. The feel of ye's a wonder. I've wanted so long to touch ye this way. I've been a coward. Ye're right, Angus. We've been fools. We've wasted too much time."

"But now we're together. And I shan't see us parted. Derek?" Angus gasps, half-breathless. "I've dreamed of things. I've pleasured myself in my hand for years now, dreaming of this, of how we might lie together."

"As have I."

"Indeed? Indeed?"

"Oh, aye, Angus! I've spent buckets of seed. Fancying yer body, yer bonny nakitness. I see the Horned One in ye, my man."

"And I see in ye the same! May I then...." Angus rolls Derek onto his back and lies atop him. "May I luve ye in some of the ways I've dreamed? Please?" Angus bites Derek's bewhiskered chin, then licks his salty neck. "Given permission, laird's son, I'll strive to bring ye bliss."

Derek cups Angus's face in his hands. "L-luve me as ye please. We'll enter this new world together."

Again the two youths kiss. "Lie back then, ye glory," Angus whispers. Sliding lower, he buries his face in Derek's black chest hair. "Ah, God. Ah, God!" He heaves a huge sigh. "It's home I am," he groans, lapping a furry armpit. "Yer scent's better than mead." Gripping the hard mound of Derek's right pectoral, he licks the nipple, the fur-swathed nub already stiff with Derek's arousal. "Yer breast is broad and strang. A warrior's breast. How I've luved to see ye stripped to the waist, working with me in the fields or fishing in Lochbuie. How I've luved to smell yer sweat."

With that, Angus begins, spitting in his hand, working their cocks with wet fists, sucking Derek's nipples, tenderly, then intensely, till the younger lad is bucking and moaning beneath him.

"Ummm, tasty!" Angus's voice is a bass growl. "As tasty as I'd dreamed. Tasty teats, my man...."

"Guid God," Derek pants, as Angus's stroking fists speed up. "Oh! Slow!"

Angus's answer is to take Derek's cock into his warm mouth. He nibbles the taut head, flicks his tongue along the shaft, and then sucks hard while stroking his own member.

"Oh! Angus! Oh!" Derek shouts, thighs tensing. He clasps his lover's bobbing head in his hands. "I'm nearly there!" Angus grins and head-bobs even faster, his hips thrusting against his own hand. As young as the lads are, as long pent-up as has been their mutual passion, they've spent within the minute, in torrents of semen and rapt exclamations of delight.

Exhausted, excited, grateful, they lie, drowsy and sweat-wet, in each other's arms.

"By the Laird and Lady, yer taste on my tongue's a dewy, milky miracle." Angus chuckles, licking his lips with a gleaming grin of triumph. "For years I've dreamt of suckling yer teats and drinking yer seed, and now I have."

Derek reaches down, gripping Angus's half-hard, slowly diminishing sex. Wiping up the semen he finds there, he licks it off his fingers. "And ye the same, Maister McCormick. A rich, sweet savor. A manly quaffing."

They fall silent, listening to thunder echoing off the mountain and rain shushing around the barn. Derek rolls onto his side, nestling back against Angus's chest. "I thank the gods for ye," Derek whispers. "Ye've always been the braver one. I might never have had the courage to...."

Angus, in response, wraps an arm around Derek, tugs the tartans over them, and pulls him closer still. "Hush. Let's get some sleep, Laird Maclaine. I'll have other ideas for us come morning."

Angus strokes his hair and kisses his shoulders. Derek drifts off in his comrade's arms, musing on the lush gifts of this world, feeling safer and happier than he's ever felt.

Both boys sleep soundly. Derek rises once during the night, to piss off the side of the loft, then gratefully returns to Angus's embrace. The rain shifts from deluge to steady drizzle. Derek wakes in the slowly mounting dawn to pleasure, strange but keen. Angus is spooning him from behind, his burly right arm wrapped around Derek's chest, fondling Derek's nipples. With the other hand, he's fingering Derek's arsehole.

Derek yawns, stretches, and groans. No one has ever played with his bum before, but the feeling has him hard already. He jacks his own sex and pushes his rear back against Angus's probing, cocking a leg so as to allow him deeper access.

"Morning, Laird Maclaine," Angus says. "That's feeling guid, is it?"

He removes his finger, spits on it, then works it inside Derek—one inch, then a second, then a third.

Derek grunts and sighs. "Ye're wanting to bugger me, luver?"

Angus prods gently. "Yer luver I am now? Aye, my laird, I want to bugger ye. If we're to be practitioners of sodomy, let's come to know all its pleasures. Am I pleasuring ye?"

"Luvers we are. That's safe to say, now that we've tasted the other's seed. Uh. Uh, aye! 'Tis a pleasure indeed." Derek bucks back; Angus's finger sinks even deeper.

"Ye're wanting to use me like a woman then? Wanting to frig my hole?"

"Nay, my laird. I want to use ye like a man. Nothing womanly about ye. Including this sweet, hot hole of yers."

"Uhhhh. A finger feels fine. But yer prick? Grand as it is? Not sure how that'd feel."

"Please let's try?" Angus pleads, moving his finger gently in and out. "God, man, many's the night I've dreamed and ached and longed to be inside ye in such a way! Yer arse is as savory a sight as this globe has to give! So white yer cheeks, and that night-black grove of fur in the crack! So, so slow I'll go. And if ye tell me to, I'll stop. I swear! Please, Derek? Please?"

"Oh, that's guid! Um!" Derek grunts, wriggling his arse against Angus's devotions. "Ahh. Who knew how grand that could feel? Aye, keep that up. Ye're doing a glorious job of convincing me. Are ye begging me, Maister McCormick? Sounds to me as if ye're begging."

"I am! I am! Please, my laird, let me inside ye! I beg ye."

Derek chuckles. "And can I do the same to ye, if I tak a mind to?"

"Ye can ride me into world's end, for all I care. Just give me yer arse!"

"Angus?"

"Aye?"

Derek pulls away. Angus's finger slips out. He whimpers with disappointment as Derek turns away from him, then sighs with relief as Derek positions himself on his elbows and knees.

"Do it. I've wanted it too. Ye inside me that way. Give it to me, brither. Be my first, and then I'll be yers."

Angus is as good as his word. He slathers Derek's virgin entrance with spit, opening him up with one finger, then two, then three. Derek kneels, marveling in the new sensations, the way Angus's fingers flick some sensitive bud inside him, causing it to well and pulse with rapture.

"May I now?" Angus says, after long minutes of such foreplay. His spit-smeared member, impatient as its owner, nudges Derek's hole.

Derek nods. "Give it to me now."

Angus pushes. Derek groans, gritting his teeth. Angus pulls out, finger-frigs Derek's arsehole more, kneading his buttocks, kissing his back, caressing his nipples, soothing him, until Derek, nodding, mutters, "Again," and they recommence. This time the cockhead slides in. Derek flinches and whimpers, his face contorting.

"Does it hurt, laird?" Angus says. "Oh God, 'tis sweeter than anything I've ever known! But if it hurts, oh God, I don't want to hurt ye! I'll pull out!"

"It hurts, aye, aye! But.... Nay, stay in...keep still...wait," Derek gasps. "God, what a fleshy dirk ye bear! So...thick. Just...wait. It burns, it burns, but...just keep still and give me a moment.... Let me...learn to tak ye."

"Oh, Derek. Oh, thank ye! Thank ye for giving yerself to me like this! God, man, I luve ye! Surely ye know that?" Voice shaking, Angus grips Derek's hips; he bends, showering his hair and shoulders with kisses, waiting for Derek's body to adjust to his own.

"I...uh!" Derek bows his head and bucks back against the impaling prick, lodging Angus's cock farther inside him. "I...uh! Oh, fuck! Oh, Angus, aye, I luve ye too. Guid God, of course I do! I'm...ready, I think. Give me all of ye now! But slow, slow, slow."

Angus thrusts his hips; Derek yelps, tugging on his own cock, rubbing precum over the head. To his surprise, beyond the burning threshold of flame waits a radiant pleasure at his root, a pleasure at being taken so entirely, possessed so completely, in a place he never thought of as empty till it was filled with Angus's flesh.

"All in!" Angus groans.

"Hold! Give me time!" Derek pleads. "The pain's nearly done. Just wait. Ah. Aye. Aye." Slowly Derek slides a few inches forward, then back again, his tight ring clasping Angus's rod.

"Oh, damn. Oh, aye!" Angus sobs.

"Fuck me, man. But slow still. S-slow."

"Is it hurting now?"

"It's...like a well," Derek gasps as Angus begins a gentle thrusting. "Like a circle.... The edges were all aflame, but now the fire's dwindling to an itch, the thinnest rim of discomfort, and now pleasure, oh aye! it's filling the center like spring water...."

"Harder, may I? Harder?" Angus moans. "It shan't tak me long, feeling this wondrous...."

"Hard as ye like now, my bonnie friend," Derek growls, bowing his head, lifting his arse, and fisting his prick. "I'm open to ye now. Ride me hard! Right me right over the horizon!"

Angus begins a violent pounding, clasping Derek's lean hips. Once again, it takes little time for their young bodies to finish the mutual delight they've begun. In a couple of minutes, they're done, Angus's semen pumped up Derek's arse, Derek's semen spattered on the tartan and filming his hand. They collapse, panting side by side on the mussed kilts, Derek's head resting on his lover's shoulder.

"Sore?" asks Angus, stroking Derek's belly, making swirls in the sweaty hair there.

"A bit. Worth it. Every time I sit down today, I'll be thinking of ye. What a strappin grandeur ye are."

"And will ye be wanting such luving again? I pray ye will, for 'twas sheer heaven, to tak ye like that. To spill my seed within ye. Had I my way, we'd do it every day. Will ye surrender yer arse to me again?"

"Surrender? Aye, I guess it was surrender. But a triumph too. Aye. Odd for a warrior to find such delight in submission. And ye were right. Nothing womanish about it, despite what the Christians say. I never would have thought it could be so sweet. As ye're soon to find out." Derek squeezes Angus's rump. "The rain's still steady, and it's verra early yet. I'm thinking after a nap, it'll be yer turn to be taken. On yer belly it'll be, big man."

"That's the pact, my laird. Ye can plow me till I weep."

Wrapped in their tartans and each other's arms, they drowse again. The rain ceases at last. Outside, the fog begins to disperse, and slants of June sun, unfettered by cloud, glitter in the wet grass. The lads wake, embrace, and recommence their ardent beard mingling, deep kissing, and prick fondling.

"And how's yer bum now, my laird?" Angus says, massaging Derek's rump. "Still sore?"

"Only a little. Welcome memento of time heaven-spent."

"I'm thinking I need to frig ye again." Angus rubs Derek's hole with a forefinger. "That was bliss beyond imagining."

Derek sniggers. "Here now, hungrysome. Yer turn to be taken. Ye promised, did ye not?"

"Aye, m'laird. Aye."

"Guid, guid. This time I frig ye," Derek murmurs. Coaxing Angus onto his belly, he burrows a spit-moistened finger between his friend's hairy buttocks, more than eager to give as he got. "Please, Angus? I need to be inside ye now."

"Now ye're the one who's begging, eh? Commence, my laird. A deal's a deal." Angus grunts and nods, spreading his thighs wider, humping the tartan blanket. Derek's just found his friend's moist hole and has begun to rub it when a familiar voice halloos in the distance.

The boys freeze, then roll apart. The voice sounds again, calling Derek's name.

"Oh, damn," Derek hisses. "My faither!"

The naked lads dress hurriedly. They're buckling on their sporrans, both sweating with anxiety, by the time Laird Lachlan Maclaine enters the barn.

"Derek? Are ye here?" The laird's shorter than his son, sporting a close, graying beard, though his hair still retains the black of his younger days. He's dressed more formally than the bare-chested farm boys above, with a cream-colored shirt beneath his great kilt, as well as high socks and elegant black shoes. In his right hand, he's clutching a polished blackthorn staff.

"Aye, sir. Here." Derek walks to the loft's edge, pinning a fold of tartan over his shoulder, trying to conceal the fright and guilt he feels. "We're both here. Angus McCormick and I. We meant to have us a wee bonfire amidst the standing stones to celebrate the sun but got caught in the storm."

"Aye? With McCormick again, are ye? Well, I'm glad ye're safe. Yer mither was troubled. Those loathly MacDonalds were carousing the countryside last night, and she thought ye might have fallen afoul of them."

"MacDonalds!" Angus, joining his friend at the loft's edge, rolls his eyes. "Those curs?" Gathering up his long hair, he binds it back in a ponytail, then buckles on his dirk. "Derek and I would have sent them howling, sir! They wouldn't dare to cross us."

Laird Maclaine chuckles. "Angus McCormick. Ye're fierce indeed. Ye're big men, 'tis true. Each lofty-tall and handy with a claymore, handier'n I ever was. But MacDonalds always travel in packs, m'lads. Ye'll always be outnumbered. If ye cross them, be sure to bring friends. Come on now. There's a big breakfast preparing at the castle—eggs and bacon, haggis and bridies—and it mustn't get cold."

With that, the laird leaves, striding down the slope toward the distant castle. The two lads descend the ladder, step out into the mucky barnyard and look out over the pasture grass, the purple thistles and spiky bushes of golden-flowered gorse. Far below, slow waves climb the beach, and summer sun glimmers on the surface of the sea loch.

"We have a secret now," Derek says, watching the figure of his father dwindle in the misty distance. "A deadly one, I think."

"Aye." Angus reaches over and seizes Derek's hand. Their fingers intertwine. "We must tak care. I'll tak guid care of ye, laird's son. I swear."

"And can ye stay at Moy Castle this even? There's some delicious ale, and the cook's making venison with blackberries. And we'll have my chamber to ourselves, up in the highest part of the keep. I intend to finish what I started this morning. Perhaps even filch some oil from the scullery to make it easier on ye." Derek squeezes Angus's hand, releases it, and pats his comrade's tartan-covered rear. "Please stay, my man."

"Ah, at home there's potatoes to tend, and much scything to do, but...John and Ewan can tak my chores for once."

"Perhaps I'll send some of that excellent ale back for them. Would that make yer brithers less likely to begrudge the extra work?"

"As thirsty as they are?" Angus snorts. "Aye. I'm thinking such a bribe, regularly given, might allow us more time together. At least every fortnight. More often once the cold comes and on the croft there's less to do."

"I wish I could move ye into my room in the castle. Or buy us a little croft of our own. Now that we've shared what we've shared, the fire I feel for ye will be gnawing my bones most bitterly when we find ourselves apart."

Angus heaves a sigh. "Even together, if we're in the sight of others, we'll be robbed of touch. How easy it must be, for lads who luve lasses."

"No choice now," Derek says. He gives Angus's cheek a quick peck. "Or, raither, we've made our choice. Our bodies made that choice together last night. Do ye want to go back, or go forward?"

"What do ye think, my raven-haired laird?" Angus says, resting an arm across Derek's shoulders. "No way back anyway. I luve ye; ye luve me. The gods will it. I'll cherish ye forever. Whatever awaits us, fair or foul, 'twill be worth it long as I can live my life, however long that might be, by yer side. Forward! I'm starving."

Down the hill the lovers race, coltish, far from sorrow, through wet pasture grass and rising wind off the sea, exhilarating in the summer warmth, the zenith of the light.

MIDWINTER 1725

Tonight, Moy Castle is crowded. They've assembled for a Yuletide feast, the septs of the clan Maclaine of Lochbuie. In the keep's barrel-vaulted great hall, long tables are lined with carousing clansmen—McCormicks, MacFaddens, MacAvoys, Blacks, and Pattons—and heaped with holiday food, with roasted oxen and swine, with crusty bread, cabbages and kale, barley and haggis, black pudding, jellies and custards, Highland cheeses, roast potatoes and mashed turnips.

At the table's head, Laird Lachlan Maclaine and his wife Claire preside, he in formal kilt-wear and she in a maroon gown. At fifty-seven, Lachlan is grayer now, though his hair is still thick, his face showing few lines. Claire is a decade younger, her black hair streaked with silver pulled back in a bun, skin tight over her cheekbones and high forehead.

To Claire's left, their eldest child Morna sits, garbed in a gown of silvery green. Married to Charles King, a wealthy Glasgow merchant, for four years now, she's escaped both her townhouse and her husband's uninspired chatter for the holidays. She's shapely, full-breasted, possessed of a regal demeanor her brother lacks. While his eyes are brown and frequently unsure, hers are an icy blue, proud, determined, confident. She otherwise resembles Derek, with her pale, smooth complexion, long black tresses, sculpted cheekbones, and full red lips.

At the laird's right hand, Derek is seated, and beside him, Derek's boon companion, Angus McCormick, both in white jabot shirts and great kilts in the red, black, and blue-green tartan of the clan. In the eight years that have passed since their first lovemaking in the barn, both men have matured, and their shared devotion has ripened and deepened as well. Their hair is longer, their shoulders wider, their arms stronger, their beards bushier. Neither can imagine a life without the other. Despite many close calls, they have managed to keep their romantic connection a secret.

Harried servants pour flagons of ale and mead, which are swiftly emptied and refilled. Tapestries flutter on the walls, restless in the wintry drafts. A fire leaps and crackles in the great hearth. Outside, sleet lashes the battlements; sharp winds rip at the bleak fields and the surface of the sea loch. High above the waters, a light snow whitens the Isle of Mull's mountaintops.

"Isn't she lovely, Lachlan? Nessa MacAvoy?" Derek's mother nudges her husband and points to the auburn-headed girl halfway down the table, seated near Angus's burly blond younger brothers, John and Ewan McCormick.

"Aye, she is," Derek's father replies. "But that Campbell girl Derek met last summer in Inveraray would make a more suitable wife. Her dowry would be considerable."

"I'm not wanting to marry," Derek interjects, after gulping a mouthful of ale.

"We must have an heir, Derek. Ye know that. The Campbells, Lachlan?" Claire shakes her head. "Is such a match wise? Everyone blames them for the massacre of the MacDonalds at Glencoe."

"Ah, Mither, for God's sake, leave Derek be," Morna sighs, rolling her icy eyes. "Marriage isn't the blessed nest that it's said to be."

"Ah, that massacre was decades ago!" Lachlan exclaims, ignoring his daughter. "Besides, we hate the MacDonalds and they hate us. The Campbells are powerful and wealthy, Claire. A bond 'twixt their clan and ours might help us build a new, modern home and move us out of this drafty medieval tower. And drive those MacDonald rovers off Mull."

"Have ye forgotten that once the Campbells seized this very castle from yer ancestors?" Claire replies. "Bonnie little Nessa there would be—"

"Nessa's a daft cow," Morna mutters. "Derek would perish of boredom if he married that cream-faced milkmaid."

"I'm not ready to marry!" Derek spears a slice of beef and plops it onto Angus's plate. "Robbie?" he exclaims as a server bustles by. "Would ye fill our glasses, please?" Beneath the table, he strokes Angus's thigh through his kilt. "My friend's here is already empty."

"Aye, sir," Robbie MacAvoy replies, pausing behind them. A distant cousin of Nessa's, he's a short, slender boy, twenty years of age, clad in kilt, jabot, and vest, with big green eyes, tousled chestnut hair, a faint beard and a shy smile. His are meek good looks that both Derek and Angus have admired. As he leans forward, pouring till the two men's mugs are full to the frothing brim, his shirt gaps open, revealing a pale, hair-dusted breast. Derek and Angus stare, look away, exchange glances, and grin.

"Guid boy, Robbie. Thanks," Derek says, nudging Angus's knee with his own. "And when pudding's served, would ye fetch us some mead? Maister McCormick here is mad for anything made of hinnie."

"Mad for yer man-hinnie, ye mean," Angus growls beneath his breath, as soon as Robbie's scuttled off. "Which I intend to tak tonight, mouthful by hot mouthful."

"Arse-full, I'm thinking. And are ye mad for Robbie's hinnie too?" Derek mutters, brow lowering in a show of mock jealousy.

Angus flashes a sheepish smile. "Ye fancy him as well. Ye've already confessed it."

"True. I'd like to grind the bonnie whelp between us. Most likely we'd break him."

"True." Angus sniggers. "Well, Merry Yule, my laird!"

The two men knock mugs. "And ye the same," says Derek. "I have a gift for ye waiting upstairs."

"Ye're always giving me little treasures. The only gift I want tonight's between yer thighs, m'laird."

"Ye'll be getting that too. Tonight I intend to tak ye captive and use ye most cruelly, just as ye've learned to like it. The gift I speak of is another thing entirely, something I found in Inveraray. All this talk of marrying me off to some—"

"Here, sir." It's Robbie again, at Derek's elbow. "Yer mead, and Tipsy Laird, and mincemeat tarts, and shortbread. And some marmalade cake, as ye asked. I know how ye and Maister McCormick favor yer sweets."

Smacking their lips, the two friends fall to. Dancing follows the pudding course. Derek leads the reel with his sister Morna. Then, at his mother's urging, he reluctantly escorts Nessa MacAvoy to the floor. Angus follows suit with his cousin Ann.

By midnight, the revelry is nearly done, drunken guests on horseback riding off into the flurry-speckled night, or clattering home in carriages, collars raised against brutal winds off the sea. Those who have traveled longer distances to join the festivities simply push the feasting tables back, curl up in kilts or blankets and sleep on the floor, after fighting for positions near the dying fire.

Derek and Angus, mildly drunk, arms around each other's cape-clad shoulders, share goodnight wishes with the elder Maclaines before weaving up the winding stairs. Derek pauses by the door to his snug lodgings near the top of the tower, but Angus urges him on. "I need some air, bitter as it is out. Let's on up to the battlements. I want to see the heavens."

Derek nods, leading Angus on up the corkscrew stairs. At the top, he throws open the trapdoor. Winter wind slams his face, causing him to gasp and swear. The men climb out, their cloaks flapping wildly around them. The rooftop is square, with chest-high crenellations along each side and turrets in each corner. For a moment, the two men stare at the spectacle: the snowy slopes of Ben Buie behind them, wind-whipped Loch Buie before them, the black arch above them spangled with stars and racks of cloud. Then, satisfied that there are no witnesses, the two men embrace at last, their breaths weaving pale banners the wind whips off.

"God, man, I missed ye," Angus sighs, wiping snowflakes from Derek's black hair. "I've missed ye so bitterly. Ye were too long in the capital."

"My faither was eager to introduce me around town. He powerfully wants me to be next chief of the clan, though I'd just as soon Uncle Hector do it. But now I'm back, and I shan't be leaving again till the spring. Are ye going to stay with us? Till after Hogmanay, I hope?"

"I'd like to. Will yer faither allow me to stay so long? I fear that he thinks ye're wasting time with me when ye could be making friends of noble bluid. I'm only a crofter's son, ye know."

"I don't care what Faither thinks. He's always been too concerned with fine society and its lacy trappings. I want ye to stay, Angus." Derek affectionately bumps his friend's chin with his own. "Ye're the noblest man I know."

"Then stay I shall," says Angus, nuzzling Derek's cheek. "After so many weeks apart, we've got some luving to do. So ye're going to make me yer captive tonight, eh?"

Chuckling, Derek clasps Angus's wrists and gently pushes them behind Angus's back. "Aye. Ye'll be quiet and ye'll do as I say, my bonnie hostage."

"Oh, aye." Angus emits a low laugh. Leaning against Derek, he bows his head with submission. "I will, m'laird. Gladly. I'll obey ye. Ye have me stick-stiff already."

The two men fall silent, rubbing cock-tented kilts together, both of them savoring Derek's dominance. "And did ye enjoy dancing with yer cousin Ann?" Derek finally says, releasing Angus's hands and taking a step backwards.

"Aye." Angus shrugs, folding his arms across his chest. "Ann's a charmer, cousin or no. And did ye enjoy dancing with Lady Nessa, yer future wife?"

"Hah! She's pretty, but she's less than clever. I shan't be taking a wife, I tell ye. If I could find a woman grand and deep as my sister, I might consider it. But none of 'em is half as brilliant as Morna or as lovely."

"I hate it when ye dance with Nessa. Ye know that, don't ye?"

Derek sighs. "Aye, my hinnie-man, I do. The gods know I'd raither be dancing with ye."

"Bet ye liked the looks of her cousin better. I know I do."

"Ah, little Robbie? The way he stares at ye, I believe he'd be glad to join us one night, if we could only broach the topic. We could ride him at both ends. Though, as I said, we'd probably snap him in half.

Nay, give me men big and buirdly," Derek says, kneading his lover's broad shoulders. "Angus?"

"Aye, sweet laird?

"Will ye do me a favor now?"

"Anything ye command."

"Get on yer knees and suck me till I tell ye to cease. Now."

"Lustie beast! Ye're always wanting to fuck and suck! Ye lairds are fore'er getting yer way, are ye not? Ruthlessly using us simple farm folk."

"Do it. Or ye'll receive a bruising punishment later."

"Punish me as ye please, ye haughty bruit. Ye know I love it hard."

"Do ye want to be frigged tonight then?"

"Aye, sir, I do. Badly."

"Then get on yer knees and do as I say, or I shan't frig ye later."

"Starved as my bum is for yer cock, ye'd deny me now?" Angus exclaims, shaking Derek by the shoulders. "Villain!"

Both men guffaw. "I luve this, man," Angus sighs. "I've missed this so badly." With that, Angus drops to his knees, slips his head beneath Derek's kilt, cups his lover's balls in his palm, and begins a sloppy cock-sucking.

"Ummm, yer prick smells and tastes heavenly," Angus mumbles in between mouthfuls.

Derek leans back against the battlements, gazes out over the loch and the stark Highland landscape, and sighs. "Ye make me feel like I own the world." Gently he strokes Angus's hair and thrusts down his throat. "Ye're the only world I want to own."

Angus's sucking grows tighter and faster; Derek's thrusts shift into a deep pounding; Angus moans and drools, nodding with hungry delight. Finally, wide-eyed and panting, Derek pulls his cock free.

"Ye got to slow down, man, or I'll spend in yer mouth."

"Sorry, luver. It's just been too long since I've tasted ye." Unsteadily, Angus rises to his feet. "Save it for my arse, m'laird. Isn't that what we both want?"

Derek pulls Angus into his arms. "Oh, aye." Slipping his hand beneath Angus's tartans, he runs his fingers over his furry bum, squeezing the buttocks and tracing the moist crack. When Angus cocks his arse in welcome, Derek digs deeper. Finding his lover's hole, he probes it. Angus shudders, nods, and leans into Derek. "I'm ready for ye, man. Let's to yer room now."

"Why can't I just tak ye here?" Derek nibbles his friend's ear, then gives his neck a nip. Turning Angus, he nudges him toward the wall, then, palm pressing against the back of his head, bends him over till his torso is resting within a notched crenelle. Derek falls to his knees on the wet stone, slips his head beneath Angus's kilt, and nuzzles his rear, licking the fur-dense crack, luxuriating in the musky aroma and flavor. Angus groans, face to the wind, staring down the tower's long drop to rock, then gazing over the black loch, snowflakes lodging in his beard and melting on his brow. Derek bites one cheek, then the other, then spreads Angus's buttocks with his palms and flicks his long tongue against his comrade's hole.

Angus writhes, pushing his arse back against Derek's soft beard and probing tongue. "Do it, man. Just tak me here. I need ye, luver. I need ye inside me. I want to tak yer seed inside me. Just put it up in me now. Oh, God, I—"

Only a sudden pause in the Highland wind allows them to hear the creaking behind them. Derek's on his feet and both men are frantically adjusting their garments and stiff cocks when the trapdoor's laboriously lifted and a man's head pokes through. It's Robbie MacAvoy, holding a lantern.

"M'laird! Are ye up here?"

"Goddamn it. Another interruption?" Derek snarls beneath his breath. "Aye, Robbie!" he shouts into the rising wind. "And what'd'ye want so late? Maister McCormick and I were just taking in the view." Derek musters a smile, suppressing a torrent of curses. He licks his lips, savoring Angus's taste on his tongue. Beneath his kilt, his frustrated balls painfully throb.

"Yer sister, Lady Morna. She's seeking ye."

"This late?"

"Aye, sir."

"Tell her I'll come to her chamber in a trice."

Robbie nods and disappears. Derek heaves a sigh. Angus pats his shoulder. "We have all night, Derek. Go on. I'll wait for ye in yer chamber."

"If I had a gold coin for every time we've nearly been caught, I could spend next summer sailing the Indies with ye."

"True. We've been damned lucky. I just can't seem to keep my mouth and hands off ye." Angus shakes his head and grins, heading for the trapdoor.

"I want ye nakit and greased and in my bed, slave, when I get back," Derek commands.

"Aye, m'laird," Angus murmurs, bowing his head in that exaggerated show of obedience that he knows his lover relishes.

In the hallway below, the men separate with a quick kiss only allowed by the lack of witnesses at such a late hour. Angus lumbers down the hall and into Derek's chamber; Derek descends the winding stone steps to the middle floor where his parents and his sister have their bedrooms.

"Come in, brither," is Morna's answer to Derek's knock.

She's combing out her lush black hair before a cracked mirror. The tapestry-swathed room is lit by a low hearth-fire and the light of several candelabra. On her dressing table a tiny glass of sherry glints.

"And where were ye? It took Robbie ages to find ye."

"Ah, up on the parapet. Getting some air," Derek says, sitting in a brocade-lined chair near his sister.

"Trying to sober up, ye mean. Ye and Maister McCormick certainly went through the ale tonight. Ye're boys of whappin appetites. Is he still here?"

"Spending the holidays with us. He'll be here past Hogmany."

"Why do ye waste so much time with that peasant, Derek?" Morna says with a wry smile. "That's what our parents wonder. Ye should be hobnobbing with other lairds, Faither would say, trying to benefit the estate, or courting well-heeled lasses in order to give us a precious, precious heir, or kissing the bums of those English-loving Lowlanders in the capital."

"Or fox-hunting with that ducal husband of yers?"

"I wouldn't wish *that* on ye. Charles is a bore, and we both know it."

"I spend time with Angus because he's strang, he's true of hert, and he'd do anything for me. He'd do anything for either of us. Ye know that."

"I do. I'm teasing ye, brither. I love the bruit too. I envy ye such a companion. All the women I know are featherheads. Have ye any whisky? Just a dram, please? This sherry is puny. Feckless tasting."

Derek nods. Pulling his flask from his sporran, he hands it to his sister, who takes a long sip before returning it.

"Dear Charles." Morna grimaces. "I rue the day our parents coaxed me into that marriage."

"Mither was disappointed that Charles didn't join us for the festivities tonight. Is he still in Glasgow?"

"I suppose. Probably in some brothel, or slavering over his account books. As long as he isn't here blathering and bragging about all he owns. So, I have something to tell ye. Can ye keep a secret?"

"Ye know I can. I have a secret or two of my own."

"I suspect ye do. And I suspect one of them is a secret ye share with that strappin farm lad of yers. A secret that's interfering with Mither's desperate yearning for a grandchild."

Derek gapes. He clears his throat and takes a swig from his flask. "And what d'ye mean by that?"

Morna chuckles dryly. "No need to speak what's better left unspoken. Just tak guid care, brither. Besides, it's I myself I want to discuss. Y'see, I'm pregnant."

"Aye? Congratulations, Morna! But why keep that a secret? Shouldn't that be reason for rejoicing? Mither will have her grandchild after all!"

"That isn't the secret. The secret is the bairn's faither. Charles hasn't touched me in over a year, the cold cod."

Derek gapes a second time. "Ye mean—"

"I'm having an affair, brither. Aye."

"With—?"

"Tyrone. He's an Irish lad who works for us. A beauty he is, with his black hair and black eyes and white skin. I luve him, I think. I'm not sure what will happen when Charles finds out I'm with child. The man's a fool, but he can count. I wanted ye to know, to be prepared, if he throws me out. Ye're one of so few I trust, Derek, and I'll need yer help badly if worse comes to worse."

"I trust ye too, Morna. Thank ye for telling me. And, well, about Angus and me...."

"Aye?"

"We do have a secret, and it's what ye've guessed. We've been...more than friends for years now. I've wanted to tell ye, but I've been afeart."

"Ha! So I was right? Ah, God. If only Mither and Faither knew what they'd bred! Sluts and sodomites!" She chuckles, rolling her eyes. "Well, I can see how ye beam when ye're with Angus. It's one more secret the world has no need to know. Go on with ye now. He's upstairs waiting for ye, is he not?"

"Aye."

"'Tis a bitter night, and I'm glad one of us has a bed-warmer then. On off! I'll see ye in the morning."

The siblings rise and exchange a hug, then Derek bounds off down the dark hall and up the stairs to his chamber. "Angus?" he whispers, after locking the stout door behind him.

"I'm here, m'laird." Angus shifts from his side to his back, pulls the heavy blankets down to his waist, and gazes warmly up at his lover.

Derek stands stock-still for a moment, absorbing what he sees, the brawny man he loves lying naked in his bed. Angus's hair is tousled, his smile white, broad with welcome. Firelight illuminates his tanned skin, the lush hair coating his chest, belly, and legs, making a glowing red-gold thicket about his half-hard sex.

"My God, my bonnie man!" Derek groans. In seconds, he's pulled off all his garments and is nestling naked against his lover.

"I'm ready for ye, laird's son," Angus murmurs, running his fingers through Derek's chest hair, tweaking a nipple. "I'm greased up down below, as ye ordered. I'm ready for ye to make me yer prisoner and give it to me as hard as—"

"In a minute, luver. Two things first. Morna knows about us."

"What?" Angus sits up in alarm. "And what will happen to us now? What—"

"She'll tell no one, I swear. She has a secret nearly as dangerous, and perhaps I'll tell ye of it one day, if she gives me permission. But I'm glad she knows. It's the only secret I've ever kept from her, and I hated to lie."

Angus lies back and sighs. "Ah, gods, when I think what could befall us if she were to tell. I wouldn't be able to protect ye, Derek. Not for long, big as I am."

"Nor I ye. But she shan't tell. Now, the other thing. As ye know, we marked Yule this past dawn with a fire amidst the standing stones. We marked the sun's return, the beginning of the light, when the mirkie days start to lengthen. It's a holy beginning. It was a beginning when we first met, my lad, and another beginning that stormy night in the barn. And this eve's another beginning." From a pouch on the bedside table, Derek fetches two small objects. When he holds them up, Angus gasps. Dim firelight glints off matching gold rings.

"Aye, luver. All my parents' talk of marrying me off to one or the other lasses of their choosing got me to thinking. When I was in Inveraray, I found these." Derek takes his lover's hand and slips on the larger ring, then slips the smaller one on his own finger. "I couldn't be more devoted to ye than I already am, but I thought it was time we had a token of what we feel. Aye? We probably should wear them on chains beneath our shirts when we're in company, but when it's just ye and I, we can wear them where they belong," he says, kissing Angus's hand.

Angus stares at the golden circle around his finger, then lifts his face to Derek's. "Oh, thank ye! Thank ye!" Tears edge his eyes and brim over.

"Ah, my big man," Derek says, kissing his lips. "Ye're weeping? No reason to weep."

"I just luve ye so much! I'd die if I were ever to lose ye!" Angus grabs Derek in a tight bear hug, wrapping his legs around Derek's own. "I never knew fear till I learned to luve ye! Fear of having to live without ye!"

"Easy, man, easy. Ye shan't lose me," Derek mutters, suddenly moisty-eyed himself. "I promise. Now, my mighty slave," he says, slapping Angus's rump, "it's time ye pleased yer maister."

"Aye, sire!" Angus wipes his wet eyes. "Do yer worst, ye horny bruit!"

"First a captive must be bound." Derek fetches rope from beneath a pillow and makes a slipknot.

"Ah, we'll see about that. Tie me if ye can!" Angus challenges. For a good minute, the two men grapple on the bed, panting, giggling, and cursing just as they did during their wrestling match in the barn loft so many years ago. Eventually, Angus gives over his titillating show of resistance and surrenders, allowing Derek to rope his wrists together before him, jerk them above his head, and secure them to the bed frame. By the time Derek is done with the knots, both men's members are stiff and hot with blood.

"Ah, by the gods, I have ye now!" Derek snarls, straddling his prisoner's great chest.

"Yes, m'laird, ye do. Now what are ye planning—?" Angus's words are cut curtly short by the long cock shoved in his mouth.

"Shut up and suck, slave," Derek growls, pushing his prick deeper. Clutching Angus's shaggy head, he pounds his lover's face till the bound man's eyes are watering and his beard and chest are moist with drool.

"Now for some arse-frigging," Derek says, pulling his cock out of the tight suction of Angus's mouth with a wet pop. "But first I need to silence ye."

Derek retrieves a rag from beneath the pillow. He swirls it into a tight band. Both men stare at the gag. Derek chuckles; Angus shudders and licks his lips.

"Please don't. No need to gag me. I'll keep quiet, laird, I swear. I'll obey ye," Angus implores, doing his best to look desperate. The big man knows how his pleading only enflames Derek more, nudging the young laird toward the ruthless, wild coupling both men cherish. After so many seasons of shared pleasure, lovemaking between the two Highlanders has become an art form.

"Ye'll keep quiet, all right. Ye need to be gagged, slave, and gagged tight." Another thrashing tussle as Angus shakes his head with protest and gnashes his teeth against the cloth Derek roughly shoves against his mouth. When Derek grips his lover's balls and tugs hard, the bigger man submits, the rag slipping between his white teeth. Derek pulls the gag tight, then tighter still, till Angus is whimpering, his brow furrowed, his cheeks cloth-creased, his lips taut.

Derek knots the rag behind Angus's head and rises. The forcibly silenced Scot heaves a ragged moan, sinks his teeth into the cloth and tugs hard on his bonds. "Ye'll be quiet now?" Derek lifts his unsheathed dirk from the nearby table. It's over a foot long, with a black wood handle and a gleaming iron blade etched with thistles. He runs the honed edge along Angus's stubble-rough neck, then with the tip carefully prods his nipples and his heaving breast. "Ye'll be guid?"

Blue-green eyes wide, Angus stares at the sharp blade, emits a short sob, and gives an emphatic nod.

"Ye won't fight me?"

"Nah," Angus moans. "Nah. Nah."

"Guid lad." Derek strokes his lover's bulging pectorals with the blade, running it along the matted crest of his belly before dropping the dirk onto the floor and taking Angus's erection between his lips. Angus grunts and bucks, thrusting up into the tight cavity Derek makes of his mouth. Derek teases him with teeth and tongue for long, exquisite moments before rising. From the table now he takes a vial of oil.

"Ye wanting me to tak ye now, my bonnie prisoner? Want me to ravish that hairy arse of yers?"

Angus nods frantically. He rolls onto his belly and spreads his thighs wide. "Now, man," he moans against the muffling cloth, lifting his pale, fuzzy rump. "Please, m'laird. Tak me! Fuck me hard!" He knows well how much it arouses Derek to hear his muted pleas, to hear him fight for speech against a rag knotted so tight. "I'm yer slave and ye're my maister. Use me now! Use my arse!"

Derek's answer is a bass beast's growl. It's been months since the men's last lovemaking; both are half-mad with ardor. Derek slaps his lover's buttocks till they're red, silently praying that his chamber's isolation will insulate the sharp sounds from the floors below. Hauling Angus onto his elbows and knees, he continues what he'd started on the parapet, making love to Angus's arse, biting his flushed cheeks, licking his crack and his furry hole till Angus is rocking and sobbing and humping the air. Derek greases them both up, opens Angus further with his fingers, then, with growling impatience, shoves his cock up the bigger man's bum and begins a hard pounding. Angus writhes and nods, mumbles and begs, slamming himself backward with equal eagerness onto the thick member transfixing him.

The juices are mounting in them now, approaching the point of no return. "Ye want me to spend, slave?" Derek grunts between gritted teeth, his fingers digging into Angus's lean hips.

"Mm huhh. Nah!" Angus shakes his head, then drops onto his belly, dislodging Derek's cock.

"Ye're right, my luve. Let's make this last," Derek says, slapping his lover's arse. They roll onto their sides, facing each other, their brows wet, their cheeks flushed. Angus grins around his gag. "Thank ye, m'laird," he mumbles, heaving a long sigh of contentment. "Ye mak me so happy."

"I feel the same." Derek kisses his brow, his nose, his bearded chin, his rag-stifled mouth. "Ah, my God, ye're beauty itself. I luve you best this way, like a bound barbarian, with that rag tied in yer bonnie mouth. Like a wild warrior I've bested and come to possess."

They kiss again and again. They doze for a time, listening to winter winds soughing in the chimney and howling about the tower, feeling cozy and warm and blessed. When Angus wakes, he's on his back, and Derek is licking his thick throat, the hair in the pit of his neck. Derek slides lower, sucking hard—an eagerness composed of both reverence and cruelty—on Angus's big nipples, then on Angus's quivering cock. Now Derek lifts his lover's thick thighs in the air, probes his hole with his tongue once more, then rests Angus's calves on his shoulders and slowly, steadily, mounts him again. A few long, luxuriant thrusts, then Derek folds the big man double, his black hair falling around his prisoner's face. Derek pounds him harder and faster, biting his neck, his shoulders, his chest, then bending down to lap his cock. Angus wiggles and yelps, crooks one leg around Derek's waist, tightens his arse-ring around Derek's shaft, and urges him deeper. Angus finishes first, thick spurts down his loving captor's throat, a load so big Derek chokes. Derek's next, heaving seed deep inside his bound beloved.

"Never. Never. I shan't ever leave ye. I need ye like bread and sunlight, man," Angus whispers as soon as Derek has unknotted the rag from his mouth. They drowse again, then wake long enough for Derek to untie Angus's wrists. Derek wraps an arm around Angus and falls into deep sleep almost immediately, his face buried in Angus's chest hair. Angus watches the fire die before joining Derek in slumber. All night it snows, blanketing the parapet of the keep, dusting the evergreens on Ben Buie and the ancient circle of stones in the far meadow beyond the castle.

MAY 1730

"No one would dare. Not even MacDonalds."

Derek takes a long draught of mead before passing the bottle to Angus. They're sprawled naked on Derek's bed, high in Moy Castle. A single taper flickers. A soft May breeze wafts through the narrow window. Flowering blackthorn branches decorate the room, and a tapestry on which is woven the clan motto, *Vincere Vel Mori*, "Conquer or Die."

"It must be grand, being a laird's son," Angus says, after a long pull on the bottle. "Always so confident. Always got the answers. Always right."

"I thought ye liked my confidence, man." Derek rolls over onto his belly, flexes his bum, and flashes Angus a cocky smile.

"Ummm." Angus flattens his free hand, lightly brushing Derek's arse with his palm, then tugging softly at the black fuzz in the crack. "I do, and ye know that. But I still think 'twould be wise to tak some of yer men with us to market in Craignure tomorrow, just to be cautious. 'Tis only been a month since I slew that dirty swine Alexander MacDonald in Oban...."

"Are ye feeling remorse? Surely not! He called our mithers piebald cunts! And he drew first!"

"And his brither, Brodie, swore revenge against all our clan. Meaning that my hot head has brought danger not only to my family but to yer mither, yer faither, yer sister, and ye, my black-beardit luve."

"Ye had no choice, Angus. Ye acted with honor and mettle. That scabby cur Alexander MacDonald and his brither have hated all of us, McCormicks and Maclaines, for years. And need I say it again? He drew first. And he did so because *I* called him a whore's son and a howlin eejit. *I* told him he had a face like a dog licking piss off a nettle."

Angus's chuckle is grim. "Yes, well said, but I was the one did the slaying." He drains the bottle, then rolls onto his back, staring mournfully at the ceiling.

"And ye defended my honor and the honor of our clan. Tomorrow we'll tak some men then. I won't have my great-herted luver worrying so. Perhaps we shan't even go, since so many men our age have sickened so in the village lately." Derek snuggles against the bigger man's side. "It's nigh midnight. Are ye weary after the cattle herding today? And the Maypole revelry?"

"A wee bit."

"The Maypole dance I have in mind we haven't enjoyed yet," Derek says with a lascivious wink. "Let's hie ourselves to the standing stones and light us a fire and call the airts. No one will bother us there, as ye well know. The stupit Christians in the village think it haunted."

"Ah, I don't know. I'm out of sorts tonight."

"Cheer up, man! It's Beltane!" Derek nuzzles Angus's full beard and runs his fingers through his pubic hair. "And that means mating. The gods themselves are said to couple on May Day."

"Ye're wanting a greenwood marriage this eve, eh?" Grinning, Angus crosses his thick arms behind his head and closes his eyes. "Always wanting to bed me, aren't ye? How many years...."

"Thirteen next month."

"Aye. After thirteen years, haven't ye had enough of me, m'laird? A clumsy old bear of a crofter's son? Dear God, my whiskers are starting to silver." Ruefully, he rubs his chin.

"Frost on birch-leaf gold. And that only makes ye bonnier in my eyes." Derek kisses the dust of gray in Angus's beard. He fists his comrade's cock and begins a slow stroking. "Enough of ye? Here's yer answer, ye daft fool. Not bluidy likely. I want this strappin thing down my gullet and up my bum tonight. And we're already wed, as far as I'm concerned." He lifts his hand, displaying his ring.

"Aye. 'Tis true indeed. All right." Rising abruptly, Angus reaches for his kilt. "Let's to the stones then." He gives Derek a crooked grin. "Sounds like that hinnie-hole of yers is hungry and in need of some luving on this holy night."

"Truer words were ne'er spoken!"

Drunk and happy, the two brawny Scots dress, buckling on their kilts and dirks. Angus slips a vial of oil into his sporran, Derek wedges a flask of mead into his, and then they descend the corkscrew stairs. On the second floor, Derek pauses by his sister Morna's room. The arched oak door is rimmed with light.

"Hold, Angus," Derek whispers, knocking, then opening the door after his sister's murmured welcome. Morna is reading a letter by the fire, her child Eamon asleep on the bed. She smiles, lifting a finger to her lips. Derek slips inside.

"Another letter from bluidy Charles. Full of threats." Grim-lipped, she shakes the letter in the air, then crumples it and tosses it onto the fire. "He drove off Tyrone, and now the toad's swearing he'll avenge the dishonor I brought to his house."

Derek rolls his eyes. "What does a merchant know of honor? Now I rue as badly as ye the day Faither arranged that marriage. Piss on Charles. He's a Jack-a-dandy and a coward. He wouldn't dare cross us. If I had the power, I'd end him for ye."

"The man's not worth dirtying yer blade, brither. Ye two are off to the stones then?"

"Aye. Might sleep there, balmy as it is. We'll see ye on the morrow."

Morna nods. "Having a rite, eh? I know what kind of prayers ye'll be praying, ye hungrysome heathens. Don't stay up too late, brither. I'm wanting ye to tak my bairn fishing tomorrow morning. Ye promised ye would."

"And I will. Angus and I both. We'll land ye a mess of fish!"

Derek kisses Morna's hand and departs, closing the door quietly behind him. The two Scots descend the remaining stairs to the ground floor. From the embers of the great hall's hearth, Angus lights a brand, and then they're out into the starry May night, taking deep breaths of cool air, both of them eager for the celebration of flesh, spirit, and spring to come.

The standing stones are only a moderate walk away, a ring of granite slabs set in a marshy meadow near the base of Ben Buie. Soon enough the lovers have lit a low fire in the circle's center. After peeling off their shirts and shoes, they lie by the flames, sipping Derek's flask, relishing the lush grass, the warm breeze off the loch and the scent of flowers, so welcome after the long Hebridean winter. Somewhere in the forest beyond, an owl hoots.

Derek stands and pulls Angus to his feet. "The airts? Together?" Angus nods. Holding hands, dirks lifted, they move to the eastern stone, then to the southernmost one, then to the western stone, finally the northernmost, calling the quarters and the elements as their ancient ancestors did. Smiling, hands still clasped, kilts hiked up, they perform the customary Beltane practice of leaping together over the flames.

The men unbuckle their sporrans and dirks, leaving them in a pile in the grass. After a long bout of nuzzling, kissing, and fondling, Derek drops to his knees before his red-gold lover. "My sweet god of light," he murmurs. Lifting Angus's kilt, he cups his balls in his palm, gently kneads them, then takes the big cock into his mouth. Angus seizes his shaggy head and spears his lips, hammering Derek's face till he's gasping and choking and Angus is panting with building bliss.

"On yer back, m'laird," Angus growls, pushing Derek from him long enough to fetch the vial of oil. "My turn on top, is it not? Time for the light to top the night?"

Derek nods. He rolls onto his back, pulls his tartans up around his waist, lifts a hairy leg with one hand, and with the other fists his prick. The two men stare at each other in silent adoration as Angus spreads oil over his member, then, kneeling in the grass, fingers oil between Derek's buttocks. Derek rests his calves over his lover's shoulders, groaning and nodding as Angus's fingers make love to his hole. Soon enough, Angus's prick has slipped inside, Derek's bent double, his knees brushing his ears, and the two men are kissing passionately, rocking together as Angus's stiff flesh thrusts in and out of his lover's bum.

"My sweet god of dark," Angus groans as Derek grips his sex from within. "My hairy Horned One. Ahh, ye're so tight. Oh, by heaven's Laird and Lady, I luve ye, Derek Maclaine. Uhhhh! Aye. Squeeze me again like that, and ye'll be getting my seed sooner than either of us wants. Such sweet is meant to last, my man. *Uh!*"

"Then let it last. Tak yer time. We have all this blessed night. I luve ye, Angus McCormick. 'Till the seas run dry and the rocks melt in the sun,' says the song. Till—"

The sound is unique and unmistakable: an iron blade being pulled from its scabbard. Derek gasps, then gasps again, first at that sinister sound, then at the sight of men moving into the firelight behind Angus.

Angus pulls out of his lover, falling backward onto his heels, then scrambling to his feet. "Goddamn ye, what'd ye want?" he snarls, fists clenched, clearly more angry than afraid.

"Thou shalt not suffer a witch to live!" one of the strangers spits, pulling his sword. A thickly built man with a bald head and a closely cropped red beard, his handsome face is twisted, eyes gleaming with hate. Derek knows his features all too well.

"Brodie MacDonald? Get off my faither's land, ye jackal! Ye have no business here!" Derek heaves himself onto his knees, eyes raking the ground for his weapon. His dirk is there, and Angus's too, in the grass, unsheathed, only a few feet away.

The snick of more blades being pulled. Already the lovers are surrounded. Derek counts them as they swiftly approach. Six. All with swords or dirks bared.

"Sodomites! Thou shalt not lie with mankind as with womankind!" MacDonald shouts, swinging his sword at Angus. Angus dodges the blade and punches his adversary in the nose. Derek's climbing to his feet when he slips in the mud. Immediately afterward, a boot slams into his jaw. He staggers forward, dazed. Another foot kicks him in the belly, knocking the breath out of him, doubling him up and dropping him to his knees.

Angus roars. Two men have seized his arms, but at the sight of his comrade's peril, he throws them off. "Derek!" he shouts. Derek watches, stunned and gasping for breath, as Angus slams his thick fist into one foe's head, elbows Brodie MacDonald in the eye, then wrests away his sword. Cursing, Angus brandishes the claymore. He's fighting his way toward Derek, fending off blows, when a dagger's shoved between Derek's ribs and, only seconds later, another sinks into the space between his shoulder blades.

Derek bellows with agony and rage; blood courses down his body. He sways; swearing, he collapses onto his side by the fire-pit. His last sight before losing consciousness is that of Angus, staring at him wild-eyed, red-gold locks falling down around his shoulders, shouting

Derek's name and swinging the claymore frantically at the crowd of enemies surrounding them.

T he smell of embers and ash. Grass moist against his cheek.

Derek wakes, burning with thirst. When he tries to rise, the pain of deep wounds flares through his frame. He slumps against the earth, then, taking a deep and determined breath, with great effort clambers onto his hands and knees.

He's alone in the fading firelight. His attackers are gone. "Angus?" he moans, remembering. Light-headed, weak, he scans the circle of stones.

There. At the base of the western standing stone. A pale heap, a slumped human form. Angus. Naked.

Derek crawls over to him, whimpering. "Luver?" he says, brushing hair from Angus's face, studying the damage with mounting despair. Dagger wounds, one after another after another after another, black with blood, pierce Angus's chest and sides. The grass is stained with blood; puddles of blood gleam a dark scarlet. Angus's breast and belly are coated with more gore than Derek has ever seen. Angus's eyes are wide, brow crumpled and mouth frozen in a snarl of hatred. His face is smeared with mud and blood.

"Dead are ye? Oh, guid God, nay, nay, nay! Not dead. Not dead." Derek shakes Angus. He wipes blood off his battered cheek. He kisses his brow, then his split lips, then his gory wounds. He bends to catch a hint of breath but can make out no signs of life.

"Angus, my sweet man, don't leave. Don't leave," Derek pants. He places a shaking hand on Angus's breast, on the curly hair above his heart, only to find stony stillness. He bends to kiss the deep wound there, where his beloved's life ran out. He emits a racked howl of grief, then, faint-headed, bows his head and begins to sob.

"You have reason to weep, lad, most certainly. Your man is dead, and soon you shall follow him." A voice, deep and kindly, sounds in the darkness before Derek. Its melodic accent reminds him of Norse traders he's encountered in Edinburgh. "Yes, boy, you are dying."

Derek wipes his eyes and snarls. "Dying, am I? Show yerself! Who the hell are ye? Did ye do this? Did ye help those fucking curs murther Angus? I'll slay ye where ye stand if ye did!" He clenches his hands into fists, tries to rise, but, gasping for breath, fails, slumping back onto his haunches.

The silhouette of a man steps from behind the western stone. He resembles an even larger version of Derek's lost lover, with long gray-streaked blond hair, a silver beard braided like a Viking's, a great kilt, and a claymore buckled to his hip. His face is deeply lined around the mouth and across the forehead.

"I had no part of this. I would have saved you both had I come in time. But I can help."

Breath is coming harder and harder to Derek now, as his wounds, unstaunched, continue their slow leaking of his life. He shakes his head, coughs, and chokes up blood. "Oh, Gods. Go away, old one." He touches his side, feeling the red welling between his ribs and knowing how little time he has left. He pants, grits his teeth, and lies down beside Angus, stroking his murdered lover's mud-caked hair, trembling with weakness, rage, and despair.

"You would slaughter them, would you not?" says the gigantic Norseman, looming over him. "The men who did this? Given life, given the chance to be whole again? I can hear your thoughts as if they were mine. '*Vincere vel mori!*' you are howling inside your head. 'Goddamn them! To die like this, like a dog in the field, to be robbed of my love and my life, robbed of any chance for reprisal, for revenge? Gods! Intolerable!' Am I right?"

"Yes, damn ye," Derek groans.

"I can help you, Derek Maclaine. I can help you survive death. I can help you take your revenge. Will you come with me?"

Derek rolls over. Light is filling his vision, as if the dawn were breaking early; a ringing fills his ears, as if Lochbuie chapel bells were tolling; his heart is pounding so hard it shakes his frame. He licks his lips and chokes out a bitter laugh. "How do ye know my name? How can ye hear my thoughts?"

"Will you come with me?" the hoary warrior repeats.

Derek gives Angus's lips a kiss, gives his cold hand a squeeze. Then he nods. In answer, the warrior lifts Derek as if the muscular Highlander weighed nothing. Derek moans, coughs up another gout of blood, and passes out.

H e wakes to webby dimness, the drip of water, the smell of stone, and an unexpected sense of comfort. He's lying on his side on something soft, in a tight low-ceilinged space; he's being spooned from behind, cradled in another man's arms, a man who strokes his hair and mutters soothing words. For a split-second, he can believe that his companion is Angus, but then memory rolls in like a black surf: the murder amidst the standing stones, the Norse stranger carrying him off into the dark.

Derek rolls onto his back, wincing from his stab-wounds. He's so feeble now, so close to death, that the merest motion is exhausting. "Who are ye?" he sighs, gazing into the green glow of the Norseman's eyes. "Where are we?" Erratic stars flash across his dying vision.

"My nest on Ben Buie. Easy, son. I have you now. You shan't perish," murmurs the man, wrapping his arms around Derek's stiffening limbs. Leaning down, he laps Derek's neck. Then something sharp, tiny twin daggers, sinks into Derek's throat, there's a savage pulling in his innards, at his heart, and he's lost consciousness again.

A warm splashing wakes him this time, a rusty dripping. It tastes like iron, like the time Angus accidentally split Derek's lip in one of their uproarious wrestling matches. In the darkness, it falls onto his face, into his beard, onto his brow, onto his chin, then in a trickle onto his lips and into his mouth. It's sweet as spring water, but warm, warm. It seems strength-giving too, as if he were an invalid being served a healing broth, for the pain of his wounds is fading, his shallow gasps for breath deepening into a hale man's respiration.

Now flesh is pressed against his mouth, the hard curves of a man's naked chest, a wet welling wound there. *Smooth breast, not shaggy like my luve's,* Derek thinks. *Bluid,* Derek thinks. Still, instinctual as an infant, Derek sucks juice from the torn torso. When he finds a nipple in that sculpted expanse, he fingers it and bites down hard. The Norseman chuckles, pulling Derek off long enough to gash the hard pink nub with his thumbnail. The young Scot suckles the giant's nipple till it breaks open like a berry.

"Ah, good. You're a savage one already." That voice again, tinged with the lilt of northern seas. A heavy hand strokes his head. The stranger rocks Derek and sighs.

The Scot has taken seven greedy mouthfuls before his mysterious savior pushes him off, only to straddle his chest and shove his cock against Derek's lips. "Other juices now. I want you strong."

When Derek resists, the stranger seizes his wrists and holds him down. "Don't fight, boy. Open for me."

Head swimming, Derek acquiesces. The giant's penis slips into his mouth, bumping the back of his throat, and begins a rhythmic thrusting.

"You wanted vengeance, did you not?"

Derek nods, mumbling an affirmative as best he can as the giant stranger cock-pummels his face.

"Then suck. My sex-sap will make you strong. I swear it."

Derek obeys. He's nearly suffocated by the colossal length and width of the man's member by the time his captor stiffens, shouts, impales Derek's throat with a final, vicious jab, and shoots his gullet full of seed. "Swallow," he commands, gripping Derek's moist hair. Nodding, Derek gulps and coughs; the giant's seed is sweet like heather honey but burns like the rawest of kettle-brewed whisky. Suddenly the young Scot's sweating profusely, his limbs afire.

Delirium pulls Derek under; he nestles into the Norseman's arms, moaning and shaking. He loses consciousness yet again. When he comes to, a finger's burrowing up his arse, a hand's kneading his breast.

"Nearly done," growls the Norseman. "A bit more moon-chrism, and you'll be death-free. Oh, you'll be a fine warrior of the night, my boy. Twice as strong as the other young ones. Master of the beasts, master of the storm...."

Wrenching Derek's arm behind him, he forces the feverish Highlander onto his side, then onto his belly. Derek feels a trickling between his buttocks, then thighs forcing his own legs apart. "Nay! Please!" he moans, but in response a hand's clamped over his mouth, the Norseman's thick cock is pushed against his hole, then into it, then up inside him as far as it can go.

Derek, agonized, thrashes and kicks. "No use to fight, son," the giant chuckles, beginning a brutal pounding. Weak as his wounds have made him, Derek's pained screams and struggles are futile, and soon the Norseman is shaking and snarling with approaching climax. He pulls out, only to slam his rigid cock back inside. His limbs spasm, and he's done, spending gout after gout of seed inside the laird's son.

Derek lies there, pinned helplessly beneath the limp Norseman, feeling a flame in his gut and a throbbing ache in his arse, in his gums and tongue, his cock rearing-hard despite himself. His limbs go tense, and then they shake like ship's rigging in high seas. The giant rouses; tenderly he kisses Derek's hair, his bare back. Rolling the Scot onto his side, he embraces him from behind, great limbs holding him close.

"Dawn's nearly here. Take your ease in my arms, Lord Maclaine. You're beyond dying now, beyond the slow gray maimings of age. And tomorrow night I will show you what I mean. I have much to teach you."

For long minutes, Derek fights the swamping drowsiness, the washing tide of weakness, whimpering with fever and fear. For a second, he can see Angus's face, smiling up at him from the barn loft's floor, straw stuck in his hair, hair red-gold as sunrise. Then the giant behind him pulls him closer still, begins a soft snoring, and Derek knows no more.

Rocking. Ship on sea. Fir limbs in winter wind. Derek awakens to find himself held like a child in the cradle of the giant's bulging arms. Night's fallen. They're outside, naked in grass near the edge of a ledge high up the mountainside. The Norseman is sitting cross-legged; Derek's slumped in his lap. Licking his parched lips, Derek stares up at the man, amazed. Dark as it already is, he can see the stranger as clearly as if it were day. The Norseman's face is smooth with youth; his braided beard and long, tousled locks are blond, without a streak of gray.

The stranger smiles sadly, blue eyes gleaming with pity. "Sea has swallowed sun," he says, indicating the scene before them. Derek turns his head and looks out over the precipice. There's Moy Castle, tiny in the distance, lights gleaming in the narrow windows, and the horizon lined with the crimson glow left by a sun just set. Stars are coming out.

Derek shakes his head with confusion. Sounds and scents crowd him: his sister's perfume, salty air off the sea loch, wash of waves up the strand, a resinous torch burning on the castle's battlements, moldy marsh grass around the standing stones, the screech of an sea eagle, a woman keening on the beach. And Angus's blood. Even this far off, Derek can smell Angus's spilt blood soaking the earth. Somehow he can sense that Angus's body is gone from the stones, that his lover's corpse lies among flowers somewhere in the distant castle.

"I know, son," the Norseman sighs. "He's gone. I'm truly sorry." He lifts Derek, pressing him to his chest. Derek wraps his arms around the stranger, grateful for such unexpected kindness. He whimpers, choking back sorrow, then breaks down utterly, sobbing against the blond giant's torso. The rocking starts up anew, the Scot weeping without check, the Norseman's soothing hands rubbing his shoulders and throbbing head. Derek wipes his face, gasps at the pink stains he finds there, then only sobs harder.

"I'm Sigurd," the Norseman says, once Derek's weeping has begun to slow. "Sigurd Magnusson." He slips out from beneath the smaller man, stands, then helps Derek to his feet. "I'm from the Orkneys. I've visited your isle many a time over the years, and many a time I've admired you and your man from a distance. If I'd known you and he were in such danger, I would have guarded you and defended you. I'm so sorry. The scent of all that blood drew me, but I got to you too late to save him. He was a grand lad."

"Thank ye, Sigurd Magnusson. Angus was a glory," Derek says. He sniffles and swallows hard, gazing with awe and admiration at the man's beefy physique. Sigurd is nearly seven feet tall, with a heavily muscled chest, shoulders, and arms. His skin is white, and smooth except for a dusting of golden fur around his nipples, across his flat belly and upon his thick legs. About his neck, a metal Thor's cross hangs on a leather cord.

"Sir, I would be dead now if ye hadn't come along. I owe ye my life." Derek gingerly rubs his side, finding not an oozing wound but an already healed-over scar between his ribs. He shakes his head with disbelief. "How can I feel so hale, so full of vigor after the stabbing I received? My wounds were deep. I felt sure they were mortal. Yet I stand before ye entirely whole. What kind of healer are ye, to knit up my hurts thus? A sorcerer, are ye?"

"In a manner of speaking. I've given you the new life and the second chance I promised, son. We're blood brothers and night-kin now. We're what my fellow Vikings used to call *draugr*. I came to this new life in 1150, when I first encountered Medb in the Ring of Brodgar, a circle of standing stones much like that in which I found you. You Scots would call her a *BaoBhan Sith*."

"A banshee? 1150? Are ye mad?"

"I told you I had freed you from death and from age. She did the same for me, the delicious trollop. She changed me as I changed you. She did it for sport; I did it to save your life."

"Changed me? How?"

"Do you not feel changed?"

"'Tis true I feel...more than myself. My senses have a weird clarity. As full of sorrow as I am, I feel...."

"Glorious? Yes. I drained what little blood your wounds had left you. Then you drank my blood and, when I ravished your mouth and arse, you took my semen. In the life-juice and the love-juice the sorcery resides. Soon you'll find yourself mightier than you've ever been, strong enough to wreak whatever reprisals you crave. It's a gift, son, though there's a price."

"To hell with the price! If I can avenge Angus, 'twill be worth it. Six of them, the cowards, taking us by surprise, cutting us down like scythed barley! I'll gut them like sea-trout!"

"Your ferocity is a lovely thing, boy. Now listen," says Sigurd, resting his big hands on Derek's shoulders. "The price is two-fold. You must live in darkness, and you must feed your thirst, a thirst that will recur again and again. It can never be escaped."

"What are ye saying, sir?"

"I'm saying that you've lost the light, that you'll be forever prey to a new and ruthless hunger, and that in return you'll be stronger than any warrior alive. I'm saying that we have much to do before the sun rises above Ben Buie."

"But my family! They might be in danger yet. They probably think I'm dead! And Angus. I must help with his obsequies, with his burial. And then I have MacDonald and his crew of toadies to disembowel."

"We'll to the castle tomorrow night, I assure you. Your revenge will come soon. But tonight you and I must talk further. You must be taught. And you must be fed. Do you not feel the thirst already?"

"Yes, I.... My head is hot, my mouth dry, my tongue scorched. Have ye wine or water?"

Sigurd chuckles. "Wine or water won't do for us, my lad. You'll feed from me tonight. Tomorrow night we'll hunt."

"Hunt? I'm grand at that. The stag, the boar. I—"

The massive Viking guffaws. "Keep silent and listen to me now. You have much to learn." Pulling a dirk from its scabbard, Sigurd cuts a Norse rune into the gleaming skin of his right pectoral. The red blood wells up and trickles over his breast, dripping from his nipple. "This is Tyr," he says between gritted teeth. "This is the rune of the warrior, boy. Come here now. Take in more power."

Derek hesitates, snuffling the air. His gums throb; his mouth fills with saliva.

"Fangs, son. There you go." Sigurd smiles proudly.

Derek lifts a thumb to his mouth. Beneath his touch, his eyeteeth are lengthening. Disbelieving, he rubs them, cutting his thumb on their newly honed sharpness.

"Come, Derek," Sigurd says, wiping his own blood up with a forefinger and licking it off. "Taste me again."

Derek's leapt upon the wounded Viking before he knows it. He laps voraciously at the man's broad chest and the bloody rune etched there, then sinks his fangs into the beefy pectoral with a whimper and a growl.

Sigurd groans. He pulls Derek off, lies down in the moss, and opens his arms. Derek slips down beside him, wraps his limbs around the Viking's frame, presses his mouth to the injury, and begins a tight sucking. Sigurd lies back, closes his eyes, and sighs, stroking the Scot's mussed hair.

nother sunset bloodies the sea. The Hebridean nightfall is clear and starry, yet high upon
Ben Buie mist is gathering. It glows an eldritch
green. Now it pours down the slope, leisurely at first, like treacle in
winter, then gathering speed, a diaphanous avalanche. Reaching the
mountain's foot, it roils over the meadow, coming to a stop about
the standing stones, veiling them in its swirling mass. Shapes congeal,
and then two broad-shouldered men in great kilts step from the dispersing vapor.

Derek kneels by the fire pit. He sifts the cold ashes between his
fingers. He stands, approaches the westernmost stone, and bends
down to touch the bloodstained grass at its foot. Straightening, he
wraps his arms around the stone, pressing his cheek against it, and
weeps quietly, ruddy drops that stain the lichen-mottled rock. When
his massive companion squeezes his shoulder, Derek nods, wipes at
his eyes with clenched fists, then leads the way across the marshy
meadow toward the castle.

Derek can smell the young man from many yards away, the aroma
of his armpits, the genital musk beneath his kilt, the tears on his
face, scents that make the young vampire's mouth water. It's Robbie
MacAvoy, sitting in the dark on a flat boulder overlooking the loch,
his head in his hands. Derek and Sigurd move with such agility and
silence that he's unaware of their approach.

Sigurd lifts a finger to his lips. Derek nods, slipping behind a bush
of blooming gorse. Stepping forward, the Viking rests a hand on
Robbie's shoulder.

The young man starts up in an instant. He whirls around, dirk unsheathed and brandished, green eyes bulging.

"What'd'ye want?" he gasps. "The castle's full of armed men! Get
back now, or I'll call for aid!"

"Will you now?" Grinning, Sigurd fixes him with his blue gaze. Robbie's mouth drops open.

"Easy, boy. I've come to help. Now sheathe that blade and sit down.
And hold your tongue no matter what you see."

Robbie pauses, blinks twice, then with shaking hands slips his
weapon back into its scabbard. "Aye, sir," he says, sitting down with
a huff of breath.

"I have good news for you, lad. The laird's son survived. Behold."

Derek steps into view. Robbie gasps. He begins to rise but Sigurd's hand falls on his shoulder, returning him to a seated position.

"Your turn, tyro," Sigurd says, addressing Derek. "Gaze into the boy's eyes. Feel his thoughts. Then squeeze. As much strength as I've given you with my blood and seed, this should be simple."

Derek steps forward, locking the boy with his gaze. Like a well-thrown dart, his will enters Robbie's wide green eyes, embedding itself in the boy's brain. Robbie shudders, closes his eyes, then opens them. He smiles weakly, nods, and stands.

"I need a boon from ye, Robbie," Derek murmurs. "Will ye give it freely? Gladly?"

"I'm so glad ye're alive, m'laird. We all thought.... Aye, I'll give whatever ye ask."

Derek smiles. "Guid lad. Come then." He opens his arms.

Robbie shrugs the fold of tartan off his shoulder, unbuttons his loose tunic-shirt, pulls it over his head, and hangs it on a gorse branch. Bare-chested, he shuffles over to Derek. His green eyes are glazed, as if they were moor-meres winter-icing over.

"Go very slowly, son," Sigurd says. "Drinking from me has dulled the desperation of your thirst, but you'll still not want to stop. Keep your aim in sight. This boy can tell us much, so spare his life. There will be others to taste inside the castle."

"I can tell ye much," Robbie repeats, grinning drunkenly. He steps into Derek's arms, resting his head on the older man's shoulder. "Go verra, verra slow, m'laird. Touch me, m'laird."

Derek chuckles softly. "Ye're so warm, Robbie. Have ye wanted me to touch ye, lad?" Again that aching in the gums as his fangs extend. He runs a fingertip down the pale skin over the boy's breastbone, flicks a hair-rimmed nipple, and probes his navel. Both men's members begin to stiffen.

"Ohhh, aye! For years now. Ye and sweet Maister McCormick. Ye're both so bonnie and so grand." Robbie exhales loudly, then bursts into tears, flinging his wiry arms around Derek's neck. "Oh, Laird Jesus, I don't believe he's gone! I've been weeping for days, mourning him. We've got to find the villains who slew him!"

"We will, I swear." Derek wraps an arm around the boy's shoulders and pulls him closer. "And ye shall help me in that task," he adds, flicking a tongue over his fully extended fangs.

Robbie whimpers as Derek sinks his teeth into the boy's pale neck. Hot wealth floods the vampire's mouth; he tightens his lips around the wound he's made, just as he once tightened his mouth's suction around Angus McCormick's eager cock. Such is Derek's hunger and his care that only a few drops escape, trickling down the lad's throat and into the sparse dusting of his auburn chest hair. Robbie rasps a low moan, pulls Derek closer, and rubs his erection against the burly Scot's own. When the boy's body starts to shake and slump, Derek releases him, lowering him onto a soft hummock of grass. Robbie rolls onto his side, curls up like an infant, musters another drunken grin, and passes out.

"Well done," Sigurd says, giving Derek's back a thump. "The thirst will be more insistent in your first century, then it will decline to proportions less deadly and more moderate. The greater your desire for your victim, the harder it will be to rein in your hunger."

"Then I've done well indeed." Derek kneels beside Robbie and tousles his chestnut hair. "Angus and I both wanted to ride this boy raw."

"And so you may, man. Just remember not to take too much from him if you want to enjoy him in nights to come."

"Speaking of such riding.... Sigurd, sir...though ye're a bonnie, mighty man, as finely featured and finely built as my Angus.... If we'd met at a different time, perhaps...." Derek clears his throat, looking up into Sigurd's sea-blue eyes. "Well, what I'm trying to say is...I'd appreciate it if ye'd not ravish me again, though I know yer strength and know ye could tak me by force if ye pleased. Not only did ye fill my arse to bluidy bursting—my hole's still a wee bit sore—but...."

"But you're grieving. But loving again, surrendering yourself so completely to another man, is something you can't imagine after losing Angus. I well understand, my boy. When those churchmen placed a binding runestone on Medb's grave, then unearthed her at dawn and pierced her with a rowanwood stake, I thought I'd never feel desire again for more than a hot mouthful of blood and a dark place to rest. But I was wrong. I've loved many humans and a couple of *draugr*, women and men, over the centuries, since I lost Medb in 1400. Now I love you, lad."

"Luve me? But we just met."

"I've been visiting Mull for centuries, Derek. I've watched you on and off all your life, since you were a black-headed brat splashing in the loch. I've had many years to learn to love you. That time you were hunting alone and got lost in the blizzard? I was the will-o'-the-wisp that led you home. Those times you fell asleep alone in the barn and woke in the morning weary and weak, tiny wounds on your neck and breast and prick and arse?"

"Ye fed on me?"

"Yes, and it was pure delight, to drink from such youth, such manliness, such dark good looks. Believe me, I never would have harmed you or parted you from Angus. You two were splendid together, and I must confess that many was the time I hovered outside the window and watched the two of you make love. The only reason I turned you was—"

"To save my life, aye! I believe ye, Sigurd, and I'm so grateful, sir, but I'm not ready for—"

"Be easy, boy. This is deep fondness without demands. If you're willing, we can sleep together during the days, perhaps sup from each other's bodies once in a while, perhaps hunt together. What say you to that?"

"Aye, Sigurd. That's all sounding like some comfort and some consolation I'll be in dire need of in the nights to come. Ye make me feel safe, as Angus used to do."

"Given time—and of that we have a plenty, may Thor and all the gods guard us!—you might yet come to care for me, boy. And you might yet come to take a human lover. As you'll see, the urge to feed often brings on the urge to fuck. Surfeiting either hunger is fine succor from sorrow."

"Another luve?" Derek shakes his head. "Fucking is one thing, but luve would be a miracle beyond comprehension."

"As you'll see, we *draugr* are extreme in all things, including lust, love and hate. Hunger like ours makes it easy to cherish the world's beauties, though it also makes it easy to destroy them, fragile and mortal as they are." Bending, Sigurd places a hand over Robbie's breast. "No need to kill kindness or loveliness. No need to stop the beating of a true heart. If you're ever of a mind to kill, there are wicked men enough to pluck like crimson bog-flowers from black mud."

"Aye, more than enough. And as for destruction—"

"Yes, lad. You're right, let's on with your revenge. I can still read your mind. Can you read mine?"

Derek pauses, cocking an ear as if thoughts might suddenly be audible. "Nay."

"You might learn the skill yet. Go on. Back to your little lad there. He's your thrall now. He'll do whatever you say."

Bending, Derek kisses Robbie's brow. "Up now, pup. Wake."

Robbie's eyes flicker open. He grunts and stretches and smiles, as if aroused from a happy dream. Feebly, with Derek's help he clambers to his feet. Derek leads him to the boulder overlooking the loch and helps him stretch out atop it before sitting beside the boy and resting Robbie's head in his tartan-clad lap. Sigurd stands beside them, listening.

"Robbie, tell me what's happened here since last ye saw me."

Robbie gazes up at Derek with adoration. Then abruptly he turns his head and looks out over the night-black loch. His lips quiver; his brow bunches up.

"Oh, God. I found him. Maister McCormick. When Lady Morna discovered yer bed empty that morning, she sent me out to the stones to search for ye both. So eager she was for ye to tak her bairn fishing. I found yer friend's body, stabbed so terribly, with so many oozing wounds. I found a trail of bluid through the grass, but ye were nowhere to be found. I took the news back to the castle." Sniffling, Robbie seizes Derek's hand. "Thank God ye're whole!"

"I'm more than whole, lad. And then?"

"Lady Morna went mad with rage. She had the bells rung to sound the alarm, then had me fetch yer claymore from yer chamber. She buckled it on, hitched up her bonnie blue skirts, and strode out across that dewy meadow like the Shadowy One herself!"

Derek chuckles. "Aye. I can believe that. We're cut from the same cloth, she and I. Continue, pup."

"The loch rang with her screams. My skin prickled at the fearsome sound. She had the men carry Maister McCormick's body in. For hours she searched about the stones, in the meadows and forest, for some sign of what might have happened to ye, some clew to who yer attackers might have been. When she found yer dirk, she felt sure that ye'd been slain and that yer corpse had been carried off."

"And Angus's body is still here?"

"Yes, m'laird. In the great hall of the castle."

"And my family?"

"Yer mither's in seclusion, nearly mute with the shock of it. Yer faither's in Craignure, to commission coffins. For ye and Maister Angus. Since ye're believed dead. He's also asking about the port, trying to discover the culprits. After what happened in Oban last month—"

"Aye, Robbie. Ye're right. 'Twas the fucking MacDonalds indeed. They ambushed us. They murthered Angus."

"That's what Maister McCormick's brothers said! 'Twas all yer faither could do to keep John and Ewan here on the estate. They wanted to scour the island for MacDonalds and slay them every one! Laird Maclaine told them that proof must be had; he ordered them to stay here and guard the castle till his return."

"And where are John and Ewan now?"

"On the parapet, keeping watch." Robbie points to the top of the tower, where firelight flickers behind the crenellations.

"And Morna?"

"In her room."

"Aye, I can smell her hair. How does she appear?"

"For a day she wept and broke anything within her reach. But now she's calm. I waited on her this morning, fetched her some milk and some bannock. Cold, cold those bonnie blue eyes of hers! She sharpens yer claymore and yer dirk; she stands by her window and looks out over the loch, waiting for word. M'laird, ye must see her! Ye must tell her the wondrous news, that ye're alive!"

"The door," says Sigurd. "Don't forget the door."

"Aye." Taking Robbie's hand, Derek pulls him upright. "Lad, I will see my sister now. Will ye lead us within?"

"Gladly."

The three men climb up the low hill to the castle. They pause before the oaken door to the keep. Robbie knocks, then responds to the muffled challenge from within. The door swings open, and Allan

Black, a brawny guard with a beard as dark and bushy as Derek's, steps out, sword drawn and gleaming in the dim starlight.

"Allan, it's the laird's son!" Robbie exclaims. Before the big guard can form a word of greeting, Derek's snagged his will and seized him in his arms. Allan gasps, leaning against Derek limply as the vampire slakes his thirst.

"Isn't he a handsome one? Not too much now," Sigurd warns. Derek pulls away, only to hand Allan to Sigurd, who takes a long draught before passing him back.

"With so much honey to taste, why drain to the dregs any one hive?" Sigurd flashes Derek a gleaming, sharp-toothed grin.

"Indeed. It's like plucking one petal apiece from a great garden of red roses." Derek burrows his tongue into the man's throat-wound, then savors another long slurp before retracting his fangs. "Now, Allan. Ye tasted as rich and rugged as I'd imagined. Are ye all right?" Derek licks the guard's thick neck and smacks his lips.

"Oh, aye, L-laird Maclaine! Never better." Allan sways, then straightens. "I p-praise the guid God ye're alive!"

"And may I enter?"

"'Tis yer family's castle! Of course ye may enter!" the brawny guard blurts.

"Welcome home, m'laird," Robbie says, pushing the door wide and ushering his master inside.

The great hall is empty, the feasting tables long removed. About the walls, candle sconces flicker. In the huge fireplace, logs crackle and crumble. Upon the dais is a bier.

Allan and Robbie guard the entrance to the hall, insuring the vampires' privacy. With slow steps Derek moves toward the bier, with Sigurd just behind him. At last Derek stands above the corpse of Angus McCormick. The big man is bare-chested and barefoot, his hands crossed on his hairy breast, his claymore unsheathed and resting atop him. His fingers are folded over the handle of the sword, his loins and thighs wrapped in his bloodstained great kilt. The habitually unkempt hair and whiskers have been combed; someone has washed the bloodstains from his body and has tried with only moderate success to smooth the grimace of rage from his bruised face. Highland flowers are arranged all about him, but their scents of spring cannot mask from Derek's newly sharpened senses the odor of decomposition.

The Scot heaves a raspy sigh, wiping bloody brine from his eyes. He falls to his knees by the bier.

"Ah, by the gods. Yer great breast's still as carven granite, yer strang arms useless as shattered swords. Yer breath's blown off like thistle-down, yer eyes harebell-blue closed forever. Ah, gods protect ye, where'er ye've flown."

He strokes Angus's hair and beard, presses his face against his bare side, then runs a shaking finger over his multitude of wounds.

"With his sword, he looks like a knight of old," Derek says. "If we'd only taken our claymores with us that night. If we'd only been more careful. Things might have been different. He was worried about the MacDonalds; he knew they might...."

Sigurd's heavy hand falls on Derek's shoulder. "It was fated, son. No one can change the whims of the Three Sisters. He loved you; you loved him. You were lucky in that at least."

"Aye. And I thank the Horned One and the Dark Lady for that. Gods, what a strength and a blessing ye were, my red-gold man." Derek lifts Angus's hand, kissing the golden ring and the furry knuckles before rearranging the dead fingers on the handle of the sword.

"I was so young, so foolish. No one would dare to cross a laird's son, I thought!" Derek's cold chuckle is ice cracking in February midnight. "And he paid for my pride."

Stiffly Derek rises. "I would be dead if not for ye, Sigurd. Would I be with Angus? In the Summerlands? Can Angus even travel over the western seas to that blessed place if he's not yet avenged?"

"I don't know, son. I don't know what lies beyond that veil any more than you do."

"If I were with him in the Land of Youth, he might have died unavenged." Derek's lips curl, exposing a fang. "I will have justice, Sigurd."

"And you shall. Soon. Do you regret this? This new life? Now that you know what it entails?"

"Regret? Perhaps later. Once all the killers are dead. But not now, sir. Now," Derek says, lapping a fang and clenching his fist, "I savor my new senses and my new strength. They are needful."

"M'laird!" Allan steps into the hall, halberd in his hand. "The guard's about to change!"

Derek nods. He kisses Angus's bare breast, leaving a few bloody tears there. He kisses Angus's brow, then the cold scowl of his lips. "I'll make ye smile again, where'er ye are, as a shade in this world or a youth reborn in the next. Goodbye for now, my hinnie-sweet man, my bonnie luver."

Derek turns, smearing tears from his beard. "Sigurd, I must see my sister now. Go back to Ben Buie and our nest there. I'll join ye before dawn."

"Are you sure, boy?"

Standing on tiptoe, Derek takes the giant Viking's head in his hands and kisses him on the cheek. "I wish Angus could have known ye, sir. He would have fancied ye. He would have found ye fair indeed. Aye, I'm sure. This is my family, my castle, my island. Ye've done enough, and I thank ye for it, but the rest is mine to do."

Minutes later, Robbie McEvoy, with two guards attending, enters the great hall to add wood to the low fire there and replace a few burnt-down tapers. All is as it was, except for the last remnants of mist swirling over the floor and a few drops of blood fallen onto the bare chest of the corpse, drops that Robbie quietly blots up with a cloth.

Derek's claymore and dirk are lying unsheathed beside their scabbards on Morna's bed. She and her child are nowhere to be seen. One candle flickers on the bedside table. On the hearth, the wood fire has burnt down to embers.

The young vampire sheathes the blades and buckles them about his waist. He moves restlessly around the room, touching insignificant items—Morna's comb, her jewelry box, her bedspread—as if saying a silent farewell to each of them. When he hears her step in the hall, he freezes. The lines of his body begin to glow green and blur, an animal's instinctual urge to hide or flee, but then he shakes his head, regains solidity, and slips into the antechamber where the empty cradle stands.

Morna pushes the heavy door open, only to pause inside. She stares at the place where the claymore and dirk used to be. Moving to the center of the room, she blows out the candle and sits in her brocaded chair. "Derek?" she says, voice level and low.

"I'm here," her brother says, stepping out of the antechamber.

"Thank the Goddess!" Morna springs from the chair. "I knew it!" The siblings exchange a long hard hug before Derek leads Morna back to her chair, then stands before the embers of the hearth.

"I heard ye've kept my weapons honed, sister," Derek says, patting the pommel of his sword. "Thank ye for that. I have need of them now."

"The fearsome dreams I had, that Beltane night. I nearly came up to the stones to warn ye."

"And if ye did, ye might have died as Angus did. Those scum were no respecters of womankind. What did ye dream? Ye've always had a bit of the Sight."

"Damned little good the Sight did either of us that night, for a true dream to come to me too late to be of any use! I dreamed ye perished, then ye crawled out of the grave-dirt and rose into the sky on great dark wings."

Derek laughs. "'Tis close enough! 'Tis close enough. And how are Mither and Faither?"

"They're both convinced ye're dead. Mither won't leave her chamber. She stares out the window and will barely speak. Feeble as he is, Faither's been in Craignure, speaking to our Maclean cousins in Duart Castle, and over to Oban, trying to discover what happened to ye two and what became of yer body."

Morna clasps Derek's hand. "Who was it, Derek? The men who murthered Angus? His brithers swear it was the MacDonalds, but the head of their clan claims they had no part in Angus's death. Faither wants to believe him."

"Laird MacDonald might not have known about the attack. That remains to be seen. But it was a MacDonald who led them. Brodie MacDonald. The other five I didn't recognize."

"Ah, Brodie," Morna hisses. "That bonnie demon. Ye, he, and Angus are—were—the finest-featured men in the Western Isles. 'Tis a pity he's a serpent-herted gutter-bluid, for all his regal bearing. Then we must start with him. When Faither returns—"

"I'll be dealing with this, not Faither. They stabbed Angus to death, sister. He died defending me. My Angus. My sweet—"

Derek falls silent. He turns, moves to the window and looks out over the loch.

"Yer sweet luver. Aye," says Morna. "His better I never met, other than ye, brither. He was yer boon companion and a member of our clan and thus deserving of vengeance. And we shall arrange it, a revenge as rich as any savored before. We'll make Brodie MacDonald and his toadies howl. But how did ye escape unhurt?"

Derek coughs and wipes his eyes. "Light the candle, Morna."

Morna rises. From the fire's embers she ignites the taper. When she turns from the hearth, she gasps. Derek stands before her, bloody tears smearing his pale cheeks and black beard.

"Derek! Ye're bleeding from the eyes!" She's fumbling for a handkerchief in her dress when his hand grips hers.

"Sit, dear one. I'm whole. The bluid ye see is only part of the great change that caught me up just this side of death."

"Death?" Morna does as she's told, sitting heavily in the chair once more. "Ye speak of death and yet ye say ye're whole? Yet ye're bleeding?"

"I didn't escape those swine. I was stabbed in the ribs and in the back." Derek raises his shirt, giving Morna a quick glimpse of the jagged scar in his side.

"Ye're scarred yet ye're already healed. How—?"

Derek pulls his flask from his sporran. "Let's have a dram or two, sister mine, and a talk. Then let's up to the parapet. We have some conferring to do with John and Ewan McCormick."

An hour later, the McCormick brothers are passing their own flask back and forth around a brazier, its warmth welcome at such a windy altitude, when the trap door creaks open and Lady Morna

Maclaine appears in the aperture. "Good even, clansmen. May I speak with ye?"

"Certainly, m'lady!" John hoarsely replies. The two men—blond and husky, with thick eyebrows, grim visages, and fierce eyes, clearly born for battle—straighten up with respect, as they always do in the presence of a lady. Hurriedly, they smooth down as best they can their unruly hair and bristling beards before John offers Morna his hand, helping her ascend the last few steps onto the square platform of the battlements.

"I'm so sorry, men. So sorry about Angus." Morna takes their rough hands in hers, hugging each of them in turn before turning to lean into the notch of a crenelle and stare out over the moon-streaked sea loch. The McCormick brothers stand stiffly behind her, confused by her effusiveness, much unexpected in a noblewoman habitually aloof.

"I have news." She turns and points toward the sky. Something winged is circling the tower, a black silhouette against the stars: soft flapping, silent veering through the spring air. "News about yer brither and mine. Do ye trust me?"

"Aye, m'lady," the brothers simultaneously exclaim. "Most surely," adds John.

"A miracle is winging its way to us. An avenging angel. But to receive it ye must close yer eyes. "

The men do so. The sound of wings grows louder, then ceases. Only Morna watches the transformation, with wide eyes and sensuous mouth forming circles of amazement. "Open yer eyes, men," she whispers.

They do so. They start and gasp, step back, and clutch the handles of their swords.

"Don't be afeart," Morna says, though the quiver in her voice seems to belie her words.

"Oh, God," Ewan rasps. "Derek Maclaine. A wraith, are ye? Returned from the dead?"

"I'm no wraith, lads. I'm solid," says Derek, spreading his arms and smiling.

"Oh, thank God!" Ewan gasps.

"My laird!" John blurts.

The two bulky warriors, suddenly wet-eyed for all their savage looks, leap forward, seizing Derek in grunting bear-hugs of enthusiasm, slapping his back, kneading his shoulders, tugging fondly on his beard.

"We felt sure that ye'd perished with poor Angus," Ewan says. "We knew ye'd never have left him willingly!"

"Gods, no, I would never have left him. Nor would he ever have left me. Angus lost his life trying to save mine. He put up a fierce fight."

John nods. "No doubt. He luved ye strang and deep. He would have done anything to defend ye. Thank God ye're unharmed, m'laird!"

"But I was harmed, lads. Verra badly. Mortally. I was stabbed and left for dead."

"Then why did we not find ye by the stones? And how are ye here, alive and buirdly-armed as ever?" John asks, brow furrowed. "Just now ye seemed to arrive from out of nowhere. Ye appeared like a spirit from the beyond. How in God's name did ye survive yer wounds?"

"And who slew our brither?" Ewan growls, gripping his sword's handle. "For our arms are strang, and we intend to make the whore-sons pay. Begging yer pardon, m'lady, for the coarseness of my language."

Morna smiles. "My brither and I already have a grand plan to dispatch those verra whore-sons. Ye two will aid us, will ye not?"

John lifts a hairy hand to his heart. Ewan does the same. "We swear!" John says. "We are yers to command. Ye Maclaines have always shown kindness and good faith to us McCormicks. We'll do whate'er ye want. Just allow us to avenge our brither."

"We'll all have a part in this vengeance, I promise ye," says Derek. "But to answer yer questions. An unco strange destiny found me dying at the stones and carried me off. A sort of magic has healed me, a dark sort of blessing. And it was Brodie MacDonald and his men who slew Angus and who wounded me so grievously."

John snarls. Ewan clenches his fist and spits phlegm over the parapet.

"Just what I thought," John shouts. "May God damn him forever! MacDonalds! The frigging curs. God *damn* them! I told Laird Maclaine it was so. He said we must have proof to act. And why do we need proof now? Yer word is proof enough! Let's to Craignure tonight and behead the scum!"

"It's Craignure he's at?" the young vampire says, lifting a bushy eyebrow.

"Aye, so we hear. In the inn by the harbor. Bluidy bastard," Ewan says before hawking more spittle over the edge. "Yer pardon, m'lady. My manners are rougher than they ought to be."

Morna laughs grimly, then spits over the crenellations too, causing Ewan to guffaw. "It's not yer manners I care about. It's yer sword arm. And I have high faith in that."

"Thank ye, m'lady. I'll tak pleasure in living up to that faith. Aye, MacDonald and his men are taking their ease in Craignure, planning to ride the ferry to Oban at dawn. That's what Davey MacAvoy told me. He also said that MacDonald has a broken nose and a blackened eye."

"Yes, Angus did that. My red-gold knight." Derek smiles wistfully. "I saw Angus punch Brodie in the face and elbow him in the eye before I passed out."

Ewan grits his teeth. "There's even word that MacDonald's been boasting in the tavern. Saying he was injured while putting down a mad dog that dared to cross him."

"Boasting, eh? Daft fool. He'll regret not taking that ferry to the mainland sooner." Derek runs his tongue over his incisors. "See ye that there?" he says, pointing to an isolate building far up the loch's shore, set back in a grove of trees.

"Yes, m'laird. Above Laggan Sands. The Maclaine mausoleum that used to be St. Kenneth's chapel," replies Ewan. "'Tis in the graveyard there that yer faither and mine plan to bury Angus. 'Tis there that everyone expected ye to lie as well. We dug the graves today."

Derek sighs. "I shan't be lying there any time soon, I promise ye. Too much to do. Tomorrow night I'll be wanting to meet ye at the mausoleum a bit after sunset. But tonight I'll be needing ye two to tak a ride. There's something I need ye to fetch me. A toothsome bit of venison, so to speak."

"Ah, grand!" exclaims Ewan. "We've had cousins in readiness in Fionnphort since Angus was found, poised to help us slaughter the MacDonalds. So we may act, m'laird?"

"Oh, aye. But stealthily. No band of cousins yet. Just ye two. No grand slaughter. No need to stir up the clans any further. The task I have in mind ye'll find most gratifying."

"And yer faither?" John asks. "Lord Lachlan Maclaine? What part shall he play? Or his men here at Moy?"

Morna shakes her head. "None. Our faither has too much clemency in his nature. He's too caught up with concerns o'er the balance of power 'twixt the clans. The less he knows of this the better."

"True, sister, true. The bluidy reprisals I plan to savor he would never condone. And my return's to be kept secret till the plan I have in mind is entirely fulfilled. Now, lads, listen here. Ye asked how I came to be here tonight so sudden and how I came to survive my mortal hurts. Before we begin to avenge Angus, there are two truths I must share with ye. One's about the bond 'twixt yer brither and me. The other one's weird and fearsome, about that strange destiny I met amidst the stones. After ye hear, then ye can decide whether to follow me or no."

"As long as Angus's killers are dealt the ends they deserve," Ewan says, "we'll follow ye anywhere."

"Speak on," says John. "What truths do ye mean?"

"In a moment. After I tell ye what I must, if I have yer allegiance still, ye two must get an hour's sleep below," Derek says, leaning against the battlements. "Use my bedchamber and I'll tak the guard here till dawn. Later, ye ride for Craignure and the port there. Ye must reach town before the ferry leaves for Oban. I'll not have our prey escape."

D usk of the following day. Swords drawn, John and Ewan walk the soft grass of the rock-walled graveyard, near the grave dug for their brother Angus. Silently they watch light die in the evening sky. They gulp the ale and consume the meat pies Morna's servants brought them for their supper, ignoring the muffled noise inside the Maclaine mausoleum. They take turns stretching out on the ground between graves for much-needed naps. Both of them are weary after their travels: the fourteen-mile night-ride to the port of Craignure, the long ride back with their wriggling burden.

All day gray clouds have thickened over the island. Now, as night gathers, a soft drizzle begins, falling in the big men's hair and on their tanned brows. Upon the shores of the loch below, upon the yellow beach known as Laggan Sands, slow waves wash up the slope, making a sad susurrus as they ascend before reaching the frothy limit of their reach and receding with a low hiss.

The light of candles and torches flares up now in the distant windows of Castle Moy. A cold wind pours up from the sea loch, bristling the hairs on the back of John McCormick's neck. A night bird calls, the leaves about the graveyard rustle restlessly, and a black silhouette appears at the edge of the woods.

Ewan McCormick swallows hard. "M'laird?"

A rough laugh sounds. "Ye sound afeart, Ewan. Have no fear of me. Despite what ye know now."

"Sorry. It's just that.... I can see yer eyes in the dark. They glow green like a—"

"A beast's? A demon's? Ye're clansmen and friends. No harm will come to ye while this particular demon is around."

Derek Maclaine approaches the two brothers and extends his hands. Both men hesitate, then, squaring their shoulders, extend their own. For a long moment, the human brothers stand there, gripping the vampire's chilly palms.

Derek releases them. "Ye have him then?"

"Aye, m'laird. He's in the mausoleum in the state ye asked."

As if in response, an outraged and muffled shout resounds inside the crypt.

"Ummm." Derek licks his lips. "And did he give ye trouble?"

"Trouble enough," John sniggers, rubbing his bruised jaw. "Caught me here with his fist. But then Ewan clubbed him in the head. We got him out of Craignure just before sunup. No one saw us, I think."

"And his men? Did the rest of them flee on the ferry, d'ye think, when Brodie went missing?"

"They'll stay in Craignure, I'm sure of it. I asked our cousin, Davey MacAvoy—he loved Angus well—to convince them that Brodie's holed up with his favorite whore in Tobermory for a day or so. And I paid the innkeeper—Alpin Patton, he's a clansman—to tell them that

Brodie had paid their room and board for the next few days. They're too greedy to suspect anything different."

Inside the crypt, another muffled roar resounds.

"Ye've done it all brilliantly, lads. Now back to the castle with ye. Get some proper supper and some good drink. Ye look exhausted. Ye're welcome to tak my bed again. Tell all to Morna, but remember, not a word to my parents. I'll come to ye before dawn and we'll plot out the next round of the hunt."

"But shouldn't we stay?" says John. "To aid ye just in case?"

"I'll need no aid tonight. What needs doing here is demon's work, not men's. I'd just as soon spare ye the sights and sounds." Derek grins, flashing his sharp white teeth.

John shudders and nods. "Demon's work. Aye. I could almost pity the bastard," he says, sheathing his sword. "Almost. Come, brither."

The McCormicks gather their things and leave the graveyard. On the path to the castle, their pace picks up. Derek stands alone by the mausoleum, listening to waves ascending Laggan Sands and the night wind soughing in the surrounding trees. He closes his eyes, concentrating. "Lord of Storm," he sighs.

The wind picks up, clawing at limbs about the graveyard, tearing off clumps of leaves. Above Mull, clouds clot and roil. The drizzle becomes a downpour, beating the loch into misty froth. Lightning stabs the sky; a thunderclap resounds, its echoes rolling down Ben Buie. Derek smiles with the triumph of a novice exercising newly acquired skills. He stands in the hard rain, face tilted up, licking drops from his moustache, water soaking his tartans. He raises his arms in rapture; another flash of lightning gouges the heavens.

Soaked now, he lowers his arms and turns. Instead of entering the medieval crypt, he strides over to the two oblong graves dug in May grass. Silently, he studies them, then he crumbles a clod of earth into one, then into the other. He wipes his hands on his kilt, enters the mausoleum, and closes the door behind him.

On the floor, there's the sound of a man's frightened grunts, a constrained shifting of limbs. What would be pitch-dark to any human eye is only a gray dimness to Derek, but still he lights a candle sconce before he hunkers down to study the prize the McCormick brothers brought him.

Naked, covered with bruises and dirt, Brodie MacDonald lies on his side on the stone floor, shivering in the dank chill of the chamber. He's a muscular, thickset man in his thirties, with a bald head, blue eyes, and a great red beard. Hair of the same color coats his body from neck to ankles. His arms and wrists are bound behind him, his feet roped together. A rag's tied between his teeth. Beneath that rag he's whimpering with terror and disbelief, staring up at the candlelit man who by all rights should be dead.

"Aye, 'tis I indeed. Ye didn't expect such a visitor, did ye?" Derek smiles. "Not after all the dagger wounds I received on Beltane night." Straightening, with his boot he gently nudges MacDonald's side. "I remember a foot in my jaw, in my belly. I remember blades in my ribs and back." Derek pulls up his shirt to display the scar in his side. "Did ye inflict any of those blows, Brodie?"

MacDonald rolls onto his back and stares up at Derek. He chokes out a sob and shakes his head. Outside, another thunderclap booms, making him jump with fright.

"No? Right. Ye were too busy with Angus. He did this, did he not?" Derek bends to run a finger around MacDonald's blackened eye and swollen nose. The man's blue eyes widen and well with tears. He nods.

"What a frame ye have. Manly and furry." Now Derek's finger strokes MacDonald's right nipple, then the solid swell of his belly. "Ye're bonnie indeed. The toast of hures and other men's wives from here to Edinburgh, I always heard." Derek's hand moves lower. He takes the man's fear-shrunk cock in his hand.

"How many harlots have ye pleasured with this wee thing?" Derek gives the member a stroke and then a vicious tug, evoking from Mac-Donald a squeal of pain.

"I've a mind to cut this off," Derek says, "and I might yet. But first we'll talk. I need some answers. Will ye give me them?"

The bound man nods frantically. Derek unknots the gag and pulls its moistened length from his mouth.

"Dear God, how can ye be here?" MacDonald gasps, chest heaving. "We left ye dead, in a pool of blood."

"I wasn't dead. Nearly but not quite." Derek unsheathes his dirk and holds it up, where it gleams softly in the candlelight. "Fate saved me for this verra eve."

"Ye're no spirit, are ye?" MacDonald says, regarding Derek keenly. "Ye're as solid as I."

"No spirit. Solid indeed. For the nonce." As if in proof, Derek lifts a foot, resting it in the center of MacDonald's chest. "I need for ye to tell me many things, Brodie. Why did yer band attack us?"

"Ye know why, Maclaine. Yer...catamite slew my brother Alexander. And because we saw what we saw that night. Sorcery and sodomy! Both are killing offenses!"

"I need to know the names of the others. I need to know who dealt Angus's death blow."

"I won't tell ye. Why should I?" MacDonald licks his lips, glaring at the exposed blade.

"Because I'll cut yer throat, ye daft mooncalf," Derek says calmly, removing his foot. "Ye took from me the man I luved most. Ye slaughtered him like a shoat."

With difficulty, MacDonald sits up. "Luved?" he spits. "I saw what kind of luve that was! Loathly! Damned! Ye deserved what ye got! No court in Scotland would convict me! It was no crime, it was obeying the word of God!"

"I'm the magistrate tonight, my man. I'd show some manners."

"Ye can't murther me, Maclaine," Brodie MacDonald snarls, struggling against his bonds. "My kin will burn Castle Moy to the ground if ye do. The Maclaines of Lochbuie are nothing against the MacDonalds, and ye know it. We were the Lords of the Isles! Cut me loose, or I'll make ye pay! I'll have yer entire clan hanged!"

"Threats in yer situation? Ye're either mad as a foamy-mawed dog or courageous beyond all reason."

"The son of the laird, calling the devil in a circle of stones! Taking a cock up his bum like a woman up her cunt! Yer family name will forever be shamed once it's told what a monster ye are!"

Derek sheathes the dirk. "Monster is it? Ye're truer than ye know."

Before the man take say another word, Derek has seized him and jerked him to his bound feet. MacDonald sways there, eyes bulging.

"If ye'd been homely, I'd merely have glamored ye, gotten the truths I needed, and then cut yer throat. But handsome as ye are, I must taste ye first. Such buirdly good looks mustn't be wasted entirely on hures. "

Derek opens his mouth, exposing his fangs. "Dear Jesus," MacDonald manages to whine before Derek sinks his teeth into the man's throat, tearing savagely at the flesh.

The drinking is long, messy, and deep, Derek growling low in his throat, MacDonald whimpering and panting. By the time Derek lowers his captive to the floor, MacDonald's breathing is shallow, his heart beating wildly.

Derek sits cross-legged on the floor beside him. MacDonald groans, rolls onto his belly, fingers fumbling futilely against his bonds, then rolls onto his side and falls still. His eyes are open, a blue glaze. His lips tremble. Blood wells up from his neck wounds, trickles that Derek daubs up with a forefinger and licks off.

"What are ye, man?" MacDonald mumbles.

"I know no word for it ye would know."

"Am I to die then?"

"Aye." Derek sighs. "Oh, aye."

"Jesus. Nay. I'm begging ye. My kin...."

"Will never find ye. I'm going to carve ye into pieces like a Christmas goose, bag yer pairts, and drop them into the sea. All save the head, which I'll be burying on Ben Buie after ravens tak yer bonnie blue eyes for their wee snacks. Yer clan will never know what became of ye."

"Ah, God. Ah, God." MacDonald heaves a great breath, then presses his face to the floor and bursts into tears. "Please, please, please...."

For a long time, Derek simply sits by his hysterical prisoner, smiling a peaceful smile, daubing up neck-blood occasionally and listening to the storm, which continues a steady drumming on the crypt's wooden roof.

"My answers, man, before I finish ye." Derek bends over MacDonald and grips him by the beard, forcibly turning his face and gazing into his eyes. "Ye'll tell me all now, will ye not?"

Wind whistles about the crypt. MacDonald gulps and nods. "I dealt McCormick's death blow. My men were directed to save me that honor. I stabbed him again and again, and then I stabbed him in the hert."

"So I thought. And the others? Kin or hired men?"

"Hired. My kin refused to aid me, since all knew that my brither Alexander had drawn first that day in Oban. They feared yer clan might stir up the Campbells against us if...."

"Aye. Their names." Derek presses his hand over MacDonald's hirsute breast, feeling his heart pound faster and faster.

"Jimmy O'Farrell...Gordon McIntyre. Gerry Gillis. The brithers, Dugal and Neil MacGowan."

"And where are they now? Craignure?"

"Aye. Save for Jimmy," MacDonald says, his voice dwindled to a hoarse whisper. "His hert was too tender for the work I paid him to do. He's devout, not much more than a boy, so right after...Angus's slaying, the little fool fled...to Iona, to seek penance there."

"And are any of them comely?" Derek grins, thumbing the sharp tip of his right incisor.

"What?"

"Are any of them handsome?"

"Aye. One. Jimmy," Brodie chokes out.

"Ah, guid! Tell me about him."

"He's...he's a...a lean, black-beardit lad from Dublin. The ladies luve him."

"As they once luved ye. The others?"

"Scabby ruffians...hired in Oban. Ill-favored, all."

Derek stands. He throws the mausoleum's door open. Gusty rain pours into the musty room. "I've given us a grand storm outside." He unsheathes his claymore with a steely ring. "It's a fine fanfare, fit to escort a villain's soul to hell. Ye're mightily sorry for what ye've done, are ye not, Brodie?"

With his last strength, MacDonald nods.

"Guid, guid," Derek sighs. "And now I can forgive ye."

Resting a foot on the dying man's cheek, the vampire lifts the sword with both hands and brings it straight down, driving the blade through his enemy's chest till the point meets the stone floor with a dull thump. Brodie stiffens; his eyes fly wide, then close. Derek pauses for a moment, listening to his foe's last breaths mingling with the soughing of storm. Then he removes the blade, only to begin, slowly, deliberately, the process of dismemberment.

An hour before dawn, the sky has found peace again. The black clouds are gone; stars glint like powdered quartz. A tiny boat, its hull spattered with blood, glides up onto the stony shingle near the mouth of the loch. Soon thereafter, a dark shape flits into a window on the third floor of Moy Castle. The McCormick brothers are snoring loudly, fully clothed, back-to-back on Derek's bed, when he shakes them awake. Yawning, they sit up, rubbing their eyes.

"Rise, lads. I have a list for ye." Derek lights a candle before lifting a small piece of paper, waving it, and placing it on a desk nearby. "I have the names. Today, ye must ride to Fionnphort and then sail for Iona. Ye have kin there who could ferry ye? Who could keep a secret?"

"M'laird," Ewan says with pride, "Fionnphort is nothing *but* sea-faring kin who can keep secrets. What will ye be wanting in Iona?"

Derek tongues a fang. "There's a Irish prize ye must fetch for me there."

"Puling twat's hen-herted." John shakes his head, cocking a thumb toward the cracked mausoleum door and the racked weeping within. "He's fainted five times since we took him and has been sabbing and bubbling like a newly ravished lassie since we got off the boat. Lady Morna's got more battle-mettle than he."

Derek chuckles. "Lady Morna has more battle-mettle than most men I've met. I'll comfort the lad, be sure of that. Here now," he adds, pulling gold coins from his sporran. "Ye two have done grand work. I visited my faither's treasury this morning before I left ye, and I pilfered for ye—"

"Payment? Nay, m'laird, nay!" John exclaims. Both brothers cross their arms across their chests. "Ye are avenging our kin, our family, our honor. We'll not accept payment!"

"Ye two are risking yer lives and yer reputations if the truth of what I am comes out."

"We're yer men now, truth or no, m'laird," Ewan says, stepping forward and gripping Derek's hand. "Ye've destroyed that MacDonald, have ye not?"

"Aye. He admitted he was the one dealt Angus's death blow. I dispatched him and disposed of his remains. He's food for the fishes now, lads, and the wild birds of the air. The eels are fighting over his wee pizzle as we speak."

"The first of the six then. The second waits for ye within," says John. "And the others?"

"In Craignure still, with any luck. Fetch them here tomorrow, the MacGowan brithers, Gillis, and McIntyre. Take the kin ye need to overpower them. MacDonald's death we must conceal from the clans, but his erstwhile henchmen are mere mercenaries. Their lives no decent man would champion and their deaths few would care to avenge."

"And so we shall," says John. "M'laird? Yer father came home today, just as we were leaving for Fionnphort. He rode a cart bearing two coffins. Robbie told us at breakfast that they're wanting to bury Angus in the graveyard here tomorrow."

"Oh, gods. Nay. Tell Morna to delay the burial a day. The thought of my bonnie man's body covered over in that hole outside...it crazes my hert. Nay. Not till we've done to death the last of the six. Tomorrow night, have them here and I'll run them through one by one. Then yer family can lay Angus to rest."

"Yer faither's mightily mournful," says Ewan. "It pains us to see him suffering so, and not to know that ye're—"

"Alive in this new manner? Are ye saying then that mine's a secret my faither should share? Or my mither? They should know what ye two do about what I've become?"

The brothers fall silent, shuffling their feet.

"I might leave Mull, boys, once the last of the killers is dispatched. I don't think I can stay, with every meadow and burn and ben reminding me of all I've lost, with my true luve in his grave. Better, perhaps, that my parents think me dead...."

Inside the crypt, another round of muffled wailing commences. Derek snorts. "My mind's not made up, lads. Perhaps ye're right."

"Ye seem like a man, m'laird," Ewan says. "Not a demon. Not a... night-walker."

"Ye're just chilly to the touch," John adds brightly. "And a wee bit pale."

Derek laughs, rolling his eyes. "And my eyes glow green like a savage beastie's! And I'm nowhere to be found in the daylight. And my thirst.... We'll see, m'lads. We'll see," Derek adds, giving their backs comradely slaps. "Now back to the castle with ye. Leave me, for I'm hungrysome. Tell my sister's what's to occur tomorrow in Craignure and have her delay that burial. Oh, and tell her to have men set pikes upon the battlements. Five of them."

"Pikes?" John says, raising an eyebrow.

"Pikes. Ye'll see."

The brothers nod. "'Twill be done. We'll see ye here tomorrow even, m'laird," says Ewan, moving off, "with the last batch of murtherers. Perhaps then our brither can rest in peace."

"As, perhaps, will I. Though I doubt it."

Derek watches them disappear around a bend. He takes a deep breath of night air before pushing open the heavy door and entering the candlelit crypt. There's a sniffling sack on the floor, hunched into a ball.

"Have ye taken supper yet, my lad?" Derek says gently, bending to touch the outline of a shoulder.

"Uh!" The bundle grunts and jolts, curling even more tightly into itself.

"Nay? Me neither. Ye're Jimmy O'Farrell, are ye not?"

Beneath the sackcloth there's the faint motion of a nod.

"Before he died, Brodie MacDonald said ye were bonnie to the eye. Let's see if he spoke truth." Derek unties the sack and pulls it down around the Irishman's waist.

"Ah! No lie." With a sudden jerk, Derek tumbles his captive out of the bag and onto the floor. As soon as the boy recognizes the Scot standing above him, he curls himself into another terrified ball and begins a shrill wailing.

"Sing out, ye rare nightingale! Aye, lad, I'm back. No grave for me yet," Derek murmurs, studying his captive with greedy focus. Jimmy O'Farrell's in his mid-twenties, with brown eyes, a long black ponytail, a chiseled face, and a closely cropped black beard. His torso and arms are snow-pale and lightly muscled, gleaming with perspiration. His hips are narrow, his long legs pelted with dark hair. He's in exactly the same state MacDonald was the night before: naked, bruised, gagged, and bound hand and foot. His wrists and ankles are chafed raw, gory from hours of panicked struggle, and the scents of his blood and sweat have Derek's fangs already extruding.

"Ah, poor lad. That keening has me close to tears. Ye're grieving yerself, are ye?" Derek bends, cupping the boy's bristly chin and gazing into his eyes.

Jimmy stops wailing. He stares up at Derek and nods, his cheeks streaked with tears.

"Brodie and I had a wee talk yestreen. Let's ye and me do the same."

Jimmy nods.

"And ye won't be shouting for help, will ye? No one's hereabouts to hear ye anyway."

When the Irishman shakes his head, Derek unknots the boy's gag, then frees his ankles but leaves his hands bound. The vampire drags him to his feet. "Come, lad. Let's enjoy the night a bit. What say ye?"

"Gladly. Master."

"Maister, that's right. Well said. Ye're a mannerly lad," Derek sighs. "'Tis a hert-pity ye're so well-favored, so pleasing to the eye, especially bound and nakit as ye are." Grasping Jimmy by his long, flaccid penis, the vampire leads him out of the mausoleum and onto the soft grass of the graveyard.

A crescent moon has risen. For a long moment they stand beneath breeze-ruffled boughs by the low stone wall. Derek gestures toward the loch, one arm resting on the shivering boy's shoulders. "'Tis a luvely night, eh? Stars and sea, bens and braes, the souch of the surf, the gorse glowing like golden candles in the dark. 'Tis a world any man would be vexed to leave. Is it not?"

"Aye, master," the bruised youth whispers.

"Look here, lad," Derek says, turning to point at the two freshly dug graves dappled with moonlight. "Whose are these?"

"I—" The boy's voice cracks. He tries again, this time with shaky success. "Yers...and mine?"

"Close enough. Were ye one who struck me that night in the stones?"

"Aye, master."

"Go on, Jimmy," says Derek, slipping his arm around the youth's waist, leading him closer to the long holes in the earth. "Tell me all."

"I kicked ye in the face," Jimmy mumbles. "Then I stuck ye in the back."

"And Angus?"

"I helped the boys hold him while Brodie stabbed him again and again."

"And why was that?" Derek asks softly. "Why did ye help Brodie MacDonald do such a deed?"

"Because I was nigh to starving, and he paid me well."

"How much, lad?"

"Twenty pounds."

Derek shakes his head. "Twenty pounds?" he groans. "Guid God. Ye slipped a blade in my back for twenty pounds? My man died because ye and yer mates needed money?"

"'Twas more than that. What we saw. Yer buggery. We...ah.... It was...."

"Continue, lad. Speak truth."

"Uggsome and unnatural. Our Lord spoke against such sin."

"I believe ye're wrong in that, Jimmy. And what did ye do on Iona?"

"I prayed in the abbey there. For my soul. For God to forgive me for the sin of killing a man, even a bugger. I'd never killed a man before. I thought I'd murthered ye."

"And did ye find absolution?"

"Nay."

"And do ye ache for absolution now?" Derek strokes the Irishman's short beard.

"Aye, master."

Derek unbuckles his sword and peels off his kilt. He unties the Irishman's bound-back hair. It falls free, black waves cascading around the boy's white shoulders.

Derek runs his fingers through his captive's locks. "Yer hair is so thick and soft, Jimmy. Lie in the grass with me," directs Derek, pulling the naked lad down onto the strip of spring green between the two empty graves. "We'll find yer absolution together."

Whimpering, the young Irishman obeys.

"There's the guid lad. Onto yer belly now. I may do as I please with ye, may I not?"

"Aye, master." Jimmy does as he's told. "D-do as ye p-please."

For several minutes, Derek lies on his side beside Jimmy, silently stroking the white curves of the lad's buttocks, fondling the fingers of his roped hands, and kneading his bunched and quivering shoulders.

"Ye can weep now, lad," Derek says. "I know ye want to. There's always much to weep for in this world."

Jimmy breaks down. Naked, Derek climbs on top of the sobbing captive, spreading his thighs wide with nudging knees. With his fangs, he gnashes his own wrist, then moistens the Irish lad's arse-crack with blood.

"Ye haven't been entered here, have ye?" Derek asks, fingering the tiny aperture in its nest of coarse hair.

"Nay, master!" the boy gasps. "Nay. P-please...don't."

"Sigurd said that feeding and fucking would go hand in hand, that hunger and its satings might save me from sorrow." Wrapping an arm around the boy's torso, Derek prods the boy's hole with his rigid prick, evoking a pained yelp. "Let's see if he was right."

He thrusts hard and fast, embedding his cock deep inside his prisoner's arse. The bound boy shrieks in agony.

"Here's yer will back, lad," Derek snarls, clamping a hand over the Irishman's mouth. "Give yer maister a fight."

Jimmy howls and thrashes; Derek thrusts and pounds. "Aye, scream all ye want," Derek pants. "Ye'll be nothing but silence soon enough." Exposing his fangs, Derek bites Jimmy's throbbing throat.

The two men rock together for many minutes, the hysterical vigor of Jimmy's screams and struggles slowly dwindling. At last the boy passes out; Derek's prick throbs seed into Jimmy's bowels just as he slurps a last mouthful of his blood. Derek removes his fangs, letting his cock slip out. He lies drowsing upon the boy, feeling his limbs spasm, listening to his heart slow and stop.

"Gods, what sweet features, and what a sweet hole," Derek murmurs into Jimmy's disheveled hair. "If only ye hadn't been so greedy for gold. I would have plowed ye and sucked ye many a night, Jimmy O'Farrell. Ye would've made a fine slave."

Rising, the Scot unsheathes his claymore. He runs a finger along its edges before bringing it down on the dead Irishman's neck. The head flies off, rolls across the grass, and bumps into a tombstone.

"One for the rooftop pikes," Derek says, retrieving it by the hair only to toss it through the open crypt door. "Tomorrow night, the rest."

He looks across the moon-spangled loch, toward the groves of forest on the opposite bank, and concentrates, remembering Sigurd's instructions. "Lord of the Beasts," he whispers, furrowing his brow and narrowing his eyes.

For a long time, there's nothing to see or hear but wind in the trees and high clouds racing in from the sea. Then, one by one, dark shapes rise from the land across the loch, making lazy circles over the water. They glide closer, revolving in the sky above Derek's head. With awkward flaps and low hissing they descend.

Derek smiles with satisfaction. The naked Scot moves among them, a hairy-breasted, shaggy-bearded wild man of the woods amidst his savage subjects, touching their bald heads and black feathers with quiet benediction. Then he sits back against the base of a tree and watches as the vultures crowd about the feast he has provided them.

S unset. Derek wakes to find his face pressed into the smooth space between Sigurd's meaty pectorals, the bigger man's arms wrapped around him in a cocoon of woolen tartans. He sits up, uneasy, peering around the cave. Naked, he crawls out of the cozy nest of kilts and over to the entrance. He shoulders aside the great flat stone sealing it, a rock far too heavy for any mortal to budge, then stands, strides to the edge of the ledge, and looks down the mountainside to the castle. From here, he can hear a commotion inside the towerhouse.

"Derek?" Sigurd pads up behind him, wrapping his arms around the Scot.

"Something's wrong, sir," Derek says, listening. "I must be off now. To the mausoleum."

"May I come?"

"Aye, friend," says Derek, heading back into the cave to fetch his weapons and kilt. "But stay in the shadows. I'll call ye if I have need."

Sigurd nods. Within seconds, two huge bats are soaring down the brae toward the distant crypt.

Shawl around her shoulders and lantern in her hand, Morna is pacing in the graveyard and calling his name when Derek strides from the shadows of the trees.

"Thank the Goddess," she exclaims, seizing his arm. "Ye must come to the castle! Faither's men just encountered the McCormick band with their prisoners and have haled them all to the great hall. Faither's going to interrogate them any minute now!"

"Damnation. Sigurd?"

The big Viking steps from the trees. Morna gasps. From the folds of her gown, she draws a dirk. "Who are ye?" she snarls.

"He's a friend, sister. Ye can trust him completely. He's the one who turned me, who saved me from death. He's kin now. Sigurd, my brither...."

"Yes, I know. I'll guard you, m'lady," Sigurd says. "Upon my word."

For a moment, Morna stares up at the blond man with fear and fascination. Then, nodding, she sheaths the blade and turns to her brother.

"Derek, go. There's no time to waste. Do what ye must. We'll be right behind ye."

A green shimmering cascades around the young Scot's body, and then he's vanished. Mouth agape, Morna watches a winged form darker and denser than the surrounding night rise into the air, make a right angle just above the treetops, and dart off toward the castle.

"I must thank ye, sir, for yer help," says Morna, offering Sigurd her trembling hand. "Will ye escort me to Castle Moy? I fear my brither will need our aid."

The torchlit hall is crowded, full of anxious muttering. Laird Lachlan Maclaine, his face pale and strained, sits on an ornately carved chair upon the dais at the hall's far end. Before the dais, a closed coffin rests on a bier. Thirty of Maclaine's men—kinfolk, retainers, and villagers from nearby Lochbuie—line the walls, staring expectantly at the open door.

Now a commotion of voices commences as the unarmed prisoners are prodded into the hall at the end of halberds and swords. John and Ewan McCormick, visages grim, stride in first, then ten of their Fionnphort relatives. Then in come Brodie MacDonald's remaining henchmen, their hands bound before them: Gordon McIntyre, Gerry Gillis, Dugal MacGowan, and Neil MacGowan, all four scroungy men in their thirties. In the excitement, no one notices a pale emerald smoke seeping over the threshold in the prisoners' wake and pooling in a dark corner.

"Be silent!" Laird Maclaine shouts. The clamor of voices ebbs to low muttering, then dies. "John and Ewan McCormick, come forward."

"Gladly, my laird," John says, eyes hard with unspoken rage. The McCormick brothers move to the bottom of the dais, flanking their brother's coffin.

"Who are these men ye and yer kin have kidnapped?"

"McIntyre, Gillis, and the MacGowan brithers! They murthered our brither Angus!" Ewan blurts, resting a palm on the coffin's lid.

"What proof have ye then?"

John and Ewan exchange glances. "We were told...." John begins, then trails off.

"Told by whom?"

"We canna say," Ewan mutters, eyes on the floor.

"Then ye have no proof to support such an accusation." The laird sighs, rubbing his white-bearded chin. "Where were ye taking these men?"

"I tell ye, m'laird, they slew Angus!" John blurts. "Ye must believe us! They stabbed him in the hert! We were given the list of killers! By someone we entirely trust!"

"List? What list? And whom do ye trust?"

"This man's a daft peasant!" McIntyre shouts. "We murthered no one, my laird!"

"They beat us and bound us, Laird Maclaine!" adds Gillis. "We're citizens of Scotland, the same as ye all! They were planning to slay us!"

"Is that true, John and Ewan?" Laird Maclaine says.

Ewan lifts his glance to the laird's face and nods. Lips curled, John takes a deep breath before replying.

"Aye, m'laird!" John hisses, bringing his fist down on the coffin lid with a bang. "We were taking them to the mausoleum as we were told. They're scum; they're assassins! At their hands yer son fell as well!"

"My son?" Laird Maclaine gasps. "Is this true?"

"Nay! Oh, nay!" Gillis shouts. "Nay! We never met yer son, m'laird! Why would we do such a deed?"

"For money, ye fucking dog!" John shouts, turning toward Gillis, fists clenched. Ewan grips John's arm, muttering, "Easy, brither."

"For Brodie MacDonald's money!" John continues. "Ye attacked Angus McCormick and Derek Maclaine because Brodie MacDonald paid ye to!"

"Ye're a liar," Gillis retorts, licking his lips. "We know no Brodie MacDonald."

"Ye're the liar, not I! Ye all deserve to rot! We'll slaughter ye yet!"

"Ye see, my laird!" Gillis whines over the renewed babble of voices filling the hall. "They indeed meant to slay us! They're the murtherers, not we!"

Lachlan Maclaine rubs his brow and slumps back into his chair. "My son's body has yet to be found. And there's no proof these men slew Angus McCormick. Why did ye brithers think ye had the right to tak the law into yer own hands? I'm the laird here, not ye."

"True enough," cries John. "But another laird, even as mighty as ye, a laird we luve like our fallen brither, we serve him now, and he—"

"Enough, John," Ewan whispers, tugging on his brother's arm. "Enough now. Say no more."

"Open the coffin, my laird!" John continues. "'Tis said that a murthered man's wounds bleed anew in the presence of his killers. Let's see if—"

"Enough!" Unsteadily, Laird Maclaine rises. "There's guilt here. I can smell it. Guards, put all these men in chains. On the morrow we'll sort out what—"

"Nay, Faither, I'll have my justice tonight."

The room falls silent for a split-second before a hubbub erupts even worse than before. Derek Maclaine—dirty, unkempt, and shirtless, barefoot in muddy great kilt, claymore buckled to his hip—has stepped from the shadows. In the dim light of the great hall, his eyes gleam green. Instinctively, men all about him back away. Brodie's henchmen stare speechlessly. Thighs quivering, they move together in a tight circle toward the wall.

"Oh, Jesus, how can it be?" McIntyre gasps.

"'Tis a specter. 'Tis a demon," Gillis wheezes.

The MacGowan brothers are too startled to speak. They simply stand there, slack-jawed, eyes bugging out.

"M'laird!" John cries, smiling with relief.

"Here's our proof!" Ewan points at Derek as the young laird moves up the aisle. The stunned retainers part before him as the sea does before a prow.

"Oh, thank the guid God!" Lachlan Maclaine groans. He totters, then sits heavily back in the great chair. "Son! Ye're alive!"

"I am, sir. And I'm here to accuse these men of the murther of Angus McCormick," Derek says hoarsely, stroking the side of the coffin. "John and Ewan were right. I was there that night in the standing stones. They stabbed Angus to death and wounded me most sorely."

"Wounded? But...."

"A healer found me in time. So which of ye knifed me in the ribs, lads?" Derek turns toward the quaking clutch of men and smiles. He catches Dugal MacGowan's eyes and lifts an eyebrow. "Which one?"

Dugal shudders, the tip of his tongue protruding from his open mouth. He gives his head a brisk toss, as if he were trying to shake off sleep. "Gillis did it."

"Goddamn ye, Dugal!" Gillis shrieks. With bound hands, he punches Dugal in the side.

Dugal coughs and staggers. "Gillis did it," he repeats, eyes wide, voice gentle. "I kicked ye in the belly, and Jimmy got ye in the back, but 'twas Gillis stuck ye in the ribs. The bluid, the bluid.... We knew that'd be the end of ye. But somehow ye're here again."

"And Angus?" Derek purrs. "Why don't ye tell us about Angus, my docile halfwit?"

"Ah, we all held him." Dugal smiles blankly. "Mightily strang he was; bellowed like an ox. Brodie pierced the bugger like a Christmas haggis. Left him full of holes, in the sloughy mud his bluid made."

"And who paid ye to do this?" Derek asks.

"Brodie MacDonald."

"Shut up, Dugal," McIntyre rasps.

Lachlan Maclaine tries to stand and fails. Instead, he leans forward in his chair, lips quivering, and points a finger at Gillis. "Man, is this true?"

"Aye, damn ye!" Gillis blurts, glaring at Derek. "This son of yers by all rights should be dead."

"And yet he's not, ye vile toad," Morna says, stepping inside the hall. "Though ye shall be soon enough."

"Daughter, this is no place for women," Lachlan mutters before returning his attention to Gillis. "Ye admit to slaying this man in the coffin here? Angus McCormick?"

"Aye! And would ye know why?"

"We've heard the reason," Derek snaps. "Brodie MacDonald's money."

"More than that!" Gillis takes a step forward. "Yer grandson here is a sodomite!"

The room explodes with shouts of confusion and outrage. Derek's eyes glitter; deep in his throat a low growl is gathering. He takes a step toward Gillis; Gillis takes a step back, bumping into the wall.

"A sodomite, Laird Maclaine!" Gillis continues, voice shaking. "Foul! Unnatural! Against the laws of God and man! Does not such willful sin deserve death?"

"What are ye saying?" Lachlan has found his feet and sways, one hand clutching the arm of his chair.

"He and Angus McCormick! The things we saw them do together! Is it not so, McIntyre?"

"Aye." McIntyre wipes his mouth, grimaces, and nods. "Yer son pleasured McCormick...with his mouth. A gruesome sight! Then he raised his own legs in the air. McCormick took him in the arse like a street-slut! We punished them as God willed us to do. Leviticus says, 'Thou shalt not lie with mankind—'"

"Derek?" the aged laird groans. "Tell me...tell me that this...."

"This can't be yer son!" Gillis blurts, jabbing a finger in Derek's direction. "No man could live after.... We left him weltering in his own bluid! This is no human being! 'Tis a demon!"

"Shut up, man! Derek, son, answer me."

"It is true, faither," Derek replies, eyes burning. "Angus and I were luvers."

"Oh, God," Lachlan whimpers, burying his face in his hands. "Son, why would ye say such a thing?"

"Because 'tis true. We luved each other the way ye and Mither have luved. And this rubbish slaughtered him. I demand justice, sir. I may be a sodomite, but I am still yer son. Will ye give me justice?"

"I.... Nay!" Lachlan lifts his face from his hands, glaring at Derek. "How could ye do this to me? To yer mither? To our name? How could ye...." He points a shaking forefinger. "Ye're not some soft fop, some London jessie! Ye're a Highland warrior! A man of Mull! From the finest bluid in the Western Isles! I've seen ye in battle! No one's a better swordsman than ye! How could ye lie with...surrender yer body to...."

"Faither!" Morna shouts from the back of the room. "Derek's kin! How can ye—"

"Silent, daughter! Oh, God, how could ye have shamed us so? First yer sister, to bring home a bastard! And now.... No! Sodomy is a crime! As foul as murther! Perhaps ye are a demon! No son of mine would do the things that ye.... Ye deserve no justice I can give!"

"Then I'll tak it for myself."

Before anyone human in the room can move, Derek's great claymore is unsheathed, and the vampire is streaking toward the clot of trembling foes. He gashes Gillis's throat with his sharp fangs, slurping a great draught of blood, then runs the shrieking man through before tossing him aside.

McIntyre is next: another flash of sharp white teeth, the carotid torn open, the sharp blade shoved between ribs, then into guts, the thump of a body—alive one minute, dead the next—against the stone floor.

It's all happened so fast that the room's dead silent yet, save for a disbelieving gasp here and there. Now Derek lifts the dripping sword again. It sings as it arcs, severing Gillis's neckbones, then McIntyre's, evoking great spouts of blood. Derek kicks the heads one by one across the floor. One bumps against the base of the bier, the other against the bottom of the dais.

"Next?" Derek says, giving the cowering MacGowans a broad smile. He licks his bloodstained lips and curls a finger, beckoning.

The long moment of silent shock freezing the room shatters. Neil MacGowan sobs, his brother Dugal emits a shrill scream, and pandemonium ensues. The braver men are shouting, drawing swords, their faces blanched, their lips trembling. The less courageous are crying "monster," crying "demon," and racing for the door. On the dais, Lachlan Maclaine clutches his chest and passes out.

Flanked by John and Ewan, Derek crouches before Angus's coffin, great fangs exposed, brandishing his sword and snarling like an enraged bear. A semicircle of terrified men wavers before him, while, behind their massed ranks, the MacGowan brothers scurry out in the confusion. When massive Sigurd materializes as if from nowhere at Derek's elbow, the armed men shout and scatter at his sudden appearance, leaving the torchlit hall to the vampires, the McCormick brothers, and the two decapitated corpses at their feet.

Sigurd chuckles. "You, my handsome student, are fond of drama, are you not? That was quite a scene."

"Guid God, m'laird," John croaks. He and Ewan lean against their brother's casket, staring at the pools of fresh blood and trying to catch their breaths.

Derek climbs the dais and bends over his father. Finding him senseless but still breathing, Derek heaves a long sigh. Descending, he gives the coffin a fond stroke, then heads purposefully toward the door. "Come, lads."

In the hallway, Derek lifts his head and snuffles the air. "Robbie! Allan!"

"Here, m'laird." Robbie MacAvoy steps out of the shadows, followed by Allan Black.

"Our task's not yet done, lads. Come here and give us some of yer youth. Give us strength for what we must do."

"With pleasure, laird." Robbie obeys, shuffling forward. Derek violently rips open the boy's shirt, tonguing a nipple before sinking his teeth into the dazed boy's hair-dusted breast.

"Join me, sir," Derek mutters in between mouthfuls. Sigurd embraces Robbie from behind. Bending, he pierces Robbie's neck. John and

Ewan stand by, staring at the eldritch scene, swallowing hard. Allan watches, rugged face bearing a vague smile.

"Off, Derek!" Sigurd grunts after a good minute of Robbie's sighing and the vampires' eager sucking. "Don't end him."

Derek nods, easing the half-conscious boy to the floor. "Allan?"

The brawny guard approaches, opening his shirt and tugging it off. In a flash, the vampires are on him, Derek puncturing his neck, Sigurd his bare shoulder. Soon Allan's eyes roll back in his head in a dead faint. Derek lowers him to the floor beside Robbie.

"A pretty pair. Now for the last two murtherers," Derek says, wiping his mouth.

"One of them I have." Morna appears around a corner, face flushed, long dirk gleaming in her hand. She smiles proudly. "One MacGowan must have freed his hands, for I saw him fleeing the courtyard on a stolen horse. But the other, the one ye entranced...."

The vampires and the McCormicks follow her down the hall. She points to the floor. There's a hatch in the stones, beneath which rises an agonized wailing.

"Ah! The pit-prison!" exclaims Derek. "Well done!"

She flicks a finger over the tip of the dirk. "He tried to shove me aside, as he and his brither were escaping the hall. 'Out of my way, ye slut,' he said."

"Ill advised." Derek snickers.

"I think he broke his leg in the fall to the floor. He sounds to be in great pain," replies Morna, sheathing her weapon.

"And I am his quietus," Derek says, opening the hatch and dropping into the lightless pit. There's a short yelp, a slurping sound, the ring of a blade pulled from its scabbard, the chunking sound of metal meeting flesh. Within a minute, Derek appears, carrying Dugal's head.

"Gentlemen, the pikes? On the battlements. McIntyre and Gillis too. O'Farrell's as well. I left his in the mausoleum. Would ye, please?" He lifts the dripping head by the hair, as if in offering.

John takes it with a grimace. "Gladly, m'laird."

"I'll have one more for ye soon enough. I'm thinking, after all that was revealed here today, that a show of bloody force, along with rumors of a vengeful demon haunting the castle grounds, will be handy in keeping order and holding power. No one will be crossing the Maclaines for long years, if I can help it."

N eil MacGowan is riding hard down the road skirting the water, heading for the village of Lochbuie, there at the head of the loch, less than half a mile distant. He can see the warm glow of windows, and the tiny chapel where salvation surely waits. Surely no demon can enter the house of God.

He's nearly to the village now. He can even smell the smoke of hearths, the yeasty smell of bread baking. Eagerly, Neil bends over his mount's neck, digging his heels into the animal's side, urging it to go faster, when there's a whirring of wings about his head. Suddenly the silhouette of a man, eyes glowing like green fireflies, appears in the moonlit road just ahead.

Neil jerks the reins. His steed rears, unseating him. He hits the ground hard, his breath knocked out of him. Something in his side feels broken. He scrambles to his feet nonetheless, moving as fast as he can toward the chapel. Behind him, he can hear deep laughter, and the first growl of thunder on the horizon.

Now May moonlight fades and vanishes as clouds teem over the sky. Neil limps into the chapel's grassy yard, past clumps of bluebells growing thick at the bases of the trees. Three crosses adorn the stone face of the tiny, steep-roofed building; the arched windows are bright with lamplight. He seizes the door handle, sighing with relief when he finds it unlocked. He dashes inside, slamming the door behind him, leaning back against the wood to catch his breath.

At the far end of the room, staring at Neil with alarm, stands an old man in ecclesiastical robes. He's got a bouquet of spring flowers in his arms, one of several he's been placing around the room for tomorrow's service. Candles glow here and there upon the altar and in the apse.

"Are ye the priest?" Neil gasps.

"I am," replies the old man, his voice high and startled. "I'm Faither Denis MacFadden."

"Give me sanctuary, I beg ye! Can this door be locked?"

"Aye. But why?"

"There's a horror after me!" Neil wails. "A villain! Lock the door!"

The old man drops the bouquet on the altar, pulls a key ring from his robe, and scuttles down the nave. "A villain?" he says, palsied hands fumbling for the correct key.

"Aye! He means to finish me! Hurry! He's right outside!"

"Laird Jesus!" The priest turns the key in the lock with a click before turning to the shaking MacGowan. "There. Ye're safe. No evil dare enter here."

"Are ye sure, Faither? He was right on my heels! He's not a man! He's a demon, a night spirit!"

"A demon, my son? What do ye mean?"

There's a flash of lightning, a crack of thunder. Both men jump. Rain begins tapping the chapel's wooden roof. Neil's about to reply when they hear a clawing sound against the door, then a low chuckle reverberating outside.

"Oh, God!" Neil shrieks, slamming his shoulder against the door. "It's him! Help me!"

The door rattles. Both men throw their weight against it. The clawing grows louder, then abruptly ceases.

Silence falls, broken only by Neil's pants. "Him? Who d'ye mean?" the priest whispers at last.

"The demon! Derek Maclaine! He's risen from the dead!"

"The laird's son? But how—? Hasn't he been missing for days?"

"My mates and I, we stabbed him to death! But he's returned!"

"Ye stabbed Laird Maclaine's son? Were ye the ones who slew Angus McCormick then?"

"Aye, God help me."

"In Jesus' name, why? Angus was a clansman of mine! He was a kind boy, a—"

A soft thudding now, behind them. The men turn. Dark shapes outside are bumping against the Gothic window over the altar. "Dear Lord, what are they?" the priest croaks. "Some huge winged—"

Thumping commences against the side windows now. Glass shatters, and suddenly the room is full of owls. Both men scream as the taloned birds swoop about their heads, plucking at their hair and eyes.

The old priest falls to his knees, crawling beneath a pew. Neil flails his arms at the birds, then covers his face with his hands, keening.

The door rattles again, then explodes. Derek Maclaine stands in the doorway, shaking shards of wood off his forearms and rubbing his knuckles. About his feet, shadowy forms slither in.

"Ye're the last, Neil MacGowan," Derek says. "Ye gave me a merry chase indeed."

Neil emits another screech of fear. Batting away owl-claws, he staggers up the nave to cower behind the altar.

Striding forward, Derek seizes the old priest's hand and pulls him to his feet.

"L-laird Maclaine?" the priest stutters, staring up into the stern face and glowing eyes of the vampire.

"Aye, Faither MacFadden," Derek sighs. "I have business here." He curls his upper lip, exposing a fang. "Ye'd best go home now. Posthaste."

"Guid God!" exclaims the cowering priest. "Is it true ye've become a demon, my son?"

"In a manner of speaking."

The old man pulls from his robe the wooden crucifix hanging around his neck and shakily brandishes it. "H-hie thee hence then. God commands ye!"

Derek regards the cross with bemusement. He taps it with a tentative forefinger. "Posthaste, I said, Faither," he says gently, slipping the crucifix back into the priest's robes and nudging him toward the wreckage of the door. "And Faither?"

"Y-yes?"

"Pray for me. And for Angus McCormick."

"Aye. Gladly," says Father Denis, giving Derek one backward glance before stumbling out into the rain as fast as his aged legs can carry him.

"MacGowan, where are ye?" Derek turns, scanning the room. From a windowsill, he lifts a burning taper, only to apply the flame to the edge of a tapestry. The cloth smolders, as if trying to make up its mind, then flame shudders through it.

"MacGowan?" Derek says again, watching the fire climb higher, finally to lap at the wooden ceiling.

MacGowan responds this time, with a shriek of pain. He staggers from behind the altar, grasping his right ankle, then falling to his knees. There's a low hissing, then he screams again, as tiny fangs sink into his calf.

"Ye've met my adders then. Well done, faithful ones, but now ye all must leave. I'll not have ye burn." As Derek, humming, applies another candle to another tapestry, the summoned shapes of feather and scale depart, slithering over the shards of door or winging silently out the broken windows from whence they came.

Flames have caught the dry timbers of the roof now; the chapel's filling with smoke. Neil slumps to the door, breaths coming short and shallow. Derek stands over him.

"Nay. Oh God. Please," the prone man whines.

"We're done," Derek whispers. "We're done." Drawing his great claymore, he plunges it into MacGowan's panting side, one, twice, three times. He licks blood from the blade before severing the groaning man's head with one swing.

Carrying the head by its greasy hair, Derek, his claymore sheathed, leaves the flaming church. The rain is cool on the young vampire's burning brow. He savors the feeling for a long moment before raising a hand. The storm disperses, and now the chapel's roof begins to burn faster. Somewhere an alarm bell sounds. Derek steps into the deeper shadows with his prize, watching the villagers' noisy and ineffectual attempts to douse the blaze, watching the three crosses adorning the chapel's façade char and crumble. He stretches a palm out toward the heat, as if he were human again, luxuriating with Angus beside a winter hearth. After the roof's collapsed, after three of the blackened stone walls have fallen and the villagers have given up, only then does Derek turn his back on the great heap of flickering embers and smoldering ash. Swinging Neil MacGowan's head, he strolls along the water toward Castle Moy.

Soon the fifth head has joined the other four on the windy battlements. Below, in the great hall, Derek sits in the dark on the steps of the dais, studying his lover's coffin. When the sky starts to lighten with approaching dawn, he stands, dries his cheeks with his hairy forearm, and raises the lid. He gazes down at the gray and angry face, still handsome despite death's slow erosion. He rests a hand on the hard, unbreathing breast. Bending, he kisses the corpse's brow and lips before closing the coffin and slowly dissolving into mist.

Midnight, the evening after the chapel fire. The parapet of the castle is gusty, as usual, and for once empty of guards. The national flag of Scotland, a white St. Andrew's cross on a blue background, whips loudly against a backdrop of scudding clouds. The heads of Angus's murderers, tongues lolling, are already in ragged shape, and eyeless, after the constant attentions of ravens. Derek moves from head to moonlit head, speaking their names. "Jimmy O'Farrell. Gerry Gillis. Gordon McIntyre. Dugal MacGowan. Neil MacGowan." Derek gazes out toward the open ocean. "And Brodie MacDonald, may ye burn in hell's foul pits till seas dry up and stars fall like cinders."

For a good hour, the vampire walks the battlements—looking out over the loch, over the braes and up to the heights of Ben Buie, toward the mausoleum and the tree-veiled cemetery containing the freshly filled grave he cannot bear to see—silently saying his farewells.

One AM. Laird and Lady Maclaine are both sunk deep in restless, nightmare-frought sleep when a broad-shouldered shadow takes slow shape just inside their window. Derek settles into a soft chair, watching their slumber, studying the crosses prominently displayed about the room, protection against the decapitating, fanged monster their only son has become. That monster buries his face in his hands, grits his teeth, and kneads his forehead. With his thumbs, he flicks bloody tears from his eyes before finally rising. He touches his mother's hand ever so softly, then shimmers and fades into mist, an agitated green that snakes under the door and down the hall.

Two AM. Morna Maclaine wakes abruptly. Her brother is standing over her bed.

"They buried Angus today?" Derek says dully.

"Yes, brither. I'm so sorry. All I can say is that ye've avenged his death most grandly."

"Grandly indeed. I've leaving soon, sister," Derek says. "With my true luve in his grave, I canna stay in a place where all reminds me of him."

She sits up, nodding. "Perhaps 'twould be best."

"What have ye to tell me? I can see in yer face a deeper sadness than before."

Morna's face contorts with disgust. "Faither, the old fool, despite his fragile health, won't stop raving to any and all who'll listen. He's denounced ye for a devil. He's blamed ye for the chapel fire and promised the good folks of Lochbuie that he'll have his men hunt ye down and slay ye. Mither is too addled with grief to eat or speak. I fear for her sanity, brither."

Derek nods. "Even more reasons to leave Mull. I plan to tak John and Ewan with me. Since they stood by me in the great hall the other night, I have them in hiding, lest they be accused of witchcraft or consorting with demons. I'll need them to watch over me during the day."

"And where will ye go?"

"Glasgow first. I plan to tak passage to America. Philadelphia, then Virginia, I think. Scotland's too full of memories. And John and Ewan are eager to start new lives in a country with such promise. Thanks to me, thanks to their devotion to me, there's nothing left for them here."

"And will ye ever return, brither? To see me? To see yer nephew?" Morna says, indicating the small bed in the corner, with her child sleeping upon it.

"We'll see. Perhaps, once I'm settled in Virginia, ye might visit?"

"Virginia? By the guid Goddess! Well, I might. Will ye write?"

"Most certainly," Derek says, taking her hand. The siblings embrace, steeling themselves for the separation both know is necessary. "But first I must ask yer approval for a certain frolic I plan to savor before leaving Scotland."

Three AM. Just inside the entrance to Moy Castle, burly guard Allan Black, off duty at last, is snoring loudly. Stripped to the waist and barefoot beneath a light blanket, he's curled up like a child upon his tiny bed. He jerks awake to find a hand clamped over his mouth and a strong arm pinning his own arms to his sides. He musters a few seconds of frightened struggle before a familiar voice sounds in his ear, soothing him. Nodding, he submits. Fingers run through his black beard, fondle his fur-matted breast, pull open his rumpled kilt and grip his already stiffened sex. He lies back, entirely acquiescent, allowing his night-visitor to take his will.

A mouth at his ear first, gently whispering directives, then at his throat, teeth piercing, lips sucking for dreamy minutes before shifting to his sex. Soon, Allan's snoring again, smiling in his sleep, his big body made lighter by several stolen ounces of blood and semen.

Three forty-five AM. Robbie MacAvoy jolts up and gazes dazedly around. In the corner, the green glow of eyes. There's his master, sitting back in a chair, thighs spread, hands folded behind his head, filling the room with silent commands.

Robbie nods. He peels off his nightclothes, falls onto his hands and knees, crawls across the floor, and kneels before his master. When the vampire nods, Robbie lifts Derek's kilt. Gripping Derek's fuzzy thighs, Robbie nuzzles and laps his master's genitals, slow and passionate attentions full of saliva and reverence. He licks dew off the taut head, then takes the thick prick into his mouth, moving his lips tightly up and down the shaft while kneading the heavy balls. Derek lies back and sighs, closes his eyes, and thrusts ever so slowly into his thrall's adoring mouth. Robbie, trembling with delight, takes his time. When, finally, with a hoarse groan his master spurts onto his tongue, Robbie gulps the syrupy seed down with a satisfied sigh.

"I will miss ye, my lad," Derek murmurs, tousling the boy's hair and wiping drool off his chin. He lifts Robbie into his arms.

"Don't leave, m'laird. Don't leave." The lad huddles on his master's lap, arms draped around his shoulders. "How can we continue here without ye?"

"Shush, boy. Allan will tak fine care of ye, just as Angus did me." Derek cradles him, savoring the boy's heat for a lengthy moment before tenderly puncturing his neck.

Four thirty AM, less than an hour before dawn. The water-soaked ruins of the chapel still smoke, an acrid stink that pervades the village of Lochbuie. After last night's slaughter in the castle and the flood of subsequent rumors, every cottage window prominently displays a cross, every cottage door is barred.

The streets are unpeopled at this early hour. Were anyone awake, he might see a wild-looking man with disheveled hair and tangled beard, dressed in a bloodstained, mud-smeared great kilt, picking through the blackened timbers and heaps of ash. The man bends, plucks charred human bones from the wreckage, and drops them into a coarsely woven sack. Then he strides down to the beach in the pre-dawn gray, onto the rocky shingle, and flings the bones one by one into the misty waters of Loch Buie. Done, the man sits on broken boulders by the water, hands clenched on his knees, watching the eastern sky grow pink. Only when the mountaintop is edged with the radiant gold of the rising sun does he heave a deep groan and streak off into the woods.

"Luver?"

Derek sits up, rubbing his eyes. He's naked, sleeping beside Sigurd in the cave, in their customary nest of moist tartans. He brushes black bangs from his eyes and stares. Angus McCormick, naked as well, his hairy breast and pale sides torn with gory wounds, is sitting cross-legged at Derek's feet. His bearded face, half-veiled with shaggy locks, is creased with a wide smile.

"Ah, by the gods," Derek gasps. "Is it ye then? Truly?"

"Truly," says Angus, opening his arms.

Derek leaps. The two men's bodies press together, then their mouths. Derek pulls away, disbelieving, licking his lips, clutching his lost lover by his wide shoulders. "Are ye truly here, my man? Or—?"

"'Tis but a dream, aye. But the dreams of yer kind are more solid than most. Tak yer pleasure, *draugr*." Angus lies back, stretches his arms above his head and closes his eyes. "Kiss my clay-cold lips, for we don't have much time. 'Tis nearly sunset, when ye must wake."

Derek, frantic, flings himself atop Angus. Growling with blood-hunger and desire, he kisses and chews Angus's bruised lips. He sinks his fangs into his neck, into his thick-muscled chest. He kisses his wounds and laps the oozing blood there. He sucks and fang-pierces his lover's fat cock till Angus's hands are clutching his head and Angus's hips are pumping his face and his mouth's flooding with the mingled wealth of blood and semen.

"Ah, that was glorious. Glorious as I remember," Angus says, pulling Derek up to lie upon him. "Yer lips, m'laird, have quite the grip."

Derek, drowsy, awash with contentment, his black beard bedewed with a few spilled drops of Angus's seed, rests his head on his lover's shoulder.

"I would have it this way forever," Derek whispers, swirling Angus's chest fur with a forefinger.

"And I as well. But our fates dictate something different," sighs Angus, stroking Derek's dirty locks. "Ye have many a bonnie bruit to luve yet."

"I'll never luve another man like I luve ye, Angus."

"No, ye shan't. Ye'll luve different. It'll be luve nonetheless."

"I can't imagine luve, only hate. They're dead, my man. The Bible-poisoned curs who murthered ye. Every snake's-son one of 'em. I'd like to scour the earth for their pious kind and dispatch the dogs, one by one."

"I know, Derek. Ye're my fierce avenger and my strappin warrior and my Highland barbarian, and ye have long years to wreak yer will on foes like that. For my sake, dinna think again the thoughts ye had this morning. When ye waited for the sun to burn ye."

"What have I to live for, now that ye're avenged? I'm so alone. I—"

"Daftie! Live for dreams like this. For the years of memories we made together. For starlight and moonlight and the life-bluid and loin-seed of comely men, for all yer sharpened senses can tak in. Most men are dull blades, rusting in corners; ye're newly honed, keen-sharp, and glittering! 'Tis not a gift to be thrown away. Ye promise me not to throw it away?"

"I do. I do," Derek mutters, nuzzling Angus's beard.

"Mak yerself content, my luve, in this new life ye have. And ye aren't alone. Ye have a fine friend and teacher, that colossal Viking snoozling there, and my brithers, ready to follow ye into that far wilderness."

"But it's ye I want, not them."

"I know, luver, I know. Yer path may yet wend itself back to me."

"Aye?"

"Aye. In some future time, perhaps, when the Old Ones choose at last to call ye away. After many adventures, many new sorrows and triumphs, we'll meet again in the Summerlands."

"And if I had died? If I had refused Sigurd's offer? If I'd chosen to perish rather than live on in this strange manner to avenge yer death, would we be together now? Did I make the wrong choice? Hate instead of luve?"

Angus wraps his big arms around Derek and squeezes him till he gasps.

"I know ye better than anyone on earth or in the afterlife, save for yer sister! Ye hated *because* ye loved! For me to die unavenged? Ye'd be pacing by my side in the Summerlands, mouth frothy with regret and outraged pride, filling eternity with yer surly complaints! Ye made the only choice Derek Maclaine could make!" Angus tousles Derek's hair and kisses him on the nose. "Now I must away. Ye know as well as I that the sun's sinking into the sea and ye must rise."

"Don't leave me, man. I'm begging ye!" Derek sobs. The hard-muscled frame beneath him is softening, sinking into the earth.

Derek wakes, his face buried in fringy softness like a bed of moss. Then something hard nudges his lips. It's Sigurd's prick, its pink tip already dripping with arousal. At the same time, arms circle his waist and a wet sheath slides over his own cock: Sigurd's mouth.

"You forget I can read your thoughts, boy," Sigurd mumbles around Derek's rigid column of flesh. "I know your plans. We must go our separate ways for now, for I'm not willing to leave Scotland just yet. I've taught you much of what you need to know. Let's feed on each other one more time ere you depart."

Derek's answer is to thrust his cock savagely down Sigurd's throat and envelope Sigurd's sex with his mouth, sucking hungrily. For half the night, the two vampires rock together, grappling and slurping, murmuring their sticky farewells.

I t's raining softly, the afternoon of the following day, as a small group of Scots says their goodbyes in the muddy yard of a cottage on the outskirts of Craignure.

"We'll tak good care of him, m'lady," says John McCormick, gripping the reins and cocking his hat against the drizzle. "He avenged our brither, just as he promised. We'll do anything for him now."

John and Ewan are sitting on the seat of a horse-drawn cart, wrapped in newly purchased coats. In the back, beneath a blanket, is their travel gear, tucked in around a long wooden crate. "We sail from Glasgow in three days' time," adds John.

Morna Maclaine reaches up, taking John's hand, then Ewan's. "Guid luck, lads, and thanks. I hear it's wild in Virginia. Frightful natives lurking in the trees."

"Ah!" Ewan flexes an arm. "We're more than a match for 'em. And if not...." He turns in the seat and taps the blanket-covered crate in the back.

Morna smiles. "Aye. Ye have quite the weapon there. Have ye enough money?"

"Aye, m'lady," Ewan replies, rubbing the fabric of his coat's collar. "Yer brither took a bag of items from yer faither's treasury, and he's spoken of a source of wealth waiting for him in Glasgow. A bank, I think?"

Morna laughs liltingly. "I know that bank. Aye."

Robbie MacAvoy and Allan Black step forward now. "Here's some food for ye," Robbie says. "Oakcakes and crowdie cheese. Some cold partridge. Some pork pies."

"And some whisky from Tobermory," adds Allan, handing up two bottles. "One for ye two, and one for the laird's son. If he still has a taste for it."

"I suspect he does." Morna pats her palm against the lid of the crate. "Off with ye," she says sternly, blue eyes moist. "Or ye might miss the ferry."

John flicks the reins and the horses clop forward. The cart heads down the hill, toward the harbor. The three remaining watch them go.

"Back to Castle Moy, lads," Morna says, once the cart's disappeared among the streets of the harbor town. Allan steps forward, helping her mount. "Will ye two tak my son fishing this afternoon? He's missing his uncle badly and could do with some recreation."

"Gladly, Lady Morna," Allan says. He takes Robbie's hand and gives it a warm squeeze before the two men mount and follow their lady down the slope and onto the narrow road leading to Lochbuie.

Two nights after Derek's departure from Mull, Morna Maclaine's estranged husband, wealthy Glaswegian merchant Charles King, is lolling drunkenly in his carriage, fiddling with his waxed moustache and waiting for a tardy servant to drive him to his favorite bawdy house, when the carriage door opens and a well-groomed man with a pony-tail and closely cropped black beard steps inside. The merchant emits a yelp of surprise, then falls silent, ready to receive instruction.

Three nights after his departure from Mull, Derek stands in the rain on a ship's lamplit deck in Glasgow Harbor. The young vampire's full and warm after a few cozy moments in his cabin with a blond-bearded steward who'd come to offer him tea. He's dressed neatly, in black boots, clean kilt, gray cloak, and jabot. The dock below is loud with longshoreman loading goods and traveling trunks. The water's vague and choppy beneath a thick fog that has delayed the ship's departure for hours and is only now dispersing.

"M'laird?" John nudges Derek's elbow. "Was this what ye wanted?"

Derek nods, taking the newspaper John offers him. Grinning, he reads the headline out loud—"Local Merchant Slain! Robbery! De-fenestration!"—before slipping the paper into an inner pocket of his cloak.

Derek chuckles. "'Defenestration.' 'Tis a delicious word indeed."

"King? Lady Morna's honkin eejit of a husband? Is this how we're traveling in such comfort then? Our cabins are bonnie, and the beds so soft!"

"Aye. The greedy bin-raider finally found a purpose. He should never have threatened my sister." Pulling a leather purse from his sporran, he hands it to John. "Ye'll need this during the days. 'Tis a long jour-ney to America."

John clears his throat. "Sir, will ye need...? If it's needed, well, Ewan and I have talked, and we...if ye need to drink during the voyage...."

Derek gives John's shoulder a brotherly clap. "Ye boys are big-herted as yer brither was! Nay, nay, bless ye, that shan't be necessary. Several handsome lads on this vessel will do nicely for seafaring supping. In fact, I've already introduced myself to one of 'em. Worry not; I shan't do any of them any lasting harm."

John nods. The two men stroll the deck, observing the noisy preparations for departure. Having reached the prow, they stand unspeaking, watching fog rise over the River Clyde.

"Cast off!" a gruff voice shouts. Chains rattle; hawsers are released. The *Persephone* slips from its moorings, hesitates, then, caught in the river's stream, slides away from the dock.

"I wish Angus were with us," John says wistfully, as the shore recedes.

"I wish the same," replies Derek, twisting the golden ring on his finger, then raising his head, as if listening to something more than the swirl of water about the prow below. "Why don't ye join Ewan below and share some supper? I'll join ye in a bit and we'll break open that bottle of whisky."

"Yes, m'laird." John moves away, then pauses. "I think I know how terribly ye miss him. Ye'll see. There's life yet for all three of us. A new home." John gives Derek's arm a sympathetic squeeze before disappearing down the steep flight of stairs leading below.

Derek strides aft. Among the far folks still lining the docks he can make out a familiar face and form, a very tall man with long blond hair and a braided beard. The man smiles, raises his hand and waves. Derek does the same. Then he returns to the prow, gazing out over the black waters as the *Persephone* moves rapidly down the river, toward the Firth of Clyde and, beyond that, the open ocean.

The Last
Crumbs of
Sacher Torte

The storm gives no sign of slackening. Autumnal, it shushes over the roof of the *Theseustempel* and trickles down the fluted columns. I stand on the dark porch, in this anomalous Austrian replica of a Greek temple, take deep breaths of wet breeze cutting across the green sward of the *Volksgarten*, and wait for the appointed time, my final rendezvous with Friedrich.

Poor boy, destitute anthropologist, he has made this year of 1897 delectable, playing smooth golden Apollo to my dark hairy Dionysus. The least I can do—on this, our last night together—is treat him to a slew of bodily luxuries he could never otherwise afford. An evening at the Hotel Sacher is his going-away gift.

I can feel him, only blocks away. He's enjoying a fine feast of boiled beef and vegetables, what the locals call *Tafelspitz*, in the grand dining room. He's admiring the walls of polished wood, the high ceilings, the heavy drapery, the candlelit mirrors and gilt. His face is flushed with several glasses of *Grüner Veltliner*; he's drunk and happy; he's looking forward to sharing dessert with me later in the elegant suite my funds have paid for.

I am very hungry. It is an appetite I have been husbanding for tonight's meeting. Since sunset, two young men I in other circumstances would have seized, dragged into the temple, and fed upon—I like my food musky, strongly built, and bearded—have passed through the *Volksgarten*, but I've abstained. Friedrich has meant a great deal to me for many months; tonight is too special to adulterate with insignificant snacks.

The wind picks up, dead leaves scuttle across the temple's steps, and Friedrich calls for me now in his sweet supplicant's tone, a voice only I can discern. He's in his room, done with dinner; the dessert I ordered has been delivered; he has found my written instructions and obeyed them. All is ready.

I shift in the shadows of the *Theseustempel*, then flit between the columns and up into November rain. My last night here, so I can't resist a giddy swooping about the city's lofty landmarks: the spire of St. Stephen's Cathedral, its Persian-carpet-patterned pitched roof of green and yellow tiles; the Gothic tower of the *Rathaus*; and finally the great dome of the *Hofburg*. Winds batter me at this height; fresh veils of rain stipple my leather and fur. Exhilaration is a fine distraction from tonight's regret. Vienna's a glorious city, one I am reluctant to leave—may the Hapsburgs' rule stretch on forever—but mountains and wilderness call me back to America, to Appalachia, where I have made my home for over a century. This urban lark is nearly done.

Friedrich's room is high in the hotel. The small balcony makes a convenient landing for winged creatures, in this case a huge, hoary bat. I shift form, take a long look at the city stretched out below, then, turning, rap on the French door. "Come in," says a hoarse voice. Given permission, I stride inside.

Friedrich kneels in the center of the ornate room, before a thickly upholstered chair. His young nakedness gleams in the glow of many candles, their flickering illumination replicated in gilt mirrors. His head is bowed; his hands are clasped behind his back. As instructed, he's blindfolded himself: a long strip of black leather conceals the long lashes and blue eyes that have besotted me for months. On the floral carpet beside him lie more leather strips, a goodly pile of them. Behind him, on a tray, are the celebratory tidbits I had ordered earlier. Tonight is, after all, a commemoration of sorts.

"*Mein Herr?*" he whispers. I stand over him, stroking his shoulder-length hair, then his closely cropped goatee. Between the pink curves of his lips I slip my thumb. He sucks me, fervently but gently.

"Sweet slave," I say, brushing shaggy ash-blond bangs from his brow. For nearly a year we have played these games. Ever since we met in that cellar bar by the Danube, even after he discovered the truth. I could have glamoured him to make him stay, but that proved unnecessary. Friedrich loves to suffer, and I have obliged him. The proof of that streaks his small, lithe body, thin scar-ridges my fangs and my whip have made during my sojourn in Vienna. "And how was dinner?"

"Oh, Derek, *liebling*, it was grand! *Dankeschön!*" Friedrich mumbles around my thumb. "*Tafelspitz!* Fine wine! How a man like I, with so few funds, a farmer's son from Styria—"

"You're more than that now, *Sklave*. A prominent anthropologist, with several monographs published. Your ambition is almost as huge as your *Riesenwurst*. Are you ready for dessert?"

"Umm!" Friedrich grunts, releasing my thumb with a pop. His face burrows blindly against my groin. "Your *Schwanz? Ja, mein Herr!* Down my throat, then up my ass?"

"In a bit, ravenous one," I chuckle, patting his head. From the floor I fetch a leather strip, and with it I bind his wrists before him. "How about *Sacher Torte* first? I know how much you relish chocolate. With champagne, of course."

Opening the bottle, I pour bubbly gold into glasses, then fetch the fat slice of torte from beneath its silver dome. I sit in the chair, my pale slave kneels at my feet, his prick half-hard and bobbing, and I feed him with my fingers. The cake is dense, a chocolate sponge coated with glossy chocolate icing, with apricot jam layered between the slices and, on the side, a big pile of whipped cream, what the Austrians call *Schlagober*. In between his eager bites, I lift the champagne flute to his prettily bearded lips; he sips, emitting sighs of satisfaction. As he drinks, I study him as if his body were a landscape I was leaving forever: the broad shoulders; the wiry arms and smooth, chiseled chest; the flat, fuzzy belly and bushy golden pubes; the prodigious cock; the lean, hairy thighs. I will miss him.

The champagne's nearly done; nothing remains of the *Sacher Torte* but crumbs. "Happy, *Sklave*?" I say, dipping a finger into what whipped cream is left and smearing it over his lips. Bending, I kiss him, nuzzling it off.

"*Ja*, master, I am. But...may I? I am famished for other food."

"Yes, I know." I rise, long enough to shuck off my frock coat, shirt, boots, and trousers. Naked, I sprawl back in the chair, anoint my cockhead with *Schlagober*, seize Friedrich by his hair, and shove my penis into his mouth. "Ah, *ja*!" he grunts before my throat-pummeling disallows further speech.

I take my time. My special coach won't be leaving Vienna's *Westbahnhof* till an hour before dawn. Fingers digging into Friedrich's white shoulders, I face-fuck him till his beard's dripping drool. He gasps, gags, chokes, and begs for more.

Finally I pull out. He pants, wipes his chin, and sways on his knees, one bound hand tugging on his long sex.

"Do you have anything to say to me, *Sklave*? Anything important you care to share?" From the floor I fetch another strip of leather.

Friedrich stops pleasuring himself. He cocks his head; above the blindfold his honey-blond eyebrows lift. "Sir? *Nein*. Only to say *Dankeschön* once more for such a glorious meal, for such a room. It's fit for the emperor himself. I don't deserve it."

"You deserve all this and more. Are you ready for more? Ready to be my sacrifice? Ready for some punishment?"

Friedrich licks his lips and grins. "*Ja, mein Herr! Mein Vampir! Bitte!*"

"And you have nothing left to say?" From the elegant tray bearing the plate of *Sacher Torte* crumbs I lift the white cloth napkin and ball it up.

Another quizzical cock of the brow. This time the slightest trembling of the hands, an alarmed intake of breath no human being would notice.

"*Nein*. I—"

"Time you were silenced then." When I stuff the cloth ball into Friedrich's mouth, he groans with arousal.

"You love that, *ja*?"

Friedrich sinks his white teeth into the cloth and nods sheepishly. This golden-headed young man's masochism has intoxicated and sweetened so many of my Viennese nights. Who knows where or when I will find such beautiful, willing submission again? Pushing back remorse, I run the strip of leather between his lips, wrap it about his head twice, then knot it behind, leaving the tail-ends to dangle down his back. Using them as reins, I jerk him to his feet, spin him around, and shove him belly-down over the end of an opulent crimson couch, beneath the dimly lit crystals of a chandelier.

White as Tyrolean snowfields, the round globes of his ass. "My Lippizaner stallion," I say, fondling a slender hip, then slapping his right buttock. He jolts, releasing a muffled yelp. Within seconds, a pink handprint materializes on the curved flesh. "Bitted and reined. Ready to be ridden. How badly you want me inside you." I strike his left buttock now, making an identical flushed imprint. "Am I right, Friedrich?"

He nods excitedly, long bangs flopping over his face. He lifts his ass, spreads his legs, and moans. I reach between his thighs and stroke the hot prick-length there. Rough treatment always gets him hard fast.

His rump is a pastry far superior to *Sacher Torte*, in my expert opinion. I spread what *Schlagober* is left over his silky ass-mounds and along the honey-haired cleft. Growling, I lap up the creamy sweet and tongue-fuck the pink drawstring of his hole. Then, unable to wait any longer, I expose my fangs and sink them into his right butt-cheek. Friedrich squeals, goes taut, and begins to tremble.

I suck hard, coaxing the hot flow. Rich human honey fills my mouth, a slow seeping I savor on my tongue before swallowing. Friedrich shivers, entranced, bucking against my mouth, humping the couch. I pull out, only to give his left cheek identical treatment, draining him of another delicious mouthful.

"Here's what you want, pretty slave," I say, wiping my mouth and standing. "Isn't it?" With his own blood, I moisten us both, then nudge my cock against his asshole. "Beg me, *Sklave*. Beg me. One last time."

Friedrich emits a long, low moan, head lolling. Frantic, he rubs his ass against me and moans again. I give it to him the way I know he loves it, fast and brutal, shoving into him, making him flinch and whine. Arms wrapped around his chest, my torso pressed against his sweaty back, I ride him hard. Sobs spill from him, a molten mixture of pain and thankfulness I have cherished since our first night together. I complete myself deep inside, a lengthy jetting that makes me shudder, jerk, and sigh.

"Time to finish you," I say, shaking off my post-orgasmic drowse. Pulling Friedrich up by the leather reins hanging from his gag, I drag him to the bed. He gives me a little ersatz fight, which only excites me more. Laughing, I subdue him with ease, forcing his bound hands above his head and securing them to the headboard, lashing his ankles together and strapping them to the footboard. He lies there, stretched out taut, panting, teeth gritted.

Lying on top of him, I lick his stubbly jaw, his leather-parted lips. "I'm going to bleed you now, and I'm going to bring you off." Tugging at the knot half-hidden in his luxuriant hair, I pull off the blindfold. Friedrich looks up at me, blue eyes wide with fear and bliss. He blinks; his lashes bead with tears.

Exposing my fangs, I sink them into his neck. Briefly I feast there, not too long yet, wanting our final lovemaking to last. Next I bite the hard swell of his white breast, worrying the tiny nipples till they give me the red flow I crave. I rake my fang-tips up and down his chest, leaving thin red furrows that well up and spill over. I cover his fuzzy belly with love-bites, then his hair-coated thighs. My passionate prisoner writhes and bucks beneath me, moaning with delight. Finally I grip his rigid penis, slip my teeth into the tender head, and steal sweet sips of blood, a copious flood I lap and lap and lap before taking the prick down my throat and pleasuring him with a tight sucking and bobbing. Soon his groin's slamming my face; he climaxes, pearly essence nearly as delicious as his blood filling my mouth.

I lie there for long minutes, cheek on his belly, watching a few lost drops of semen mingling with the blood-ooze on his golden-fuzzed belly, like the red strawberries and white cream he savored on our shared summer nights. I lick that pink amalgam up. Then I rise on my elbows, only to wrap my arms around him and drink from his neck again, this time more deeply.

His struggle is no longer feigned. I've never taken so much from him before, and the woozy weakness no doubt swamping him alerts him to that fact. He twists beneath me, pleading. I hold him down and continue the feast. When he screams, I press a hand over his mouth and keep sucking. When finally I pull out, his limbs are limp, his eyes are glazed, his cheeks streaked with tears. I tousle his hair, then unknot the leather strap between his teeth and tug out the sodden napkin.

"*Mein Herr*....W-why?" His lips are trembling; he tugs feebly on his bonds and whimpers like a sick puppy.

I grip his bloodstained cock. From the tip, the aftermath of rapture oozes. I lick it off, then kiss him, smearing his lips with the juice.

"You shouldn't have written that new monograph, Friedrich," I sigh, licking clotted blood from his right nipple. "Damn you. *A Treatise on the True Facts of Vampirism*? Why did you do that? *Dummkopf*."

Friedrich musters a low gasp. He closes his eyes, shakes his head, and licks his lips.

"How long have you...?"

"Only a few days. Long enough to put my affairs in order. I'm leaving Vienna tonight."

"But the manuscript?"

"Is in my coffin, for more leisurely reading later. You're a real stylist and a fine researcher. You could have become world-famous, yes. Your publisher, sad to say, is waltzing with the fishes in the blue Danube."

"And I?" he whispers.

"Blue and gold, my boy. Blue and gold and white. Your white, strong body. Shaped like a demigod. You're staying here." I run my hand over his chest, rest my palm over his fluttering heart. "I watched the storm from the porch of the *Theseustempel* tonight. Did you ever hear the story of Theseus and his boon-friend Pirithous? They risked everything, descending into the Underworld to abduct the Queen of the Dead. They sat on stones, and they grew fixed to the stones. They were trapped in the darkness. Heracles rescued Theseus. Pirithous never returned to the light."

"Oh, no," Friedrich moans.

"I would have done anything for you, my boy, my *Sklave*. My beautiful *Sklave*. Why, oh why did you have to...." When I bend over Friedrich, a drop of blood splashes his chin.

"Derek, you're weeping," he croaks. "I didn't know you could weep."

"Not often, *Schöne*." I say, licking tears from his rough cheek. "A few times a century. Forgive the weakness." I brush golden hair out of his terror-wide blue gaze. When I kiss him, he kisses me back.

"Close your eyes," I say, and he does. I bend once more to his neck.

It takes only minutes. I leave him still bound to the bed, a Grecian sculpture of white marble and blood-rust. Good to be leaving this city. The classical statues of gods worked into Vienna's façades would remind me too much of that slender, finely formed figure on the bed.

I pace around the room, snuffing candles, wiping my wet face. From the plate, I scrape up the last crumbs of *Sacher Torte* with a finger and lift them to my lips. An alien, bitter taste, brewed from a tropical seed. Nothing like the native sweetness my slave surrendered.

There's a mouthful of champagne left. I take up the glass; I sit on the edge of the bed, and, as I have so many nights, watch Friedrich sleep. Later I will unbind him, carry him onto the balcony, and shift, gripping what's left of him in my claws and taking to the winds. The Danube awaits. But now I finish the champagne. I climb into bed and stretch out beside him. I kiss his brow, I kiss his mouth, I kiss the wounds on his neck. Then I pull Friedrich to me, wrap him in my arms, and wait for the last of his warmth to fade.

Hemlock Lake

The water has returned, like the appetite of a warrior whose wounds are slowly healing. Were there starlight tonight, I could see the Pleiades floating on the black surface, like portents in an obsidian mirror, and Orion, with his broad shoulders, sword belt, and glimmering blade.

Hemlock Lake is cyclic, emptying itself every century, then, slowly, over a season or two, refilling its depths till it once again laps the dock. It was low when it was first discovered, when, new to America, I followed that band of eighteenth-century explorers to this mountain, feeding on them abstemiously, taking a dram from one man one night, another man the next, sleeping by day beneath great stones, curled in with the timber rattler or the bobcat. Its waters were low at the turn of the twentieth century, when an academic conference on the Greek god Dionysus convened here. I lost control then, and so one handsome classics scholar was found floating face down in what was left of the lake.

Tonight, renewed by long rains, Hemlock Lake is high and hungry. The red spruce stumps are submerged now, and the yellow-green grasses of the meadow that grew in years of low water around the dock. Submerged, what finger bones and skull shards the archaeologists have not found, the sacrifices that renegade Indian tribe fed to the water, provoking its present thirst.

Silence and holiness in the thickening fog. The power is palpable here, the presence. Gods in the greenwood. Stag horn and wild grape. The forest's glittering eyes. Lap of lake water against sandstone. Night dense as muscle, blacker within the rhododendron groves.

And now the scent of Scotch and smoke, the spice of armpit sweat. I turn toward the massive lodge where it stands, mist-veiled, on the slope above the lake. Music ended at last, lights winking out, the wedding party retiring. He has slipped his mandolin gently into its velvet-lined case, with the tenderness he touches his wife or child, and now he descends the foggy path, boots loud on gravel, stopping every fifth stride, hesitant, for he has not chosen this meeting

I wish I could see Hemlock Lake by day, as he can. For power, we pay what price we must. His heels echo now on the dock's planks. He meets my eyes. Power determines who does the choosing.

For me, they have fixed the wedding at dusk. Spencer is so grateful to me—after all, my publishing company has helped forge his present reputation as a novelist—and so, when I explained that, due to my work schedule, I could only arrive at nightfall, he and his acquiescent bride-to-be kindly timed the event so as to allow my presence.

What church has a more beautiful view? Standing on the porch and looking out over the darkening mountains of Southwest Virginia, great humps of black still rimmed with red, the tiny lights of distant farmhouses twinkling on, again I wish for sunlight—the light I abandoned in 1730 on the Isle of Mull. Well worth the loss—to escape the mortal death that my enemies thought they insured by many dagger wounds, to revenge the death of my lover Angus with claymore, dirk, and flame. Still, how majestic these hills would look in October sunlight, the first yellow gleaming in tulip trees, the first scarlet in sumac, dawn-frost glittering on the fall-frowsy grass.

Masochist, focusing so often, so perversely, on all that's lost forever. But the wedding music brings me distraction. Or, rather, fascination, in the form of this bearded musician. Fascination dismisses the past and insists on the present.

A small crowd here, in Brandywine Memorial Church, halfway up Hemlock Mountain. Spencer looks aristocratic, flushed, in his tuxedo. Angelique looks both sensuous and elegant in her misty trails of seed-pearl satins. As I know better than most, it is easier to find a mate when you are not a monster.

This is not the traditional ceremony. Writers so often prefer to do it differently. Thus the poetry by Mary Oliver and Kaye Varley. Thus the bluegrass band: guitar, upright bass, and mandolin. Thus the heat suffusing my face, my groin, as I study the mandolin player.

Local mountain boy, from his looks. Thick brown hair falling over his brow, trimmed brown beard framing an intelligent face. Dark eyebrows over hazel eyes. The type that looks best in jeans, flannel shirt, and cowboy boots, though tonight he is dressed semi-formally for the occasion, in brown corduroys, tan dress shirt, and dark blue tie. Before the ceremony, he'd bent over his instrument, hand flickering over the strings, the tip of his tongue occasionally showing as he hit the highest notes. Now that the wedding's begun, he stands there, attentive, cradling his mandolin against his chest. He seems to listen not to the minister's words but to the sound, beyond the church's open door, of autumn wind in the sugar maple boughs outside.

I am listening to the wind too, the vast night encompassing this crowd, this church, this mountain. And, at the center of night's black sphere, his heartbeart. I imagine, beneath the formality of his dress shirt, animal fur covering the mounds of his pecs. I imagine the aroma of his armpits, maddening combination of salt, leaf meal, and cider press. Inside him, the black blood courses and laps like a lake fed by underground springs and hard rains. Moon on the water, fragment of moon I cup up in my hands and slowly sip, drinking the sun's reflected light.

A fine reception on the mountaintop, in one of the spacious conference rooms of Hemlock Lake Lodge. Dancing with the bride, sipping champagne, watching those partial to solid food as they dine on prime rib, roast potatoes, pasta salad, and pecan pie. And, always in the background, the music. A beefy bear of a banjo player has joined the bluegrass trio from the church, and all evening they rollick through cheerful dance numbers, interspersed with a few slower songs for more romantic dancing.

Spencer thinks my interest purely musical, and so I garner from him all the pertinent facts. The band, Hardscrabble Hill. The mandolin player, Tim. Twenty-eight years old. Playing weddings and festivals all over Southwest Virginia, struggling to make ends meet. Liable to be leaving around midnight, skipping the last set, heading home to help his wife with their new baby.

The band ends the third set with an instrumental version of "Green Grass It Grows Bonny," an excuse for the straight folks to slow-dance. Spencer and Angelique begin, and soon several couples are shuffling together across the dance floor.

Difficult for me to imagine—I, a man burdened with double stigmas, a thirst for blood, a lust for men—difficult for me to conceive of a cosmos in which my desire is public, in which my hunger, my aesthetic, meet approving eyes rather than suspicion or hatred. How often an outsider's status propels him into fantasy. This is not the world in which I can take the mandolin from its handsome owner, gently pull him into the dancing throng, wrap my arms around him, feel his thick hair on my cheek, press my lips to his brow, his eyelids, his neck. For the ravenous, for those whose hunger makes them exiles, how wearisome are the limits of possibility and propriety.

Instead of dancing with whom I desire, I softly sing the lyrics the band is wisely not singing, words far from appropriate for a wedding reception, a song whose melody is etched in air by Tim's high strings. Old song, one I heard versions of in Scotland, during my human years with Angus.

I wonder what's keeping my true love tonight?
I wonder what's keeping you out of my sight?
I wonder if you know all the pain I endure?
And yet you stay from me this night I'm not sure.

At dawn, I will return to the great heap of boulders at Hemlock Mountain's very top, to sleep where I slept in 1740, when this lake was first discovered. I will sleep alone, curled against cold rock, and I will dream of Angus McCormick, lost to me that Beltane night at Lochbuie, and Mark Carden, lost to me at the Battle of Chickamauga. But tonight, before I return to the stony niche of my self, I will absorb what I can of human warmth.

"Scotch?" I offer, holding up my flask.

Tim's a little drunk already. He turns away from the urinal, zipping up, and he stares at the Celtic swirls etched into the pewter flask. Swirls like dark water draining from the lake, a vortex into the subterranean, bones of the drowned slowly swallowed by silt.

Then he looks up at me. I smile. I enter his eyes, and then his brain. Hard rain seeping through the soil, into thirsty root hairs and down to bedrock. Leaching into the deepest layers, where desire is shaped and will conceived. I reach those depths. Gently, I find a purchase, and then, gently, I twist.

Tim closes his eyes, shakes his head. He staggers a little and leans back against the restroom wall. Then he meets my eyes and takes the flask from me.

"Thanks," he says, and swigs.

"Derek Maclaine," I say, proffering my hand.

"Tim Graham," he replies, gripping my hand hard and taking another mouthful. He stands unsteadily under the florescent light, our stares locked together like stag antlers or sword blades, our palms still skin to skin.

He's afraid. This desire is not natural to him, but it springs up nevertheless, dicotyledons of seedlings pushing up from rich earth, from the seeds I have planted.

"I.... I've got to leave now. Got to get home. My wife's expecting me." Confused whisper, heartbeat like a bodhran, the fast rhythm of the battlefield.

The hard and proper handshake transforms, as I slide my fingers through his fingers and pull him to me. Our brows bump, my goatee brushes his lips. His eyes are fixed now, like stationary stars. Fixed on my face. Satellite losing its freedom, gripped by gravity, hurtling toward the earth.

Calluses on his fingertips, sweat filming his palms. "Put your hands behind your back," I whisper, and he does.

The monarch butterfly probing milkweed blooms. I aspire toward such tenderness, opening his mouth with my tongue. He sighs against my lips, then sways, then falls against me, head on my shoulder.

With my left hand, behind his back I grip his wrists together. With my right, I find the stiffness of his nipples beneath his shirt's fabric. I stroke them, then press each between thumb and forefinger. With my thigh, I rub the sudden density between his legs, beneath his corduroy pants.

"You will not leave now," I say, lapping his ear. "You'll play till the party's over. After the music ends, you will meet me on the dock."

Against my shoulder, he shakes his head. "No," he grunts, but again I fill his mouth with my tongue, my fingers press deeper into his chest's flesh. I release his wrists now, and his arms wrap around me and hold me close, his head still shaking refusal.

"I can't. I can't," he groans, and I'm about to unzip his pants when a footfall outside the door resounds. Gently I push Tim from me, turn toward the sink, and begin washing my hands.

T he hemlocks after which this lake is named are dying. A foreign parasite, the wooly adelgid, is eating their needles, season by season. Another in a long line of extinctions. I remember the great chestnut trees that used to fill these forests, and the graceful droop of the American elms, before the diseases that wiped them out. Tonight, waiting on the dock, watching the fog thicken, the cold fog promising hard frost, I stroke the feathery boughs of the hemlocks, their twigs already crusted with the insects' white fuzz. What good is power if it is not enough to rescue what you love? What good to be a survivor when again and again you are left with nothing but litanies of loss?

Then the scent of him, his heels on the dock. Fear, lust, uncertainty. He fought me for an hour, during the last set, meeting my eyes across the room as he played, then looking nervously away, sweat staining his shirt's armpits. He knew his wife was at home, worrying and wondering why he was late, waiting uneasily for his return. *I wonder what's keeping my true love tonight?* Perhaps, solicitous husband, he called her with some excuse.

No matter. Now he is here. I was far from certain that he'd come. It is hard to divert the natural course of a stream. But, young and strong as he is, I am stronger.

He stops three feet from me, summoning up his last resistance. He's wearing no jacket. The cold fog wraps its ropes around him. He hugs himself and shudders.

"What do you want?" he whispers.

I smile, lift one hand and beckon. A pity to mar Spencer's wedding with a mysterious death. But Tim is so handsome, and I am so hungry. And I have fed this lake before.

He shudders again. He stands still, avoiding my eyes, staring instead at the black water beyond me, as if it offered some escape.

"I've got to go home. Jen's waiting for me." When he speaks, the heat of his words weaves its own mist. He half-turns and takes one step toward the hotel, the distant glimmer of its few lights feathered with fog.

"Tim," I say, and he stops. It's been years since a man put up such a struggle, presented such a delicious challenge.

He turns toward me again. I step forward, clasp his hand, pull him to me. Beneath his clothes I can feel leanness, the hard curves of muscles, the harder angles of bone. Hard and resistant, like his will, like the scattered chips of femurs and phalanges at the bottom of Hemlock Lake. He's shaking violently now, from the chill and the fright, and I hold him in my arms, as if his welfare were all that mattered, as if I had human heat to lend him.

The tree's as young as he is, a red maple sapling growing deep in the rhododendron groves. He stands against it as I've ordered. As I've ordered, he crosses his wrists behind the slender trunk. Slowly I unknot my tie, pull it out of my collar, and with the silken length of it I tightly bind his hands together.

He's shaking still, panting now with a barely stifled panic, beginning to realize what danger he's in. With his belt, I cinch his elbows together behind the sapling. I unbutton his shirt, pull the ends of it out of his pants, push the collar back till his chest and shoulders are exposed to the night air.

"Please," he gasps. Pleas for release, yes, but neither of us is certain which release he wants the most. The artificial lust I've planted in him still battles with the natural fear. The crotch of his corduroys still bulges.

Now I unknot his tie and push it against his lips. He fights me for half a minute, gritting his teeth and twisting from side to side, and this I allow, for I relish a man's struggle, I savor a man's strength as he's subdued.

Then I speak his name again, and instantly he submits. The cloth slides between his teeth, and in a few deft seconds I have his tie knotted behind his head.

The beauty of sacrifice. I stand back and study him. Broad shoulders, pale in what minimal light the woodland allows, pale as October fog into which his life tonight may well disperse. Thick brown hair matting his muscled chest and lean belly, torso arched forward by the angle of his bound arms. Beneath my gaze, in this silent tabernacle of trees, he hangs his head, ashamed to face, in my smile and the depth of my eyes, the fact of his helplessness made complete.

I step up to him, cup his bearded chin in my hand, and lift his face to mine. Above the dark silk tied between his teeth, his eyes are wide and wet with a growing terror, the terror of a man who suddenly realizes he's met his murderer. No one will find us here, in the middle of the night, in this dense forest, on this mountainside. Neither he nor I know whether he will survive the night.

When I run my tongue around his gagged lips, he starts to pant again, and when I kiss his forehead, he begins to whimper. "Ssshh!" I whisper into the thick hair falling over his face, but he's breaking now, the terror has him completely, banishing the last remnants of that desire my mesmerism demanded. When I wrap my arms around him, a seismic tremble runs along his limbs like lightning down the bole of an oak.

Suddenly, Tim jerks himself out of my embrace. He does what any animal scenting its own death would do: he tries to escape. He tugs furiously at the belt around his elbows, the tie about his wrists, growling like a dog into the fabric knotted between his teeth. He twists and curses, twists and tugs some more. The maple tree shakes beneath his frantic efforts. A few red leaves, dislodged, fall about us.

He shouts once—a silk tie looks good in a man's mouth, but it doesn't make a very efficient gag—and that's when I slap his face hard, stunning him. I seize his shoulders and slam him back against the tree.

Another red rain of maple leaves. One wet leaf sticks briefly to his bare shoulder like a crimson handprint before continuing its descent.

His struggle's only confirmed his helplessness. He sags in his bonds, in my grip, faces the black earth between his boots, and starts to sob.

The violence of his tears surprises me. Most mountain boys prize their courage, their stoic manhood, and refuse tears in any extremity. It takes great fear to conquer a man's pride. It takes great grief or terror to overcome his shame and permit such unabashed weeping. Tim's crying now with the sort of force with which winter winds tear off tree limbs on this mountain's bleak height. Tears like the steady gray descent summer thunder leaves in its wake, drumming on the tin roof, waking the sleepers, cutting rivulets into hillsides.

Gently I stroke his temple, but he pulls violently away and keeps sobbing, head down, determined to refuse any comfort from his killer, aiming his muffled sorrow into the leaf meal at his feet, the black rot of centuries.

I step back then, and slowly I unbutton my shirt. No need to ruin another outfit. I have waited long enough. I am hungry, he is beautiful, he is a coward, and that triad of facts has decided his fate. On a mountain laurel bush I hang my blazer and my shirt, listening to his sobs retreat like tides, gather force and breath, and then renew themselves.

Enough. I slam my palm over his mouth and push his head back against the sapling.

"Shut up," I say. "You don't want to die weeping."

Beneath my grasp he shakes his head, and, within seconds, the sobs grade into soft groans against my hand, and then into silence.

His eyes are closed, his chest heaving. He's chewed and fought his tie till it's soaked with spittle. Tears streak his cheeks like sugar sap from a broken maple twig, glimmer in his beard like rain clinging to tamarack needles. Who could resist? I lick the salt, the hot seawater, from his cheeks, from his chin.

"You're going to be brave now? You're going to be quiet?"

He nods. He opens his eyes and stares at me, stares at the fact of his end. Then his glance shifts to the forest behind me, as if acknowledging some invisible witness. His breath slowing, he closes his eyes again and mumbles something that my hand and his gag render unintelligible.

With a handful of his hair I pull his head to one side. The skin of his neck glimmers as if it were dusted with mica. That bodhran beat again. Soon the drummer will weary, the rhythm will slow and stop. Now my fangs lengthen, and I press one sharp point against the thin skin separating my thirst from his great artery's generous throb. His own thumping fright will pump him halfway dry, will hasten the welling of that underground spring. Only at the end will my mouth need to pull from his body the thickening, dwindling juice, the hot black wine lowering, lowering, till the chalice is empty and his abandoned body gleams against leaf mold like a cold point of quartz.

A wind's worrying the treetops, like the wind that, during the wedding, soothed the maples beyond the church door. He slumps against me, all hope gone, prepared at last to die with courage, a pleasant transformation after those torrents of unseemly tears. I press my fang harder—slowly, slowly, savoring this moment as I savor every entrance, every conquest—and the skin's resistance splits. The first drops of blood wet the corner of my mouth, prelude to the rich flood to follow. I will bury the body beneath boulders on the hill, or I will simply slip the corpse into the lake.

His blood is tinged with pot and Scotch, and it wells into my mouth. I press his head against my bare shoulder, gulp the first mouthful, listen to the leaves rustling overhead, listen to his mumbling. He's limp, all struggles over, passing in my arms from passion into peace.

They often mumble when they die, prayers or curses. Few of them go without words of some kind, a soft speech trailing off and disappearing like the wake a ship writes on water.

I lift my hand from his mouth, place it across the muscled mound over his heart, and I take another swallow. I want to feel his heart slow and stop beneath my touch. I run my fingers through his torso's thick fur, over a nipple hard with the autumn chill, hard as a seed. I will leave him here till the hour before dawn. I will leave him gagged and bound, slumped like the Christians' savior against his tree. I will sit on a stone, drink Scotch from my flask, and watch his limbs stiffen, study the fog as it thickens about him, painting gray frost across his chest hair. He was not brave enough to deserve life, but he is beautiful enough to deserve a wake.

His blood is surging freely now, so hot and sweet my head swims. Greedily I gulp and gulp. A few more ecstatic mouthfuls, and his life will be over, his future will be entirely consumed.

By my ear Tim's muttering on, and suddenly, without the added obstruction of my hand over his mouth, his muffled words come clear.

"Jenny," he says. "Jenny."

Mouth full of blood, I hesitate. His mutter subsides to a whisper. A name repeated once, twice more, before his head falls against mine and he passes out.

I gulp down the sweetness, the hot honey that makes half-human flesh of my marble. I withdraw my fangs and wipe my beard with the back of my hand. His blood pulses still, trickling down his neck, staining the edge of his shirt.

Beneath my fingers, his heart throbs faintly. Against my neck, his hot breath continues.

Tim is so easy to carry, arms and chest hard as a laborer's, but belly flat with youth and poverty. Still stripped to the waist, I stand by the water, this young musician slumped in my arms, and I hum "Green Grass It Grows Bonny," the melancholy tune played only hours ago at the wedding reception.

Hemlock Lake rustles against the dock at my feet, wanting its share, wanting more flesh and bone to join the offerings that came before. It has waited so long. I know how it feels, that ravenous, impatient ache. I remember how eagerly its dark fingers swarmed over the sinking corpse of that classics scholar, just over a century ago.

Tim is sleeping too deeply for the cold water to wake him. How gently I might slide him from my arms and into the lake, and how silently, how painlessly he would drown, face down in the dark. No chance then that he might resist my mind and remember this night.

Local legends say that the lodge is haunted by the old woman who had it built, and I believe it, for tonight there is an interior mistiness that matches the fog outside, a gleaming mist that hovers by the reception desk. Employees have sometimes glimpsed the vague form of a woman, in gray dress and white shawl.

She would approve of mercy, I think. She would approve of life, a lover's last-minute reprieve.

Four AM and the foyer is entirely empty. Carefully I lower Tim onto the leather couch by the fireplace. Sweet survivor, waylaid wedding guest. Someone left to pluck Scottish melodies from the mandolin, someone to admire, as I cannot, the way October sunlight loves Hemlock Lake.

I mistook his tears. Not fear but grief fed them. He wept not for himself but for her.

His shirt is still unbuttoned, and I kiss each of his nipples, warming their hard points with my mouth, giving back the heat I stole, before covering him with a rough Indian blanket I pull off the back of the couch. Someone will find him soon. His memory will be vague, crazy fragments blamed on alcohol and a bad batch of marijuana. His wife will scold him relentlessly. He will be dogged with nightmares for months.

The spectral mist gathers about us, lingering and glimmering. Tim groans and shifts beneath the blanket. I kiss his lips, stroke his soft beard a final time. I slip a wad of bills into his shirt pocket. Then I rise, salute the mist, and stride through the door.

Outside, night fog has left a killing frost on the broad lawn before the lodge. Tomorrow, all about Hemlock Lake, the scarlet leaves of maples will break loose from twigs, ride wind onto water, and float in the sun for hours before joining their forebears' muddy molecules on the lake floor. On the couch, Tim will wake, hold his throbbing head in his hands, and wonder how blood came to be on his shirt, why the tie stuffed in his pants pocket is so moist, as if it had been soaked in dew.

The water is bitterly cold. Already it begins to rob me of what little warmth Tim's blood lent me. Naked, I am as pale as he would have been by dawn had I not heard her name.

My body might appease the lake for a while, though it is a morsel the misty water must relinquish before dawn. Soon, from the entrance to my makeshift tomb, I will watch the mountain's edge bleed with the coming day. Soon I will return to the high water mark of my hunger, sleeping within my stony cave, dreaming of passions mutual, not manipulated. Dreaming of Tim, hairy and naked, his warmth curled against me, grateful and loving, rejoicing in my touch.

Till then, dead silhouette of ivory set in an onyx oval, I float on the surface of Hemlock Lake, listening to lake water rising, listening to hemlocks dying. I raise my hand, and above me the prompted fog swirls, thins, and parts, revealing the stars. There is Orion, the brave one brandishing his sword, averting his fate, the rushing width of heaven set between him and the sting of the Scorpion.

Saving Tobias

(FOR TIFFANY TRENT)

T obias Crockett has good taste in accommodations. The Tabard Inn is quaint and historic, full of antiques, paintings, and well-heeled sorts chattering over meals and cocktails. All a bit noisy for me, an undead introvert accustomed to the high, forested silence of West Virginia's Potomac Highlands, so I'm sitting as far away from people as possible, here in a dark corner of the parlor. The ceiling's low and dark-beamed, like the Cape Cod tavern where I used to hunt in the mid-seventies. Tonight's February-gusty, so the big fireplace is in use, flame-light flickering over glossy wood-paneled walls. The few table lamps are turned low, creating an atmosphere of dim intimacy. Perfect for sipping red wine and studying Tobias across the room.

His name befits him. *Tobias.* It's Hebrew for "God is good." God has been good to him indeed. So far. Handsome blond giant, wealthy, talented, powerful, he's as magnificent as Oedipus must have been a few hours before the truth, before the kingly fool thrust the pin of his mother's brooch, his wife's brooch, into his eyes. The truth can do that, certainly. Put out the eyes, splinter the soul, castrate, eviscerate, shatter. The truth is what I bring tonight.

I've had my sights on Tobias for several years now. But with immortality to enjoy, why rush the consummation of a passion? Back during his country-music days, he was one of few men who brought out the bottom in me. His bulk and rough-rebel persona were the reasons, I think. I would examine the images on his CD covers—blond goatee, blue eyes, pouty lips, cowboy hat—and wish he were on top of me thrusting away. When I attended his concerts with my country-boy lover Matt, who's an enthusiast of all things Nashville, I'd watch Tobias swagger the stage, finger his guitar, gift us with that resonant baritone and those macho bad-boy lyrics, and imagine him pushing me over a sawhorse and ramming me with the yee-haw vigor of the Virginia farm boy he used to be. It would be a heady pleasure to be filled up by a man that burly, that much bigger than I. I might even let him come inside me before I turned on him and put him in his place.

But Tobias has, alas, put music behind him for politics. That's his fatal misstep, his *hamartia*, as Aristotle put it when analyzing *Oedipus*. That's what he's doing in DC tonight: using the good looks and charisma that made him a country-music superstar to network with Republican hangers-on and sycophants. A long way from his Wytheville roots, his glamorous years in Nashville. Now he's a member of Virginia's General Assembly, a busy senator moving back and forth between Richmond and Washington, a power broker planning the move from state to national politics. The five middle-aged men sitting with him and guffawing by the fire are probably congressmen. All quite wealthy, judging by the cut of their business suits. And all right-wingers, no doubt of that.

My handsome Tobias should have stuck to songwriting. If he had, the fantasies I entertained about him wouldn't have shifted so radically and moved into the sphere of practical planning. I wouldn't be here tonight, only yards away, admiring his face and body, sipping this cabernet, readying the scourge.

What a fine specimen he is. He leans back in his leather-upholstered chair, drinking beer, grinning at some colleague's joke. His eyes are as blue as the photos on his CD's. He has a full head of curly blond hair, and his goatee is golden brown and neatly trimmed, bespeaking carefully controlled wildness. His lips are very full, the lower one so thick it contributes to the surly look he's known for in the press, a pout made all the more dramatic-dark by the rare gleam of his arrogant smiles. The jeans and muscle-shirts of his Nashville days have been replaced by slick politico suits, though he has yet to relinquish his cowboy hats and boots, just to retain the good-ole-boy image that appeals to so many of his conservative constituents. Expert at studying clothed male physiques and discerning how those forms might look stripped bare, I can make out the wide shoulders, thick chest, and beer belly of a well-fed ex-athlete. At his age, mid-forties, the bulk's as much fat as it is muscle, a proportion that has always appealed to me, bear aficionado that I am. Big as he is, he'll keep me snug and warm tonight, after our official meeting.

My kind—Scots Highlanders, mountain men—we love to tell stories. I order a second glass of wine from a lean young waiter with hairy forearms and an angular Mediterranean face shadowed with beard—a muskily aromatic boy who, due to my plans for Tobias, will be spared my sharp attentions tonight—and I think about those whose stories brought me here. Karen, Charlotte, sweet little Chet: three of my handsome senator's ill-fated constituents. Vivid narrative often makes for the most convincing political advice. Once Tobias retires for the night, we'll begin that summit discussion.

As if on cue, Tobias checks his watch, orders a bourbon nightcap, knocks it back, and says goodnight to his little crew of sartorial vipers. It's approaching midnight, and he has early morning meetings, he explains. No distant human ear could pick out his words over the chatter of the parlor, but I can. I can smell him too. As he passes me, heading for his room, he leaves a lingering scent of spicy aftershave, and the sweat-smell of a big man whose deodorant gave out by late afternoon. I lick my lips. Beneath the table, I nudge my hardening cock with the back of my thumb. He will, without a doubt, taste as fine as he smells.

I have had several hundred years to learn the subtleties of strategy, and so I wait for a bit once Tobias leaves. After what will happen to him tonight, I don't want anyone remembering me as a suspicious character who directly followed him out. Instead, I finish my wine slowly. I think of Karen walking into the barn, Chet standing by the creek, Charlotte gasping in the hospital bed. I study the waiter, whose shirt is open one flirtatious button too many to be truly professional, and I make out, in the cleft his open collar makes, the black chest hair I've tasted on so many Middle-Eastern, Greek, and Italian men. Perhaps, upon my next trip to DC, I will have to sample him, though carefully and abstemiously, considering his frail build. With a man as hefty as Tobias, my appetites will have significantly wider range.

It is time. Leaving my asocial nook, I stand by the fire to take in the heat and finish that last sip of wine. Cold as I am, cold since 1730, I gravitate to fireplaces, to any flame, those restless substitutes for the sunlight I am denied. Matt, sweet husbear, pants away summer afternoons stripped to the waist, chopping oak to fill the woodshed, and by the time I rise with dusk, he is richly rank and tastes of sweat-salt all over. With those hard-won cords of wood, he keeps the hearths hot all winter in our snow-swathed Mount Storm farmhouse. Every night, as hard wind rattles the panes, he fixes us hot Scotch toddies, strips us both and pulls me into bed to curl with him beneath the quilts. He wraps his big arms around me, presses his hot, hairy chest and belly against mine and sighs, head lolling dreamily, as I carefully and blissfully feed on him. Sweet boy, he has never entirely reconciled himself to what happens when my rages and my hungers go untrammeled, but he certainly understands my need for erotic and culinary variety, and, as grief-stricken as he's been lately—sobbing on my shoulder every night for a week—I think he understands the necessity of this mission I'm on tonight. The nation, after all, stands in need of improvement.

Outside the Tabard, thickening snowflakes scurry down N Street like swarms of white flies. In order to visit Tobias with complete discretion, I must indulge in a little shapeshifting. That's the ability that Matt has always most envied in me, ever since he found out what I really was, a wintry night much like this one, down by Kanawha Falls. My paranormal powers delight him, especially when I gently pluck his adorable, furry mass into my claws, spread my wings, and give him a ride up to the top of Spruce Knob to take in the summer stars.

So, were there onlookers—and there are not—they might see, striding into tonight's dark DC alley, a tall man dressed in a long black Western duster, sporting unruly, grey-streaked hair and a silver beard. They might see, flying out of the alley, an unnaturally large, hoary-backed, black-winged bat, a bat that methodically hovers by window after window of the Tabard Inn, front and back, looking for ingress, some escape from the cold. To those hypothetical witnesses, the size of the bat would be odd enough; odder still, its presence in midwinter, when it should be hibernating.

Here is Tobias, in a top-floor room in the back of the inn. He's chosen it for its spacious privacy, its relative isolation, desires that conveniently dovetail with my intentions tonight. I perch on the sill, swaying in the cold wind, hungry darkness on the edge of the light, savoring the warmth so soon to come. He's pulled off his blazer and tie, unbuttoned his dress shirt a few notches, and rolled up his sleeves. The light of a single lamp glints along his forearm fur. He sits at the desk, big fingers working over his laptop. He uncaps a bottle of Scotch, fills a water glass with its amber, slugs it down, and sets out his clothes for tomorrow's meetings.

And then Tobias strips for me. Not that he knows he has an audience. He stands, tugs his shirt over his head, and tosses it on the couch. He pulls off one cowboy boot, then, hopping around, pulls off the other. He unzips his charcoal-gray slacks, shucks them and his boxers down his thick, hairy thighs. For a few seconds, as if aware he has an admirer, he stands naked in front of an ornately framed antique mirror. His back to the window in which I peer, he grins at himself, knowing his power. He grins and lifts his glass to his own reflection. The world is his. His charm knows no limits. Tonight, he sleeps only five blocks from the White House, but in the future, perhaps....

Tobias is built just as my careful study of him in the parlor led me to believe. In the mirror's depths loom his huge football player's shoulders, his chunky pecs, his solid, muscled arms. Only a little blond hair around his nipples and over his sternum, to my disappointment, though there's a decent thatch across his tastily broad, gone-to-seed beer belly, honey-blond fur the color of broom sedge that whispers over abandoned pastures back in Appalachia. His back, turned to me, is wide and muscled; his ass is beefy, smooth, curvaceous, and very pale. It will feel like volcanic velvet beneath my cheek. He's the perfect combination of occasional weight-lifting—my guess is his ego demands that he stay in some kind of shape—and regular gastronomic indulgence—a poor boy who grows up to live high on the hog just can't forego good food and drink.

Ripe, ripe, mature, ripe. Other than the sad sparseness of his chest hair, he's exactly my type.

The proud gentleman from Virginia gulps the last of the glass and steps into the bathroom, beyond the line of my sight. There's the rush and splash of the shower; wafts of steam curl around the frame of the bathroom door.

Time to focus. My membranous darkness and silvery fur dissolve. As glowing chartreuse mist, I hover about the window, find a slight opening between brick and frame—these old buildings are always blessed with expedient little gaps—and enter. Time for Tobias' surprise.

By the time tonight's lover has finished his shower, I'm naked too, cozy coverlet pulled up to my belly, propped on thick pillows, hands behind my head. If he were gay, he might perhaps—if he were into leatherbears instead of twinks—enjoy the sight of me, my thick beard, my hairy chest and armpits, my tattoos. But he's straight—a nasty homophobe, in fact—and besides, it takes him a few seconds to notice, in the low light, the silent stranger awaiting him. Oblivious, he fumbles about for his robe in a closet at the other end of the large room, pulls it on, belts it, pours himself another shot of Scotch, and then turns toward the bed.

If I were in his shoes—well, his situation, I should say, since he's barefoot—I might drop the glass in shock. He doesn't. He simply gasps. He tightens his grip on his drink and, born fighter, starts assessing. You can tell from his song lyrics that he was quite the redneck bar-brawler in his day. He's bigger than I am, he figures out fast. I'm naked; I have no weapons in sight. His initial second of fear metamorphoses almost instantly into anger.

Tobias backs up a step and says, low, intense, "Who the fuck are *you?*"

I smile. I stare into his wide blue eyes and start feeling for a purchase in his thoughts. He shakes his head and takes another step back.

"Bad manners, Senator Crockett. Aren't you going to offer me a drink?" I arch luxuriously against the flannel sheet, run my fingers through my silver chest hair, and keep smiling. "I prefer single malt, but I'll settle for that blended you have there."

Two more steps back, then three to the left, and he's put the Scotch on a dresser and pulled a gun out of his suitcase. *That does it,* he thinks. *Checkmate. I was born to take control.*

"I asked you a question. Who the hell are you? And why the *fuck* are you here?" Tobias levels the gun at me. I level my glance at him. I take in that heaving chest, the heartbeat speeding up with adrenalin, the soap-scent of his crotch. I would have preferred him unwashed when I took him. I like to carry a man's dense musk in my beard after we part.

Our eyes lock. I continue to dig. Sensing an intrusion he's never encountered before, he shakes his head again and again, trying to dislodge me. Big man, big will. It's like arm-wrestling. But he's only had forty-some years to gather his strength. I've had centuries.

"Put down the gun, Tobias," I say quietly. "I know you're an avid gun-toter, but those days are over. Put down the gun."

He shakes his head. His big hand begins a fine trembling.

It's intoxicating when they fight me. It makes overpowering them all the more thrilling. Forcing strength and beauty to submit: that's a quest worth the dedication of many lifetimes.

I rummage through his brain, trying to find it, the place from which to rule. Rare is the human whose will I can't subdue. Like wrapping my hand around an uncut diamond, like holding a man's heart-lump in my grasp and squeezing ever so tenderly. The fulcrum with which Archimedes suggested we might move the world.

Here. Here, I think. I press down. Tobias blinks, staggers back, lowering the gun.

"Why don't you put down that gun and fetch me a Scotch?" I'm stroking my beard, smiling at this latest in several centuries of triumphs. And, just when I think my fingers have sunk deep enough to encircle, enslave, his will flexes—an abrupt expansion, a hardening, like the sudden strain of an athlete's biceps. His eyes grow wide, and to my amazement, he shakes me off. He raises the gun, pointing it at my face.

"You tell me who the hell you are, you bastard, and what you want, or I'll blow your head off."

"So you're one of those," I say, sitting up. "You really are remarkable. In all these years, I've met only a handful of men who could do what you just did. Warriors and heroes, every one of them. A magnificent will to match a magnificent body."

"Get the fuck out of my bed, asshole." Tobias waves the gun. "And do it slow, or I'll shoot."

"Yes," I say. "Gladly." I obey. I stand in front of him naked, a mere yard's distance between us.

"What the hell?" Tobias stares down at my erection.

"This is what beauty inspires," I say. "Your fault entirely."

"What are you? Some kind of fucking—?"

That's all he gets out before I leap. I'm on him before he can lift his eyes or draw another breath. In a split-second, his grip's broken, his gun's on the carpet at his feet, and my hands are wrapped around the pulsing trunk of his neck.

"How—?" he gasps, before I dig my thumbs into the flesh over his windpipe and cut off his breath. His big hands claw at mine. His robe falls open as we sway and circle. "Jesus," he croaks. His eyes bulge and water. His face reddens. He's very, very strong; even robbed of air, he weakens slowly. It takes more time and effort than I ever would have expected to force him backward, step by straining step, to the bed's edge, to force him down and then back onto the sheets.

"And I was trying to make this meeting as cordial as possible," I say, lying on top of him, his nakedness so warm beneath mine, so moist with terror's sweat. "But of course you're a fighter. I should have known you'd opt for troublesome."

All that blood, pounding in his neck as he bucks beneath me. "You're only making me harder," I say, wrapping my legs around his to subdue his panicked kicks. He's been too proud to try to summon aid, but finally now his fear overcomes that pride. Too late, too little breath left. His cries for help are no more than frantic wheezes. I gaze into his eyes, studying the rapid flickering of his long lashes as he pries futilely at my fingers.

"Please," he says, such a small whisper from such a large man.

"We're not done yet," I say. I kiss his full lips, lightly, then strike his temple with my right knuckles—one sharp rap to the skull, as if his head were a door. He grunts. His blue eyes close. Beneath me, he goes limp.

I leave him there, slumped across the bed. For a few minutes I stand by the door, listening. Silence in the hall, no one roused by the brief struggle. Fetching his abandoned Scotch, I stand by the window, watching the snow sifting down outside. When I'm certain there will be no interruptions, I light a candle, place it on a side-table, and search among his belongings for what's needed next.

Tobias is ready now. Many hours yet till dawn, so I can take my time, I can savor the Scotch, stretch out in this big bed beside him, relish the sight of him sprawled unconscious on his back—brawny, handsome, and entirely helpless. He's naked now in the candlelight, sleeping his next-to-last sleep. I tousle his blond curls, rub his bearded chin, run a hand over his broad breast. Such a splendor; such an evil. Such a pity that I must erase one in order to erase the other.

With the terrycloth belt of his robe, I've tied his big wrists together in the small of his back. Not snug-tight, the way I like to rope up my sweet lover Matt, but hurtful-tight. Tobias' politics require it. With a leather belt found in his suitcase, I've bound his arms behind him so tightly his elbows almost touch; I want his big muscles contorted, his joints racked. With another leather belt I've cinched his ankles together. To stop his speech, I've tied two dirty white gym socks together at the toes, stuffed his mouth with the fat, foot-sour knot, and secured the ends behind his head. He's exceptionally beautiful this way. The world will be less one loveliness tomorrow.

Tobias shifts beside me, coming awake. Bending over him, I lap his chin. His eyes flicker open, blurry blue. He groans, rolling onto his side. His eyes wander, fall on me, and focus. He grits his teeth around the gag, growls deep in his throat, and tries to rise. He fails. His muscles strain. Awareness of his thoroughly powerless position fills his eyes. Truly delicious, such frantic surprise. The trammeled thrashing and stifled shouting begin.

"Keep still, Tobias. You'll hurt yourself," I say, but it's too late. Wide as the bed is, his struggles are so violent that he rolls off the edge, landing on the floor with a thump and a grunt.

I slip off the bed to fetch him. He lies stunned, on his side, knees drawn up in a fetal curl, fists clenched against the small of his back. When his struggles recommence, as do his muffled shouts, I stand astride him, then lift a foot and press it hard against the side of his face.

"Be quiet and keep still, or I'll crush your skull."

He obeys immediately.

"You're going to do what you're told?"

Tobias hesitates a second, then nods. How it must pain him, that reluctant recognition of superior strength.

"Good boy." I bend, heaving him upright. He sways there on bound feet, glaring down at me, panting into the cloth stuffing his mouth, then loses his balance and topples into my arms. I catch him, lifting him beneath shoulders and knees. I can feel him stiffen with shock as I carry him to the window.

"Look. It's still snowing," I say, gazing out into the restless sheets of white, then down at him, folded up in my arms as if he were my son. I smile. "You're wondering how a man so much smaller can pick you up?"

He sucks in air through his nose and nods. Shudders course through him.

"I have a secret," I say, "and some stories to tell."

I carry my captive to the bed, gently lower him onto it, and slip onto the sheets beside him. I gaze down at him, at that well-muscled bulk trussed up tight and panting in candlelight. He stares up at me, eyes moist with terror. I love it when they want to sob but their masculine sense of shame won't allow them. Their eyes grow wet at the edges like a farm pond's ice giving way with spring thaw.

"Take a look at you now," I say, dragging a finger over the delicate pink flesh of his gagged lips. "The Virginia senator has nothing to say?"

Tobias shakes his head slowly. How badly he wants to look away or close his eyes, but he can't. Never in all his most agonizing nightmares could he have imagined himself so powerless.

His shuddering is even more violent now that we're in bed together. Plus the building's old, the room's drafty, snow's swarming the windowpanes.

"Are you cold?"

Tobias nods. "Poor boy," I sigh. Stretching out on my back beside him, I pull the covers over us, lean back on the pillows heaped against the headboard, and say, "Put your head on my chest." Bound as tightly as he is, it takes a little squirming on his part, a little nudging on mine, till the weight of his big head rests over my heart.

"Isn't this sweet?" I sigh, wrapping an arm around him. "You feel so good against me. Comfortable?"

Tobias shakes his head emphatically. Behind the sock-knot a grunted "Huh uh."

Chuckling, I play with the hair fringing his nipples. He stiffens against me; jagged trembling runs through him.

"You hate this, don't you? My touching you?"

A slow nod. More trembling.

"Good. Would you like to know why I'm here? Other than to do this?" I tug at his belly-hair now, squeeze the thick muscles of his shoulders and arms, the thick meat of his chest. "Other than to pay homage to your considerable might?"

"Ummm mmm," he mumbles into the socks, breathing heavily through his nose. I pull him closer, sip my Scotch, and stroke his head of golden curls.

"Let me begin with this," I say. Even after these several centuries, I can't keep the sorrow from my voice, stern as I might want to sound tonight. "In 1730, my lover Angus and I were caught making love, attacked by a gang of men like you. Men who thought their God hated us. Angus died. He was stabbed to death. I was saved for another life."

Tobias emits a low, long groan. His shaking grows more violent.

"Do you understand? This is why I am stronger and faster than you could ever be, why my skin is so chilly against you."

Tobias shakes his head. He gives a small sob.

"You're still shivering. Are you still cold? I am as well. Here, let me hold you closer." Rolling him onto his side, I curl up against him, his broad back to my chest. My left arm pillows his head, my right arm I wrap around him.

"Better. Ah, you're so, so warm," I say, caressing his beefy chest beneath the blanket. "Tobias, do you remember that hateful amendment you helped pass? The one outlawing same-sex marriages in Virginia? The one insuring that 'any contracts between same-sex couples that might approximate marriage would be illegal'? I think that was the wording. Tonight really began there. And with three people with whose fates I'm familiar. I wish you could have known them. Perhaps then you and I would never have met."

I rest my palm against his breastbone. His heart drums madly beneath my hand. I nuzzle his nape, smell the blood coursing beneath his thin, fragile skin, and lick my lips.

"There was Charlotte, a bar-buddy of my lover Matt's. She was driving home one night when a drunk driver hit her head-on. Her lover Grace was barred from her hospital room. Thanks to your amendment, Grace was not considered family. So Charlotte died alone. Can you imagine that?"

Another choked sob. A gag-muffled "No," a shaking of the head.

"Then there was Karen, Matt's friend from college years ago. Her ex-husband swore to identify her as a lesbian in court if she fought him for custody of their two sons. She hanged herself in her barn. That's the kind of world your laws help create, Tobias. Can you see that?"

"No, no." Muffled, but louder.

"And sweet little Chet, Matt's cousin. Just sixteen years old. Thanks to your adept political maneuvering and all your fundamentalist friends, his high school wouldn't allow a gay-straight alliance. No sympathy from his parents, who told him he was a damned-to-hell monster. The boy drowned himself in Peak Creek last week. My lover's been weeping on and off ever since."

As I whisper in Tobias' ear, I press my hand over his brow, and inside his skull I cause them to appear, the consequences of his demagogical bluster: the bloated body hung off creaking rafters, the pale limbs splayed in gray water, the woman sobbing in a hospital waiting room. Beneath my palm, the images cascade through his brain, on and on, on and on, the pain, the deaths, the fear he's helped create.

Enough. I lift my hand from his forehead, and the stream of stories stops. "They were my kin. Now do you see why I'm here?"

This time a nod. This time a sock-muted "Yes." This time an unchecked trickle of silent tears I wipe from his face with my thumb.

"Good." For a full minute I stroke his streaming cheeks, tasting the salt, the remorse, the appetizer of brine. Suddenly, roughly, I roll him onto his belly, climb on top of him, and clamp one hand over his gagged mouth.

"What a Christian," I say, stroking the fuzzy crevice between his buttocks. Tobias gasps beneath my grip; his broad shoulders heave.

"Here's your salvation," I say, spitting into my palm, then moistening us both. "Here's your forgiveness." I burrow a wet fingertip into him, and his sphincter muscles spasm against me. Manly beauty has always inspired in me an urge to possess, dominate, punish, and control. But the combination of beauty and hatefulness that Tobias embodies sparks in me a sadism no human can long survive.

Were I to give him the benefit of the doubt, I might assume that these sobs wracking him are born of guilt in the face of the destruction I've shown him, the misery he's helped create. I suspect, however, that what's really evoking his tears is the certainty of what's about to come, as well as the bodily pain I'm causing as I roughly push my finger deeper. Men I respect, men like my lover Matt, I take slowly, solicitously. Tobias, well, I'm using very little spit and very little patience.

"Sweet country boy, virile Virginia virgin. You're so tight and sweet and soft inside," I sigh, wedging a second finger in. He jerks and whines. Sobs shake him like winter rattling the windowpane.

"If you were fat and old and homely, like most of your right-wing colleagues, you'd be spared this," I say, pulling out my fingers only to nudge my moistened cock against his tightness. "This is what comes of being so proud and handsome," I say, pushing into him an inch.

Now he goes wild beneath me, screaming against my hand, tugging on his bonds, thrashing and bucking. I love such resistance. It only highlights my own supernatural strength. Wrapping an arm around his torso, I let him flail and shout for a moment or two before shoving my cock's entire length into him and simultaneously burying my fangs in his sweaty neck.

I pump into Tobias, Tobias' blood pumps into me. Contrapuntal rhythm. Ass full, mouth full. Spilling not a drop, I gulp down his strength, his will, his youth, his manhood; my gray hair, beard, and chest pelt slowly blacken in answer. Beneath my hand, he keeps screaming for a while. Beneath my weight, he keeps thrashing for a while. Then, as the tide of his blood recedes, the screams slow, dwindling to barely audible pleas, and the struggles slacken.

Practice allows me perfect timing: I retract my fangs just before he passes out but well after he's too weak to put up any further fight. He simply lies there now, wheezing beneath me with each cock-thrust, bound hands fumbling at nothing, brushing my belly hair as I ride him hard. Occasionally, in response to a particularly savage slamming, he manages a muffled groan. This is a judicial ecstasy I've been long yearning for, so, as much as I would enjoy prolonging this, I'm soon done. Wrapping an arm around his throat, I shove into him one last time, shudder, grunt, explode.

I wake with a start. Sated, I've been happily drowsing on top of him. It is, I sense, about four hours before daybreak. The candle has burnt low. Snow still fills the windowpanes with busy, silent static.

I roll off Tobias and lie beside him. His bonds and gag are still in place; he's still breathing, still conscious. Eyelashes fluttering, slowly he shifts his stare from the sheet to my face. In the candlelight, his cheeks gleam with tears. I kiss his gold-brown goatee and his blood-ied neck. I press my lips to his big ass, lap the smooth, pale skin there, then spread his buttocks and push my tongue inside him to harvest violation's crimson ooze. What might he have been without evangeli-cal poison in him, the Christians' vicious piety?

He's perfectly still as I untie his elbows, hands, and feet. When I prop him up into a sitting position, he slumps against me. When I heft him with eldritch ease into my arms, huge man that he is, his head falls against my face, his arms bounce loosely.

"It's time to end this, Tobias," I whisper. Around the knot of the sock-gag, he takes a deep breath. Exhaling slowly, he nods acquies-cence against my beard.

The bathroom is even colder than the bedroom. It's spacious, with a marble sink covered with the tentacles of potted plants, with a window of glass bricks against which the thickening snow bats. The shower is simply a tiled corner without a curtain, with a big floor-drain down which I might later rinse any scarlet stains my hunger misses. Carefully I shift docile Tobias from my arms to the floor, turn the water on, adjust its temperature, then drag him into the stream-ing wet warmth. On the floor I sit cross-legged with him in my arms, his heavy linebacker's body cradled in my lap. I nuzzle his gagged mouth, then loosen the socks, let the silencing circle of knotted cloth fall around his neck, and kiss him tenderly on the lips. I caress his rapidly moistening curls, his nipples, his fading heartbeat. His head sags against my shoulder. He hasn't strength enough to groan.

Warm water sluices through my shaggy dark hair, running through my beard to drip over his face. It runs down his thick torso, his hairy belly, and mats up his pubes. I cup his flaccid cock in my hand. "Warm enough?"

His lips move silently. Another long draught and he'll be done.

"I'm Derek Maclaine," I say, apropos of nothing.

"You are so beautiful," I sigh, rocking him in my arms. "You were so strong. You could have been so good, so true. Why did you listen to them? What a warrior you could have made. What a brother-in-arms. I would have been proud to love you."

Lifting his limp right hand from the tiles, I hold it in mine. When I squeeze it, with what life he has left he returns the pressure.

I gaze down into Tobias' glazed blue eyes for a long time. "It's all right," I say, smoothing curls off his brow. "Sweet boy."

He smiles up at me sleepily. He lifts his free hand to touch the barbed wire inked into my upper arm, then, with a visible effort, reaches up to brush my tangled black hair and beard before his fingers droop and his hand drops exhausted into his lap.

"Here You are," he whispers in disbelief, words so weak even I can barely discern them. "It's You. You. Oh, Lord, oh, Jesus, I been waiting for You."

Together we listen to the snow-wind beyond the walls, holding hands in the steamy rush of the shower. Prisoners of necessity, we are both late for different destinations, and it is nearly dawn, nearly time to part, but let us sit here for a while yet, pressed together in this warm womb hemmed in by winter. I will stay with Tobias till he closes his eyes, till his hand releases mine, till, soon, soon, he needs me no longer.

Whitby

(FOR ANGELIA R. WILSON)

It's hard to name the color of his eyes, even in bright café light. They're brown from one angle, hazel from another. Now they're gray, as he cups his hands behind his head, arches his back, stretches hugely, and yawns. His thick biceps bulge, cresting like Highland hills. His T-shirt tautens over his chest, highlighting the curved meat of his pecs, the promontories of his nipples. Down the long length of him, he grins, staring at me over his ale. The bastard knows how hungrily I'm soaking him in. He's putting on quite a show.

I sip my pint of Tetley's bitter, stroke my bushy goatee, gone silvery since my last meal, and grin back. It's a tight grin, meant to hide lengthening fang-teeth. That's a surprise I'll save for later, once we're alone. My gaze rakes the dense ink of his twin tattoo sleeves—black, gray, and purple thistles and thorns—then returns to his chameleon eyes.

"How much?" I ask, as the waitress places before Robbie a steaming plate of fried cod and chips. He gobbles a good quarter of the fish in about ten seconds, wiping tartar sauce from the bearded corner of his mouth. "Two hundred quid an oor, mate," he says, before taking a big swig of ale and then munching a handful of potatoes. There's a tiny chip marring his right front tooth, a detail that adds to his overall air: rough-and-tough, yet boyishly endearing. "Normally one hundred, but extra since ye say ye like it kinky."

The iPhone my partner Matt bought me this last Yule has certainly proven handy in locating feasts during this most recent of my UK visits. It's found both this cheery restaurant, the Magpie Café, and this fetching Scots hustler. "Butch Glasgow Top. Hairy, bearded, built, tattooed. Age 30, horny and hung," said the profile, beside a tiny photo of Robbie grinning and flexing one burly, inked-up arm. Perfect source of warmth on this cold March night in northern England. I love the accent, that Glaswegian burr. I love the breadth of his shoulders, the dark fur foaming over his T-shirt collar, the trimmed brown beard, the long brown eyelashes. The boy's built like a full-back, considerably bulkier than I, with thick-muscled arms and torso and just the beginning of a beer-gut, all self-consciously and seductively displayed in a skin-tight white T-shirt. Exactly what his profile advertised, exactly what I'd hoped for.

I'm not even trying to hide my predatory stare. "Ye fancy ma look, eh, Mr. Maclaine?" Robbie's got more tartar sauce in his beard. If we weren't surrounded by noisy tables of diners, I'd offer to lick it off. He takes another big gulp of ale and finishes the first of the three pieces of fish.

"Yes, I do. You're even hotter than I expected. A physique like Hercules. How long since you've eaten, by the way? You seem ravenous."

"Ah, I'm always hungrysome. Ma dad calls me the locust." Robbie wipes grease off his lips with the back of his hand. "Mind if I order pudding? They have my favorite, roly-poly. It's verra fine here."

"I don't mind. Stuff yourself. You'll need the energy for later."

"I vow to plow ye fine, mate," Robbie says with a wink and a crooked grin.

"So you're from Scotland? I grew up on the Isle of Mull...a long time ago. How do you make a living, other than offering escort services for lonely gentlemen like me?"

"Auto mechanic," says Robbie. Lewdly he tongues the tip of a chip, then slides the fried slice of potato slowly between his lips. "I'm handy with engines of all varieties. Yers need some attention tonight? Some lubrication, eh? Need me to drive ye home? Ile up your parts?" Another big swig of beer, this one leaving a pale smear in his moustache, foam he laps off with a leer and a flourish.

His clumsy double entrendres and suggestive gestures make him even more appealing. Blue-collar vulgarity, it's a lagniappe. Reminds me of my sweet lover Matt and the other potty-mouthed country boys I've doted on back in Appalachia. As if a man this throbbing-hot needs to waste his energies on seduction.

"Let's just say that I'm mightily hungry and grateful you weren't already booked tonight. Someone like you is bound to make me feel younger." I can't resist a few double-edged expressions of my own. "Bound to satisfy."

"Ye'll get yer money's worth, Mr. Maclaine, I promise, though y'might be walking a wee bit crooked come the morn. I'm verra thick, if ye catch ma meaning." Robbie pats his thigh and arches an eyebrow. "Wouldn't want to hurt ye," he says, voice low and husky. "I'm too much for some blokes. Ye think ye can tak me?"

I chuckle. "I'm sure I'll manage. I have no doubt you'll quench my thirst. But first, satisfy my curiosity. What's a Glaswegian mechanic doing in Whitby, other than making a little money on the side?" My eyes keep returning to the chunky curvature of his chest, the points of his nipples, the hair curling over his collar. The boy must be hairy as a bear.

"Ah! I'm gled ye asked!" shouts Robbie. He gulps the last of his pint, unzips the backpack resting on the floor, and jerks out a paperback. "*Dracula*! *Dracula*, mate! Part of it was set here, ye know! Whitby Harbor was where the vampire's ship ran aground after he left Transylvania! He lowpit off the ship in the form of a wolf! He hidit in the suicide's grave! Here he took his first victim in England!"

One minute a seductive hustler, the next an overgrown, enthusiastic kid. Robbie's so loud and excited that folks at several tables about us turn to stare before returning to their food. "Right," I say. "I remember. Lucy Westenra. He fed on her in St. Mary's churchyard, right across the river." Delicious. Exactly where I should take him later on tonight. It will be a literary lark. "But what does that have to do with—"

"Ah, I'm a *writer*, mate! I'm here to research ma novel. Being a mechanic pays the bills, but writing's really what I do. Y'see, ma book's gaun to be a sequel to *Dracula*! It'll sell whappin big! Y'know at the end of the novel they never staked him, right? They just cut his throat and knifed him in the hert. No wooden stake, y'see? So what if the bruit survived, eh? What if—"

Robbie chatters for forty minutes straight, through the last of the fish and chips, through three more pints, a scotch, and an order of roly-poly pudding with custard. If he weren't so visually luscious, he'd be intolerable. Typical would-be author's attitude, this pure self-absorption. Perfect candidate for a ball-gag. His writerly ambitions, however, have given me an idea. Greed is so easy to manipulate.

Fairly well sauced by now, if his slurred burr is any indication, Robbie finally winds down. "And so what I nee's a bad dream. Like Stoker. Y'know he got his idea for *Dracula* from a nightmare? Ate too much dressed crab, he did, and dreamed of the count. So that's how *this*"—Robbie waves the paperback at me—"got started! Fuck all! I just need ridden by a nightmare. For insp'ration!"

I choke back a snicker. Bending forward, I take a deep breath of him—some sort of woodsy cologne, olfactory patina atop his body's warm musk, and, bass note beneath that, his lifeblood. Below the table, I grip his knee. "I'd like to see the churchyard, Robbie. Why don't you give me a tour?"

W e're both bundled against the damp chill of northern England, Robbie in a jacket of brown rawhide, I in my black Western duster. It's a cloudy night, with a sharp breeze off the North Sea. St. Mary's churchyard is a long walk from the Magpie—along the river, across the bridge, and up, up, up the 199 steps to the hilltop, where the church stands, and, behind it, the crumbling walls and Gothic arches of a ruined abbey. Young and well built as he is, Robbie's panting by the time we reach the top, his breath fogging the night air, his gait a little unsteady on all that alcohol. He's too self-absorbed to notice that, despite the long and strenuous climb, my breathing is unaffected. Amazing stamina is one of several gifts I received that night in 1730.

All about the squat-towered church eroded gravestones jut. We wander among them before taking a seat on a bench. It's very dark up here, but below us are the lights of Whitby, spilling over the steep slopes of the valley channeling the river Esk, and the harbor, a widening where the river meets the sea. In the distance, the sheer Yorkshire headlands recede, breaking waves a recurrent gray against their feet. To our right, the churchyard's edge drops off into sea cliff. A good place to toss leftovers, were one to have a mind to.

"Here, I think," I say, resting an arm across Robbie's wide shoulders.

My delicious escort's mind is clearly stuck on Bram Stoker rather than tonight's assignation. He misreads me. "Aye, right, mate, Mina saw Lucy from over there," he says, pointing across the valley. "Lucy was in her nightgoun sitting on one of these kirkyaird benches and something daurk was bent over her. The count! Mina ran across the brig we just crossed and all the way up those bloody stairs, for fuck's sake! She saw the count's fauchie-pale face and glistering red eyes! She found Lucy here. The next day she noticed the bite on Lucy's throat. In ma novel, I think I'll—"

"Did you bring lube?"

Robbie turns to me, thick eyebrows knitted. "Aye, in my jaiket."

"Good. It's time you shut up and strip," I say. "I want to fuck you."

Robbie shrugs my arm off. "Here? It's too cauld. And *I'm* the Top, ye recall. No, Mr. Maclaine, le's go back to ma hotel. Ye're *strappin*, an eesome bonnie bloke, but ye'll look even better with yer lang shanks in the air. I'll stuff my briefs in yer gab and haimer ye till ye sab, mate, I'll—"

"No," I say evenly. "Here. Tonight I think you'll enjoy being the bottom. Surely a man as handsome as you has been ass-fucked before? And I don't think I'll need to pay you. I have something else you want more than money."

Robbie stands up, fists clenched, face grim. "Look, wanker, are ye mental? Are ye an *eejit*? Do you want a *bleachin*? We agreed—"

If I were mortal, a man this large and angry might be intimidating. But as it is, I'm simply amused. I stand up, smiling. I could try to mesmerize him or I could simply overpower him, but this is more fun. It's always entertaining to turn a man's greed against him.

"Lucky for you that we met. I'm a publisher," I say, pulling out my wallet and producing a business card. "I own a publishing company in America. How'd you like to get your vampire novel published?"

Robbie's mouth drops open. He takes the card from me, peering at it in the darkness. "Too mirkie to read," he says.

"Trust me," I say. "Are you willing to forgo such an opportunity?"

"Ye'd publish me?" Frowning, Robbie folds his arms across his chest. He's shivering. Tight T-shirts are good for pec display but not too handy at keeping a man warm in England's late winter.

"If your book's any good at all."

"Why would ye do that?" Suspicious, dubious, hopeful. Delectable.

"Because I'll owe you. Because you're going to do exactly what I say now. You're going to please me all night in every way I require. Am I right?"

"Yer word, mate. I need yer word."

"You have my word. And my card." I slip it into his back pants pocket, then pat his big ass. "Now strip."

Robbie hesitates, still disbelieving. "I'm na sure. What if ye're a psycho?"

"You aren't afraid of me, are you? A big-muscled man like you? The Glaswegian Hercules?"

Pride pricked, his frown deepens. "Afraid? Nah! But what if ye're conning me?

"All right," I say, moving toward the path on which we came. "Good luck with that novel."

I've passed only five time-stained gravestones before Robbie shouts. "Wait, Mr. Maclaine! Come back. Aye, I'll do it! I—I'll do what ye say."

I turn. He's shucked off his jacket. By the time I've returned to his side, he's peeled his shirt off. He stands before me, bare-chested and trembling, hugging himself. My fangs lengthen again, beginning to throb. The wind picks up, rolling off the jet-black sea.

"All of it," I say. He sits on the bench, unlaces his Doc Marten's, tugs them off, peels off his army pants, then his skimpy briefs. He stands before me, clad now in nothing but white socks and a thick metal cock ring.

"Very fine," I say, licking my lips. "Put your hands behind your back. Keep still and keep quiet. Scenery this mouth-watering deserves some study."

Robbie obeys. Our eyes lock for a few seconds, but then he can take my gaze no longer. Shame-faced, he hangs his head. I circle him, taking in the details. Stocky as a barrel, thickset as an oak trunk. Sturdy arms entirely etched in ink. The dense chest- and belly-pelt I'd expected. Big nipples stiff and prominent with the cold. A broad, round ass, cheeks and crack coated with more delightful hair. And, between his substantial thighs, a short fat cock, standing erect in its pubic nest.

I laugh. "Hell, aren't you pretty?" I stroke his cock. Robbie shudders. "Seems like you savor submission all of a sudden," I say, thumbing a drop of precum, smearing it over the head. "And I thought you were all Top."

"Mostly," he mutters. "Na always." He shuffles in the dead grass. He clears his throat. "Sometimes I bottom if the bloke's hot and butch and willin' to pay extra."

I drop his cock and step behind him. From my duster's pocket I fetch the cuffs. He jumps at the sudden chill of metal about his wrist, but before he can react further I have both hands locked together behind his back.

"No, no, mate!" my captive gasps. He tries to turn, to pull away, but I wrap my arms around his quaking frame, pulling him close.

"You're not going anywhere, Robbie," I say, holding him firmly against me. "A man as handsome as you needs to be bound. My rapture requires it."

"Don't hurt me. Please, Mr. Maclaine. Don't—"

I lick the fan of hair between his shoulder blades, the furry patches capping his shoulders.

"What? You're going to scream for help like some Victorian damsel? I won't hurt a man who does what he's told. All right?"

Robbie nods; his struggles subside. When I run my fingers over his hard nipples and torso-thatch, he gives a little groan.

"Suck me," I say, releasing him. Sitting back on the bench, I pull my very hard cock from my jeans. "Now."

Robbie needs no further direction. Dropping to his knees, he takes me into his mouth's hot grip. For a supposed Top, he's a surprisingly fine cocksucker, tonguing my slit, gently gnawing the head, deep-throating me till I begin to pump his face hard. He chokes and gags, then rediscovers his rhythm, his beard tickling my balls, his saliva moistening my shaft and dripping onto my lap. I sigh, looking out over the harbor, the dark and distant bluffs that drop so steeply into sea. I take Robbie's big pecs in my hands and knead them, tugging on the thick hair there. When I pinch his nipples, he groans around my cock, nods, and bobs with even more vigor on the stiffness stuffing his mouth.

"Like a little hurt, huh?" I chuckle. For long minutes I give him the rough tit-work he clearly relishes, his slurps alternating with excited sighs. "Now for your ass." Pulling my penis from his eager suction, I lift him to his feet. "You're the one getting fucked tonight."

"Ma novel? You swear?" he says. He staggers a little, beard dripping wet.

"Yes," I say, pulling a ball-gag from my duster pocket. "Now let's make you even more helpless."

His eyes widen. He emits a little gasp as I push the black ball between his teeth. "Umm umm," he mumbles in protest, shaking his head like a dog, giving me some fight.

"Behave, or the deal's off," I say. Instantly he submits, allowing me to buckle the straps behind his head with no further trouble.

"You were quite the chatterbox this evening," I say, leading him behind the bench, shoving him forward, bending him over the back of it. "I've been wanting to shut you up for a while now. In my considered opinion, men as hot as you should be kept naked, bound, and gagged most of the time."

Robbie shakes and grunts as I brush my silvery goatee over his ass-cheeks, then tug at the hair in his crack with my teeth. "You like your hole eaten?" I whisper, raking a fang gently across one cheek, then the other.

My hairy Scot nods. His groan is long and low, much like a foghorn, as I clench his broad cheeks, spread him, and work my tongue up inside.

He's opening now, like a pink peach blossom, and, if his happy nods and ecstatic grunts are any indication, he's having quite the fine time. I tongue-fuck him for a good while, savoring the tasty ass-amalgam of musky, salty, bitter, and sweet, nipping his butt-cheeks every now and then.

"You ready to be ridden?" I say, running my fingers over his ass and down the wet cleft.

This nod's more enthusiastic than any before. The bigger and butcher the man, the hornier and hungrier the bottom, 'tis true indeed. So much for his Top pose. In a flash, I've fetched lube from his jacket, dropped my jeans around my ankles, greased us up, and am pushing my cock against his hole.

"You want me inside you, don't you, Robbie?"

He nods, fists clenched in the small of his back.

"Beg me to fuck you, Robbie."

He pleads and mumbles around his gag: unintelligible syllables, ball-muffled, spit-wet, compliant.

Robbie whimpers and winces as I work the head in, apparently hurting a bit, head tossing like a Highland pony. His is the kind of ass I love most: rarely used, almost painfully tight. Slowly he opens further, my brave boy. He keeps mumbling and nodding as, by slow degrees, I slide inside him and begin moving in and out, a rhythm of cresting sweetness. Soon, he's spread his legs wider and pushed back against me, driving me deeper into him, his flesh gripping me hard from inside.

"Does that feel good?" I growl, gripping him by his hair, pounding him harder. "Do you want more?" I can feel, tight around my cock, the throbbing of his blood, the racing of his heart. Cold as the night is, his back's growing faintly silver with sweat. "Uh huh!" he murmurs. "Uh *huh!*"

The bench creaks beneath us as I ride him. I stroke his gag-taut-ened lips, saliva smearing my hand. I fist his hard cock, dig my fingers into his nipples, grip his pec-meat and tug. I gaze out over the twinkling seed-pearl lights of Whitby, down at his broad back, his tattooed arms, his cuffed, fumbling hands, out again to the harbor and the sea. Beautiful man, beautiful vista. I can't recall a more pleasing combination.

Another few minutes of bucking and grunting in flawless unison and we're finished, I up his hole's snug sheath, he in my hand's tight stroke. I lie atop him, licking up sweat-beads along his spine. When he's caught his breath, I help him up. We sit side by side on the bench.

Heavily he leans against me. I wrap my arms around him, lapping first drool from his beard, then his semen from my hand.

"In a little while, I'm going to take you back to your hotel room," I say, "and warm you up. I'm going to cuff your hands in front of you, tape your pretty bearded mouth shut, take you to bed, and cuddle with you all night. Just before dawn, I'm going to hoist your legs over my shoulders and ram your hairy ass again. Would you like that?"

Robbie nods, his breath slowing, his shivers renewed by the sea breeze.

"Say please," I coax, bumping his chin with mine.

"Pleh," he grunts. Bubbles of saliva fleck his lips.

I nuzzle his neck, licking the throbbing column of his carotid artery. Now that one hunger's been answered, it's time to sate the second. "Didn't you say you needed a nightmare? I'm ready to give you that."

Robbie has time only to lift one curious brow before I've bared my fangs. Gripping his hair, I yank his head back. His eyes go wide, twin terror stars. His frame stiffens against me. His scream's a well-dammed torrent.

My teeth sink into his neck. Against the rubber ball, Robbie keeps screaming and screaming. His thick body thrashes against me. I hold him close, gulping and growling, lips clamped to his neck. Within minutes his youth has flooded and filled me with its luminous liquid. His blood's thick and sweet as wildflower honey; in it are the salt of Northern seas, the metallic tang of swords.

I pull away as soon as Robbie passes out, before any lasting damage is done. A few centuries of such supping has taught me that skill. Lowering my captive gently onto the bench, I sit by him, watching his broad, hair-dark breast rise and fall. A light rain has begun, falling upon my head and in my beard, upon Robbie's naked form and the old gravestones about us. I could lift him to me and drain him completely, fling his husk over the sea cliff, be on my way. That would be expedient, uncomplicated.

That would be weak. The world needs all the loveliness it can get. Droplets of rain are beading the matted fur of his torso, belly, and groin; the slow wash of rain thins out the blood oozing from his wound. With a fingertip I trace the thorny swirls of his extensive tattoos. It will be grand to own him.

Robbie groans. His long-lashed eyes flicker open. He stares up at me without fright. His glance is fond, familiar, acquiescent.

I help him sit upright. I unbuckle the gag, unlock the cuffs. "Thanks, mate," he mutters, listing limply against me. I rub the stiffness from his jaw, from his wrists. I lick the last crimson from his neck.

"What happened?"

"You fainted. Get dressed," I say.

He does so, slowly, wobbly from blood loss. The rain thickens about us. Out on the sea, a mist creeps toward the land. The distant head-lands grow vague. Far up the coast, a lighthouse flashes.

Clothed, he stands before me. "Robbie, you have a choice," I say, straightening his collar. "If you want, I can make you forget this night. Do you want to forget?"

Robbie gives me a puzzled smile. "Yer hair and beard are black now," he says, stroking my face. "Na, sir, I don't want to forget ye. Who would want to forget such a royal plowing as ye gave me? And that fiery kiss?"

"If you invite me to your room, I'll hold you till dawn. Tomorrow night, if you choose, I'll come to you again, here among the graves, or by your bedside. Whenever I return to this land, you may serve me, be my boy, my slave. I'll care for you well."

"I need na choices, Mr. Maclaine." Robbie runs a hand across his rain-spattered brow. "Dinna understand it, but I know I'm yers now. Come callin' whenever ye tak the mind. I'll be ready and eager. To open for ye, if ye catch ma meaning." He steps forward, wraps his big arms around me, and rests his chin on my shoulder with a sigh. "Sir, the room I'm lettin' is on Crescent Terrace. Help me back there, will ye? Seems I'm a wee bit dizzy. All this cauld and damp, I guess."

"On the way, let's stop for some single malt by a pub fire," I say. "That should warm us up till I get you naked again. Meanwhile, here's a little advance."

Pulling out my wallet, I peel off a thousand pounds and lay the bills in his palm.

"What's this?"

"For your novel. Have you had sufficient dreams to inspire you?"

Robbie stares at the money. "Well, fuck me." He pockets it, then gives me a quick kiss. I can smell my own musk in his beard.

"First round's on me, mate, master, Mr. Maclaine."

The fog's reached the coast now, swallowing us in its deep chill. I grip Robbie's hand, leading him through the gravestones. He stumbles once, across a broken bit of statuary, but his stride has steadied by the time we reach the stairs and begin our descent, through the lowing of a distant foghorn and the thickening mist. Wrapping a protective arm around him, I help him down the wet steps, leading him from the dark hilltop of the dead into the warm yellow lights of town.

Wolf Moon/ Hunger Moon

I.

"He won Best Butt at the Roanoke Bear Run," Matt whispers. We're watching our waiter's ass with avid fascination as he crosses the café to place an order. I can smell the boy from here—my vampire senses are almost always an advantage, unless I'm around garlic or that Appalachian equivalent, the wild onions called ramps that folks hereabouts love to feast on in the spring. Something about his aroma is abnormal; there's a feral whiff I find both arousing and worrisome. I can smell animal in the musks of most men, which is why I like my prey unwashed—no damned colognes for me—but this boy's scent is wild in a way I haven't smelled in a very long time.

"Woof!" Matt says, grinning. "I'd sure like us to make a sandwich out of that cub! You didn't see the Butt Contest, since it was held in the afternoon, and you were sleeping, but, man, I did. They had the contestants strip down to underwear and then doused 'em with water and had 'em bend over, and, Lord, that waiter. Big ole chunky rear! Through the wet boxers you could see the hair all over his cheeks and in his ass-crack." Matt smacks his lips. "No wonder the lil' bastard won."

My husbear's as horned up as ever, and I love it, whether the object of his lust is myself or other men. We've been together for ten years; his age is finally showing a bit. He's forty-five, as muscular as ever but thicker around the middle. His shaggy hair's stippled with gray, as is his bushy goatee. When he grins, there are faint lines around his hazel eyes. He's never been handsomer, more desirable, but still I recognize the signs, the slow way he's leaving me. I too age when I haven't fed for a while—tonight my black beard and ponytail are silver-streaked as well—but after several deep draughts of blood, I'm young again, I look like I'm thirty again, the age I was when I was turned.

"I know what you're thinking," Matt says, flashing me that fur-framed grin that made me fall in love with him. "You're thinking how damned black that hot little waiter's beard is, compared to my grizzled-geezer look, and how much you'd like to tie him to our bed and pump that plumpcious rear of his."

"'Plumpcious?' Great! Actually, I'm thinking that I'd like to have you two roped down side by side, so I could take turns riding your butts. He looks like a younger version of you." I sip my wine and look out the café window: January flurries dusting the streets of Monterey, Virginia.

"Yeeow! That would be a hot scene!" Matt rubs his hands together. "Might try to arrange that. Let me lay on my hillbilly charm! Hasn't failed me yet!"

Matt's enthusiasm is adorable. His earthy, untrammeled sensuality is one of many reasons I cherish him. "Or I could mesmerize him," I say, "if you want him that bad." My knee bumps his. It's always been fun being Matt's conspirator in seduction. Four-fifths of the time his good looks and aggressive appeal are enough. "Though I doubt we'll need my powers of glamour. You're a long damn way from being a geezer, and you know it. With your charisma, you can still land any stud you want."

"Hm." Matt strokes his beard and chuckles. "Such flattery. I love it! Well, don't know about charisma, but I will say I look a little younger every time you bareback me. I'm thinking that...the human lovers you had before, did you notice that—?"

"Yep." I take a sip of red wine and grin, flashing a split-second of bared fang. "Regular ass-loads of vampire semen do seem to prolong a mortal's youth."

"Well, then, how 'bout later tonight you inject me with a little of that fountain of youth, Daddy?" Matt's whisper is husky. Beneath the table, his Carhartt boot rubs mine. "Get us a fire going in the bedroom. Cuff me and cuddle with me. Work my nips some. Stuff a jock in my mouth and—"

I savor listening to Matt's hoarse butch-bottom requests as much as he savors composing them, but his lusty whisper's interrupted by our waiter, who reappears with a solemn look and a heaped tray. There's something tense about him, an anxious aloofness.

"Here we go," he says flatly, doling out a plate of cat's head biscuits and a bowl of beef stew for Matt, plus more wine for me. "Hope y'all enjoy." His bass voice is almost absurdly deep. The cub half-turns to leave, giving me a meaty profile of pec- and belly-flesh filling out the front of his black t-shirt.

Matt's not about to let this shy find get away so easily. "Donnie, right?" he says, breaking open a biscuit. "I saw you at last summer's run. The one the Virginia Mountain Bears put on."

The boy turns back to us, running a nervous hand over his buzz-cut. He's short—several inches less than Matt's five foot eight—with broad shoulders and a burly frame. Not more than twenty-five, I'd wager. Can't recall the last time I saw skin that pale, eyes that dark, a beard so black. Or arms so hairy. The fur starts at the wrists, coats his forearms, and continues on up to beefy biceps before disappearing beneath the sleeves of his t-shirt.

"The run? Really?"

"Really. I saw you win that contest too. You deserved it." Matt stares at him. "Finest butt in the New River Valley, I'd say."

I may be a preternaturally powerful member of the undead, but Matt's infinitely bolder when it comes to flirtation. The boy blushes furiously, the stern look breaking into a sheepish grin, a glint of white teeth, before returning to tense solemnity.

"W-Whoa, man. Thanks, thanks," he stammers, dark brown eyes sidling sideways. For a guy so handsome, he seems painfully shy. "That run was fun."

"I'll bet you had a slew of admirers," Matt says. "Not much in the way of queer nightlife around here, I'll bet."

"In Monterey?" Donnie snorts. "Hell, no. Nearest, uh, nearest bar's Roanoke."

"Yeah, we get it," Matt replies. "We're small-town boys too. I'm Matt Taylor," he adds, offering his hand.

They shake. The contact continues about two seconds longer than it would have if they were straight.

"Strong grip," Donnie says with a wince. "Now that you mention it, I remember you too. And you too, sir. Are y'all partners?"

Sir. I love it. "Yes indeed. I'm Derek Maclaine." I offer my hand. Donnie's grip is firm and warm. His feral-scented musk washes over me. It seems familiar; it makes my cock harden and the hair on the back of my neck prickle with unease. "Have a seat." I pat the booth beside me. "If you have time."

Donnie looks back at the kitchen. "Well...." he murmurs, then half reluctantly scoots in. "Thanks, bud, uh, Mr. Maclaine. I, uh, I got, uh, a few minutes. So what y'all doing here? Do y'all live around here?"

The booth's narrow; Donnie's denimed thigh is a warm pressure along mine. "We live up in West Virginia," I say, "in German Valley. About half an hour away. Big mountaintop farmhouse we call Mount Storm. I telecommute—I'm in publishing—and Matt here works for the Forest Service."

"Yep," exclaims Matt. "And I'm a damn good cook, if I do say so myself. Y'ought to come up for dinner sometime. We got a fireplace and a hot tub. Bring your boyfriend if you'd like."

"Uh, I'm single as of, of yet," Donnie mutters, an admission that causes Matt to break into a pleased grin. Donnie drops his gaze and brushes a crumb off the tablecloth. "But, well, uh, sure, man. Sometime. Do you like, do you like our little café?"

"Derek here, he works days, so he don't make it down much, but, hell, I'm here at least once a week gobbling up your all's pintos, chow-chow, and cornbread. Plus I can't get enough of these cat's head biscuits! How come I ain't ever seen you in here before? Good-looking cub like you I wouldn't have missed."

Donnie musters another blush and clears his throat. "Thanks for the compliment, bud. You all are, you all are a handsome couple, for sure." He looks intently, first at Matt, then at me before yet again dropping his eyes. "Uh, well, I'm new 'round here. Just moved to the area. I rent me a little trailer near Head Waters."

Matt takes a deep breath—I can feel him gathering his energies, preparing to make an even bolder move—when Donnie abruptly rises. "Well, look, Mr. Taylor, Mr. Maclaine. It was real nice, it was, uh, real nice to meet ya. Y'all seem like real cool dudes, but, um, I better be getting back to work."

"Whoa! Hold on! Here!" Matt fumbles out a business card and pushes it into Donnie's hand. "E-mail's on the back. And there's my cell phone number. What's your number?"

"Thanks, man. Gotta go." He hurries off, our gazes once again affixed to his butt.

Matt's stew and biscuits are soon scarfed, my wine soon done. We rise, tugging on our coats. Donnie's avoided us the remainder of the evening, save for shyly leaving our bill, then taking our money with a stuttered thanks and averted eyes. I leave a big tip nonetheless.

We step out into falling snow and head down the street to Matt's four-by-four. "Shit," Matt says, cocking his WVU cap over his eyes. "I thought for sure he was into us. So much for my hillbilly charm, huh? Next time, Derek, use your glamour. Man, we gotta get us some of that!"

A week later. Matt's got a wood-fire going when I enter the den, refreshed from my day's sleep in the cellar. Long used to my undead rhythms, he gives me a hard hug and a wet kiss on the cheek. "Here ya go, honey," he says, handing me a tumbler of Tobermory, my favorite single malt, from the Isle of Mull, home during my mortal life so long ago.

I can smell bread baking. "Making me some pumpernickel to go with sausages and sauerkraut," Matt says, rubbing his belly. "My Germanic ancestors have bequeathed me certain appetites. Wish you could eat some. But I guess I feed you in other ways." He gives me a salacious wink and rubs his butt against my crotch.

"Vulgar hillbilly!" I say, squeezing a pec.

"Damn right! Ain't that why you love me?"

I sit back on the big leather couch; Matt sits at my feet, stein full of beer, his head resting against my knee. Loreena McKennett's new CD fills the room. Beyond the windows, the flurries continue; a full moon rises, breaking every now and then through clouds to silver the snow-pale lawn. Unspeaking, we watch the fire flicker and leap. Ten years together have made our companionship as much comfort as passion; it's a precious balance, something that, before Matt, I hadn't had for over half a century. I still miss him, my last human lover, Gerard McGraw, that sweet, cocky boy who died in World War Two.

"Bread's done." Matt rises. In the kitchen, he gobbles a quick supper of pumpernickel, sausages and kraut, then returns to the den with another beer. "Look here now," he says, tossing me the newspaper as he settles once more at my feet. "Today's *Pendleton Times*. Ain't this odd?" He points at the headline.

I skim it fast. Over the last two nights, a bunch of dogs have been killed in the southern end of our county, Pendleton, and down in Virginia too, in Highland County, around Monterey. A few dead deer as well. All maimed by something sharp-toothed and savage. A rabid coyote, they surmise, an especially large one.

I fold up the paper and run my fingers through Matt's hair. Finishing my Scotch, I stand. "I'm going out for a bit."

"Honey? What's wrong? I know you. What's up?"

Matt rises and grabs my shoulders. "Do you need to feed? You don't need to go out for that. Here." He unbuttons his flannel shirt, shucks it off, and peels his thermal undershirt over his head. He stands before me, naked to the waist.

I can't resist him—his rich smell, his fur-matted chest, his rounded redneck belly, his prominent, very hard nipples—and he knows it. My little mission can wait. Matt laughs, softly, triumphantly, as I hoist his burliness over my shoulder, carry him up the stairwell and into the bedroom, and lower him onto the big four-poster. He winces and sighs, clinging to me as I sink my teeth into his breast and begin a long, slow, carefully measured supping. He's weakening by the time I pull out and begin lapping his neck. He looks up at me, sleepy, with a lop-sided grin. When I sink my fangs into his carotid, he emits a tiny gasp and a soft sigh before going limp.

Matt's still passed out, after my cautious blood-feast, tucked beneath the quilts. He'll sleep till morning, giving me time to enjoy a little reconnoitering around the Potomac Highlands. I brush tangled hair from his face, kiss his nose, and leave him. Perfectly safe, slightly drained, and snuggled in, that's how I like my husbear to slumber.

I step out onto the porch, then down onto the snowy lawn. Mountaintop winds slam me; above the stand of spruce trees back of the house, the full moon breaks free from cloud. I break free from human form, spreading membranous wings, and take flight.

Exhilarating, to cruise over these sparsely populated mountains and the great valleys in between, to dip over snow-heavy boughs and ice-edged creeks. I move southwest, veering in and out of cloud-shadow and moonlight. The Wolf Moon, that's January's. Apropos for tonight's jaunt, for, reading those headlines, I was able to remember where I'd smelled a scent like Donnie's before.

The lights of Monterey glimmer below. Of course he won't be on duty tonight. Not if I'm right. It takes me exactly five minutes to shift form in an alley, glamour the hostess at the Allegheny Café, get Donnie's address, and once more take flight. Up over another mountain range, the winds fierce up here, battering me, then over the tiny hamlet of McDowell, across the black bulk of Bullpasture Mountain, and there's the white church at Head Waters, the moon-shimmering creek, the holler, the tight cove, and the trailer in a stand of pines, a ramshackle car parked beside it.

Shifting again, I stride onto the stoop. The place is dark, but, yes, I was right, here are tracks in the snow—misshapen amalgam of human foot and wolf paw—and more of that animalistic scent.

I mist-sift under the door. Convenient to have outgrown, after my first couple of centuries, that pesky need for an invitation to enter. I explore. Heaps of dirty clothes. A banjo with a broken string. A couple of pizza boxes. Piles of books on the kitchen counter and on the floor: *Leaves of Grass*, *Oedipus*, *The Consolation of Philosophy*. CD's: Led Zeppelin, Old Crow Medicine Show, Alison Krauss, Gillian Welch. If it weren't for that wild smell filling the trailer's stuffy space, it could be any literature-loving country boy's messy man-cave. I pick up a pair of dirty underwear, take a long sniff, and lick my lips.

It's when I mist-sift back outside and re-congeal in human shape on the stoop that I hear growling. Ah, good. Let's see how this were-cub fights.

There he is, on the edge of the woods, a short, stocky silhouette. He moves closer, stepping into the moonlight, hunched, the snarls growing deeper and louder. Pretty much the shape of the boy in the café—threateningly muscular—except he's bare to the waist and covered, as many a legend would lead one to expect, with shaggy black fur. And he sports dangerously large fangs, much more prominent than mine. He bares them at me and rumbles with rage.

"Donnie," I say, moving toward him a step, staring into his wide golden eyes, deep-set beneath bushy brows. Might as well try a little mesmerism. It didn't work the last time I encountered one of these beings, but that one was much larger and much older. "Donnie. It's Derek. Remember me? Calm down, were-cub."

My mind reaches out, fingering for a way in. Human minds are full of little creases, inconsistencies, internal conflicts, self-doubts, and confused desires, more than enough room to wedge in my will. But, shit, just like that older lycanthrope, in this one too the mind is solid and hot, like charred, smoldering wood. When I try to manipulate it, it burns me.

No time for further attempts at mind control. Now the were-cub leaps. Very fast, but I'm faster, sidestepping. He crashes into a snow bank. Snarling, he scrambles to his feet, crouches, and leaps once more. Again I step aside. This time he smashes into the wall of the trailer and falls to his knees.

Predictable critters. Their rage addles them, making them less than graceful in their attacks. I stride forward, grip the unkempt beast's head in my right hand, and make ready to slam him into the trailer wall again.

As if to prove me wrong in my assessment of his agility, the furry fiend turns and sinks his teeth into my left forearm. "Cur," I hiss, trying to shake him off. Damn, I'd forgotten how strong they were, how much their saliva stings. Now the little monster's beginning to gnaw, and it fucking hurts. Teeth that sharp, he's about down to undead bone.

I punch him in the right eye, then the left. His jaw goes slack; his teeth release me; he staggers back.

"Troublesome brute," I spit, shifting into mist. "I'll be back for you."

He leaps again, lunging through my smoky wake, sinking wolf-teeth into vapor.

From mist I move to dark wings. The eastern horizon has that warning flush. I'm on my way home, flapping fast to beat yet another dawn. My flight's crooked, slowing my course. That damned werewolf saliva throbs through my left limb. If I were human, such a bite might eventually transform me. As it is, I'm going to be sore for days, and surly too.

I reach home just in time to check on my sweet Matt and his stentorian snores before taking to my cellar coffin. I fall asleep plotting my revenge. I'll taste that bad dog's blood yet.

"You were right," Matt whispers. A few days later, moon waning, we're sitting in our favorite booth at the Allegheny Café. "He's gotta be that wolfie-beast. The boy has a helluva set of shiners."

Donnie's more sheepish and aloof than usual. "Howdy, guys. What y'all want?" He flips open his order pad.

"Other than your phone number? So where'd you get those black eyes?"

"I'm, uh, I was boxing. With my cousin," Donnie mumbles, exhibiting his customary blush.

"Boxing, huh? Sorry, man; don't mean to be nosy. Well, you're still sexy as hell. Makes you look dangerous. Wild, y'know?" Matt gives Donnie's shoulder a soft punch. "Downright ferocious."

Now that we know the cub's secret, Matt seems even more interested in bedding him. "You like it rough? We can give it to you rough," Matt says with a wicked grin. "When you going to come to dinner, bad boy?"

Donnie's pale face grades into flustered amusement. He ruffles his order pad.

"One of these days. Uh, I cain't, uh, talk now. So what y'all, what y'all want to eat?"

"Wow. Ain't you a tease? And here I thought I was irresistible." Matt shakes his head and emits an exaggerated sigh. "Derek just wants some Merlot. I want macaroni and cheese and the pulled pork sandwich. And how's about a slice of that coconut cream pie in the pastry case?

Donnie scribbles without looking up. "Slaw on your sandwich?"

"Slaw? God, yes. What Southern boy don't want slaw with barbeque?"

"Thanks, bud." Donnie turns and trundles off. Again we watch his broad rear-end recede.

"Wow," Matt repeats. "First time I've ever wanted up a werewolf's butt. Ten years cohabitating with a vampire, and now this. So how did you know?"

"His smell." I chuckle. "And keep your voice down."

"*Really?* He just smells like a hot lil' guy I'd like to fuck. What do you smell?"

"Animal. Wolf. I met one of these before. The scent's very distinctive."

"Yeah? Where? When?" Matt bends toward me, eyes gleaming. Years cuddling with the undead have made him more fascinated than fearful when it comes to the supernatural.

"Russian steppes. I encountered him during one of my nightly wanderings. He'd killed a goodly number of cattle in a village and a couple of villagers too. He was a mite stronger than I was, though not as fast. We fought pretty much to a standstill. It was his territory, though, and I was just passing through, so I let him be after that. This boy, he's not as strong as that one, but he bites deep. My arm still burns."

"So whatta we do? He's dangerous, right?" Matt rubs his forehead; his eyes range over the unaware inhabitants of Monterey enjoying their meals. "We don't want him prowling around our neck of the woods. What if he hurts folks we care about? What if he comes after us? He's gotta be pissed that you blacked his eyes."

"I doubt that he remembers what happened. Probably doesn't even know how his eyes were blackened or that it was me he encountered while he was in wolf form. Lycanthropic memories are spotty that way, or so the esoteric literature indicates. Wait till the next full moon, sex-pot. I'm going to conduct a little experiment, and, with luck, you might end up with an unusual Valentine's Day present. We have a farmer's almanac at home, don't we? I need to consult the schedules for sunset and moonrise."

II.

February's Hunger Moon rises like an enormous opal over the eastern ridge. The sky above Donnie's trailer is cloudless. The wind's still bitter and strong; evergreens sough around me; old snow below me gleams with a hard crust of ice. I claw-cling to a spruce bough, wings folded about me, and wait. Tonight, I intend simply to watch, just to be sure beyond a shadow of a doubt that our hot waiter-cub is indeed what we think he is.

The moon rises higher; its light slants through the forest, creeping across the snow, and soon it's bathing the little trailer. Inside, the lights go off; something shatters. There's a mounting series of whimpers that rise to an agonized crescendo. Then silence. Then a low growling. The door flies open; the hunched black shape lopes out, sniffs the night air, and darts off.

I follow him for hours, watching from above. His movement is leisurely and mindless. He zigzags over pastures empty of everything but blue snow and broom sedge; he circles a pond; he skirts houses, snuffles around a barn, causing many a terrified whinny from the horses housed inside; he tracks, chases, and brings down a deer; he inspires hysterical barking from a farmyard blue-tick hound and makes a quick messy end of it, bounding off with a bloodstained gnashing of teeth when the dog's owner comes to the back door and releases a round of buckshot.

I've seen enough. He is what we thought. When my stocky were-beast sprints into a deep stand of pines, I veer off over a nearby ridge. Been a while since I've visited my favorite redheaded weight-lifter/ historian Kent in McDowell. I'll need the full complement of my powers tomorrow night, and that calls for a hearty meal this evening.

L ast of the three nights of transformation the moon's fullness allows. I have to move fast. Talk about cutting it close: sunset's at 6:05; moonrise is 6:51. I leap from my coffin and rush up the basement stairs. "Careful!" Matt shouts as I tear past him onto the porch and take flight.

As rapidly as I sky-speed toward Donnie's trailer, I have to sacrifice a good minute on his porch to catch my breath before knocking. Panting would, after all, compromise my vampiric dignity.

"Who is it?" Donnie shouts through the door, customary bass rumble turned anxious tenor.

"Derek Maclaine," I say.

Clicking of locks; the door opens a crack; overheated air pours over my face. Donnie's face appears, dark eyes wide with fear, his beard-black jaw set. "What are you, what are you...doing here, Mr. Maclaine? You got to go, bud. I, uh, I got, uh, a crisis I got to deal with, so you got to go, okay? Don't mean to be rude, but"—he chews his lip, stealing a quick look over my shoulder at the eastern horizon—"you really, *really* got to go."

"We don't have time for this," I say, staring into his eyes. "Look at me."

He may be impossible to manipulate in lupine form, but right now he's just a terrified young man. It takes me exactly five seconds to swallow up his will in the maw of mine. "Open the door, Donnie boy."

He obeys instantly. "Why, sure." Smiling blankly up at me, he steps aside, and I enter.

The boy's wearing nothing but boxer shorts; I take in the black mat of hair coating his thickset chest and belly and lick my lips. His feral smell is even stronger tonight.

"I've come to help you." I grip his bare shoulders. "I know what you are. Will you trust me? Will you come with me?"

He tenses beneath my touch. Glamoured he may be, but waves of fear, shock, and doubt contort his face nonetheless. "You know? How?"

I rub a palm over his buzz cut. "I've encountered your kind before. Is the change deliberate or uncontrollable?"

Donnie bursts into tears. "Deliberate? God, no! I never chose this!"

"Ah, kid," I say, pulling him to me and wrapping my arms around his wide shoulders. He clings to me, sobbing.

"Okay, I guess that's my answer. Family curse it is. Look, boy," I say, tipping his wet face up to mine, "we can talk later. We've got to go. The moon's due to rise soon."

Donnie pushes me away. From beneath the trailer's sunken couch, he pulls a pair of handcuffs. "Here!" he says, tossing them to me. "Please? I don't want to wake up covered with blood again! Please!"

I toss them back. "Cuff yourself," I whisper, "and I'll take care of you till dawn."

"You promise?" he says. "You'll keep me from killing?"

I nod. Donnie takes a deep breath. "Thank God," he says, clicking the metal around his right wrist.

"Behind your back," I order. "Then I'll take you somewhere you'll be secure."

A second clicking of ratchets, and now he's sweetly caught, thick arms locked behind him. "Damn, don't you look pretty? Come here, cub," I murmur, beckoning.

Donnie steps forward, leans against me, and presses his face against my chest. I embrace him for a full minute—the boy's clearly in powerful need of comfort—before sinking my teeth into his neck.

He gives a little cry and a moment of weak fight before he faints. I gulp and growl, savoring him for the few seconds I can spare. His blood's rich with manliness and youth, downright delicious, but I can taste a musty under-tang to match his aberrant scent. Retracting my fangs, I lift his limp body into my arms and step out into the snow. Along the eastern ridge-top's a pale glow. The moon will rise within the half-hour.

First, my hasty return to Mount Storm, captive clutched in my great claws—somewhat of a workout, for between cub-fat and cub-muscle, the boy must weigh nearly two hundred pounds. Next, dashing down to the basement dungeon, a windowless play-space equipped with assorted pieces of BDSM furniture and toy-filled cabinets. Next, locking the great steel door behind us, so that Matt will be safe no matter what happens. Finally, applying the many yards of chain in dim candlelight.

I finish with only minutes till moonrise. Donnie lies on his side at my feet. He's still out cold, hands still snugly cuffed behind him. A thick section of chain stuffs his mouth, pulled between his white teeth and locked around his head, the silver links glinting against his black beard. Since there's only Matt in the house to hear his inevitable protests, it's an aesthetic touch, I admit: I most enjoy a captive gagged. Longer, thicker lengths of chain are padlocked around his furry torso and arms, around his thick thighs, around his knees. A chain fastened around his neck is secured to a ring in the wall; further chain fastens his ankles to the opposite wall. He's stretched taut, like a spider's snack. I never thought, when I built this underground room, that it might serve to detain a werewolf, but, as it is, this is the perfect space.

Bending over my plump prisoner, I stroke the hard curve of his belly and sigh with lecherous delight, relishing my complex link-and-lock handiwork. Few things are more beautiful than a masculine, muscled man in tight, thoroughly inescapable restraint. Well, no human being could escape all this chain, but an angry werewolf, we'll see. That might be another matter. I could have a ferocious fight on my hands if the monster breaks loose.

The boy-not-quite-yet-brute whimpers; his eyes flicker open. When he tries to move, he finds himself nearly immobile. He tenses against the tight circles of chain, then gives a deep groan: discomfort, I'd guess, mingled with relief. The panic in his face softens.

I kiss his cheek. "I said you could trust me."

He nods. He stares up at me, gaze aglow with gratitude, body relaxing into precious helplessness.

"You're not going to hurt anyone tonight. We're underground, in a locked room. Even if you break all this chain, which I seriously doubt, the door behind me—"

No time to finish. His face distorts; his eyes widen. Teeth gnashing the chain, he gives a series of sharp sobs before beginning to thrash.

I watch it all, the weird, panting devolution. It's fascinating, horrible, exhilarating, as I'd expected, to see a boy so desirable shed his humanity and return to our communal source in savagery, re-achieving tooth and claw. A slower process than I'd thought, the black hair already plastering his human form growing thicker, coarser; the dull fingernails curving into spiky weapons; the jaw metamorphosing, lengthening; the nose darkening and moistening; the beard bushing out to join new hair around the eyes and across the brow; those blunt human teeth that grit the chain sharpening into a dangerous animal's. The eyes, the brown-eyed human terror fading, replaced by glaring golden malice. And the smell, that savage scent, so adulterated in Donnie's human form, so pure and distilled in this trammeled being before me. The reek's rolling off him, stink of dens inside the earth.

I keep my distance for a while, watching the beast writhe, listening to him snarl. Blood-foam builds up between his teeth as he champs the chain; he rolls, jerks, kicks, squirms, batters the floor with hairy heels. I let him exhaust himself. That Russian wolf-prince of the steppes might have had the strength to tear himself free of these fetters, but my were-cub Donnie seems to be fair and squarely caught, just as I'd hoped.

He lies limp at last, clearly exhausted, emitting a deep, continuous growl. The growl grows louder as I approach. He begins thrashing again; I seize his shoulders and hold him down. Scarlet drool mats his chin.

"Risky, yes. But I can't resist this," I say. I breathe in his scent, extend my fangs, and puncture his throat.

Crazing syrup hits the back of my gullet, a flood rush, a black smolder. I close my eyes, sucking hard. Red flickers across my eyelids; manic shakes seize me; my chest tightens. It's intoxicating and sickening all at once. I could drink him dry, or I could vomit it all up now.

I'm about to take another draining draught when the dim memory of that handsome boy in the café flits across my consciousness. Sweet, awkward, scared. His present monstrous state is not his fault. If I don't pull out now, I might kill him.

I retract my fangs. Part of me curses, aching for more. I lap his bleeding neck, and then I stand, swaying. The creature beneath me shudders, jerks, and falls still. I wipe my mouth, lean against the wall, close my eyes, and pass out.

I wake to a pounding. A dual pounding: my head and the locked dungeon-room door. The sun, I can sense, has set.

I'm lying on my side. I sit up. The room's a mess: St. Andrew's cross splintered, paddle bench torn to pieces, candelabra smashed, toy cabinets tipped over. There's Donnie, in human form again, only a few feet away. He's naked, his bonds still in place, his boxer shorts torn to shreds. He's staring at me, brow creased with anguish, face frantic and tear-stained, teeth clenching the chain. His chest heaves. Against the stifling links of steel, he moans my name. He's lying in a smelly puddle of his own piss and weakly tugging at his chains.

I right myself. Unsteady yet. *Ufff.* I unlock the door.

Matt rushes in, giving me a bear hug. "Oh, God, I thought he'd killed you! Damn it, Derek! How fucking stupid—?

"Oh, shit!" He releases me, hurrying over to my prisoner. "Oh, damn, poor kid! Help me let him loose! Where are the goddamn keys? He's been chained up for twenty-four hours! Derek, what the hell happened in here? Who the fuck wrecked this room?"

"Uh, I guess I did. I don't remember doing it. Maybe his blood, uh, maddened me?" Head bent beneath my husbear's righteous harangues, I unlock our captive. Beneath the long-applied metal of cuffs and chains, his neck, mouth, wrists, and ankles are rubbed raw. His limbs are so sore he can't walk, so I carry him upstairs to the bedroom. I'm nauseous with both guilt and were-blood by now, and—no fucking help at all—Matt won't stop cussing me. When I try to make a joke of it—"Sorry I left you chained up so long, but it serves you right for biting me last month"—Donnie sniffles, again on the verge of tears.

"Hey, hey! Easy, easy," I mutter, tucking him into our bed. "You sleep, and Matt will fix you some food." The boy's out by the time I close the bedroom door behind me.

I straighten the dungeon room and trash-bag the wreckage. Shit. Drinking were-blood = mindless destruction and blackouts. Nice to know. I believe I'll limit my future Donnie-feeding to times other than the full moon. Matt whips up a salad with blue cheese dressing and some spaghetti carbonara. We wake our guest, who takes a shower before shuffling stiffly into the den clad in one of Matt's robes. Matt bandages the cub's chain-chafed wounds. They eat and drink in silence on the leather couch by the fire; I watch them, sipping wine. By the time they're through with supper, both men are buzzed, talkative, and in better moods. They're also touching one another—casually, briefly, but frequently, the way guys who are flirting do. Here a pat on a shoulder, there the rub of a thigh or the nudge of knee against knee. This evening might end far more happily than it began.

"I'm truly sorry," I say, adding a log to the fire before lighting candles around the room. "I never meant to leave you bound all day. I meant to free you when the moon set. But I drank from you and, uh, well, kind of—"

"Ran amuck and passed out. Like a goddamned frat boy." Matt rolls his eyes, scoots closer to Donnie, and wraps a protective arm around him.

"Drank from me, you said. So you're...sort of like me? Not exactly normal?"

"Well, let's just say that bondage and blood sports are among my favorite enthusiasms. Let's just say that the good folks of Highland and Pendleton counties would approve of me about as much as they'd approve of you...if they knew the truth."

Donnie smiles weakly. "Pitchforks and torches, huh?"

Matt pats Donnie's knee. "Derek was turned in 1730. He's a vampire."

Our guest's dark eyes widen. "Uh, well, so, so." He stares into the fire, silent.

"Derek and I have been partners since 2002," Matt says. "He can, well, he can be dangerous, but mainly just to assholes, people who hurt folks he cares about. He fucking hates fundamentalists!"

"Hell, me too!" Donnie grins. "Y'ought to kill off as many of them as y'can!"

Matt snickers. "Yeah, I get that! Several nasty homophobes have, shall we say, gone missing. With other folks, well, when he feeds, he's learned to be real careful." Pulling his shirt collar back, Matt displays the red mark on his throat.

"You fed on me in my trailer, right? When, uh, after you had me cuff myself?"

"Yes," I say. "And you tasted mighty fine. I'd be grateful for another sip sometime if you're willing."

"Speaking of feeding." Matt slips a hand inside Donnie's robe and rubs his belly. "Ummm, *mmm*, love all this hair. Hell, even hairier than me! Did you have enough to eat?"

"Yep, yep, you bet!" Donnie smacks his lips. "I'm single, bud; I'm used to fast food or canned pork and beans! That meal was a fucking, a fucking, uh—was much 'preciated, thanks!"

"You want some deeeeeees-sert? I got some apple crisp needs eating."

"Uh, that sounds great. But first, I just wanna know.... Uh, say, buddy, can I, uh, can...."

"Spit it out, cubster." Matt hooks an arm around him. "God, just spit it out!"

"I, uh. I'm sorry I was so standoffish at the café. I've just been so afraid of getting close to people. 'Cause, well, with a secret big as mine, but, well, now, so...now you know, and y'all have a big secret too, so, look, you all are so.... I ain't never met guys that.... Look, you're *hot*! So can I spend the night? Between you two? Will, uh, y'all hold me all night?"

Matt and I exchange big grins. We all finish our wines; we all rise.

"Got a goodly number of hours yet till dawn," Matt says, taking Donnie's hand. They head for the bedroom while I blow out candles and close up the fireplace.

W ind shakes the farmhouse, muttering in the chimney. The bedroom's lit only by the wood-fire my husbear's started on the hearth. We're all three naked now, lying on our sides. Donnie's cuddled between us, facing Matt, a leather dog collar buckled around his sturdy neck; Matt's whispering in Donnie's ear, caressing his beard, lavishing him with deep kisses; I'm kissing Donnie's back, nibbling his shoulders, pinching his prominent nipples, fingering his moist butt-crack.

Donnie trembles and sighs, his face pressed against Matt's. "Please, won't y'all, won't y'all both fuck me? Please? Please? I need a plowing awful, awful bad."

"With pleasure," I say, rolling Donnie onto his belly and spreading his thighs. His butt bare is just as beautiful as we'd imagined: beefy and broad, firm cheeks plastered with black fur. I feast on his ass for a long time, my face buried in that wild crack-fuzz forest, easing him open with my tongue, fang-nipping and kissing his buttocks. He's opened up a bit, but he's still tight, hurting some when I stretch out atop him, lube us up, and start working my cockhead up his hole.

"Yeah? *Yeah?* Like that?" Matt murmurs, stroking his face. "That dick can really fill you up, cain't it?"

"Yeah, but, *hhhhuhh*! Hurts some. Uh! Wow. Big!" Donnie winces, pressing his face into the flannel sheets as I slide farther inside.

"Slower, Derek! And Donnie, easy now, just relax!" Matt takes the boy's head in his hands and silences his pained whimpers by pushing his tongue into his mouth. I ride Donnie slowly, starting with shallow strokes before fucking him harder.

"Yeah, yeah. Take it, boy!" Matt growls. "You're so damned hot, you hairy little bastard."

"Oh, yeah, that's feeling real, real good now, Derek!" Donnie gasps. "Uh, Matt, man? Fuck my face, bud. Please, bud?" Donnie begs, fumbling for Matt's cock. "I want you guys to spit-roast me, okay?"

"*Hell*, yes!" Matt rearranges us: Donnie on his hands and knees, me giving it to the cub from behind doggy-style—appropriate for a werewolf, I guess—and Matt stuffing Donnie's bearded mouth with dick. My husbear and I bend together over our guest, kissing one another while filling him at both ends. Donnie groans and slobbers around Matt's cock, nodding with happiness, and bucks back onto my cock.

The boy's asshole is so tight it doesn't take long. With a shudder, a grateful groan, and a final thrust, I finish deep inside him. Matt's turn now. He takes his place behind Donnie, applies lube, and pushes into him.

"Oh, my *God*, you're tight!" Matt pants with wonder. "Superlative hole!"

He gives Donnie's buttocks a series of sharp slaps before commencing a vigorous in-and-out. I slip in beneath our were-boy, lapping his fleshy chest, finding a nipple in that wilderness of midnight-black fur, slipping in my fangs, and nursing from him, lush mouthfuls of blood.

Donnie doesn't resist; the pain my teeth inflict seems to excite him. He rocks back and forth above me, hissing with pleasure as Matt slams him.

"Man, oh man, you two sure know how to fuck a hole," Donnie sighs.

I feast on his other nipple, then slip lower, first to nip that luscious overhang of a belly, next to take his fireplug cock in my mouth.

"Oh, man!" Donnie groans.

Matt plows him harder. I nibble Donnie's cockhead, then slip in a fang.

"*Oh*! I love, uh! I'm gonna— *Oh*!"

Donnie bucks against my face. Semen mingles with blood, filling my mouth with blended sweet and bitter, like the elderflower. Matt finishes immediately thereafter, plunging to the hilt inside Donnie, climaxing with a blissful yell.

"Can I, uh, can—?" Donnie's voice is tight and low, almost a whisper. "I really love it here. And you guys are great. Can I, can I, uh. Can I come back?"

The room's dim with ebbing firelight. I lie between my hefty boys, arms around both, Matt's head on my right shoulder, Donnie's on my left, quilts pulled over us. We are, this combination is, I realize, both irony and miracle: a long dead man sandwiched between the doubled treasure of fleeting human warmth.

"Course you can come back. Right, Derek?"

"God, yes," I say, kissing the top of Donnie's head. "You're adorable."

"How 'bout next weekend?" Matt says sleepily. "Bring your banjo, and I'll git out my guitar...w'can work up a few songs. I'll cook us up some bourbon-barb'que ribs. And some tater salad. Some braised kale, maybe some deviled eggs. Y'like all that?

"Ummm, oh, yeah."

Their fingers fumble over my belly, meet, squeeze, and interlock.

"You hillbilly boys are always hungry, aren't you?" I run my fingers through Matt's unkempt locks and fondle the whorl of Donnie's ear. "You're welcome here anytime, Donnie-boy. You can keep Matt company during the day. And maybe, next full moon, since I've drunk from you, I can control you in your other form. If not, we can keep you in the dungeon room."

"Yeah," Donnie mumbles drowsily. Matt's already snoring. "Don't wanna hurt anyone...."

Now Donnie's snoring into my armpit.

"Always wanted me a pup," I say to no one. "Yep, a pup. A husbear and a were-pup. Goddamn, I must have done something right. You two are a plethora of riches. Couldn't ask for anything better than this."

I lie there for hours, watching them sleep, my two burly, insensible mountain men, their arms flung over my undead body. Sleet spatters the windows; hard wind grumbles down the chimney; the fire slowly dies. There's something calm inside my chest tonight, something sated, a warm swelling, like a snowdrop, an apple bud in spring, as if my heart had never known rage or loss, as if the regretful gods had decided to give back some of what they'd robbed over the centuries.

When dawn approaches, I slip out of bed, doing my best not to disturb their slumbers. Donnie rolls onto his side; Matt pulls the smaller man into the circle of his arms. Donnie grunts, Matt mumbles, both smile in their sleep, sigh, and start up snoring again. I rearrange the blankets over them before heading downstairs toward the cold room where my coffin waits.

Black Sambuca

I sense him before I see him. He radiates power the way a glacier exudes cold or a woodstove heat. There, that broad-shouldered silhouette, that gleam of pale hair and skin beneath a leafy canopy of vines, on the edge of Piazza Viminale. *Ristorante Strega*, says the sign. He's sitting back in the quiet shadow of a remote corner—as my kind tend to—watching happy humans as they feast al fresco on aromatic Roman food and wine in the warm summer night. When a shapely waitress bustles over to seat me, all I have to do is murmur his name and she escorts me to his table. A man well known in Rome, it appears.

He rises, smiling down at me, and shakes my hand. Though, like me, he appears to be in his mid-thirties, I know he's much, much older than I. He's several inches taller too, easily six and a half feet, and more mightily built. "*Buona sera*, Derek Maclaine," he says. His grip is strong, very strong. It makes me want to wince. Already he's reminding me of my position. He is the lord here, and I the suppliant. Not only is he older and stronger, but this is his territory. I am a mere tourist.

My centuries in the American South have made my manners immaculate, despite the displeasure I'm feeling at being the less powerful in our exchange. I meet his blue-fire gaze, then drop my eyes. "I much appreciate this audience, Mr. Colonna," I say.

"Call me Marcus," he says, still gripping my hand, then turns to the hovering waitress and orders for us both. "My guest will have

Romana Black, and I my usual." Off she goes to the bright lights of the bar, leaving a hint of jasmine in her wake.

"She wears that scent for me." Marcus turns to me, face shifting from an expression both stern and impassive into a barely perceptible smile and then back again. "Welcome to Rome, Derek Maclaine," he murmurs, giving my hand another painful squeeze before releasing me and taking his seat. "Sit," he says, and I do. The man was once a Roman senator. He's accustomed to swift obedience. And in order for me to get what I want, I suppose I too must obey him.

As handsome as he is, my obedience might be more pleasure than pain. "Thank you, Marcus," I say, studying the high forehead, sharp cheekbones, and shoulder-length ash-blond hair. His lips are red and full, his chin cleft, with the shadow of a goatee about his mouth. "It's mighty fine to be in your great city at last."

"Isn't she luscious?" Marcus says, voice smooth as rose petal yet embroidered with a growl. "Roma, yes. But our waitress too. *Bella, bella*. Her breasts and hips.... She is, as you Americans say, my type. Her name is Nigella. One night I will have her. But why rush?"

I smile. "I hadn't noticed, sir, but yes, she is beautiful." I can't recall when I last called another man other than my father "sir." Before I was changed, back in 1730? No, there was that Russian lord in St. Petersburg...and that Greek in Santorini, and, of course, Sigurd, the massive Viking warrior who turned me.

"Ah, yes. You are a sodomite. Which will make your payment easier on us both, I suppose. I myself enjoy both the sexes, as lovers, slaves, and prey. What is your type, Derek Maclaine? And do you have a lover?"

"Yes, sir, I do. A human one, back in West Virginia. His name is Matt. He's my type. One of my types. Shorter than I, burly, hairy, with a bushy beard. A country boy. From the mountains, like me. What we in America call a butch bottom. We've been together for a decade."

"What is his age?" Marcus says. The waitress arrives, placing a slender glass of yellow liquid before Marcus, a similar glass filled with black liquid before me. "*Grazie*, Nigella," Marcus says, voice soft. She smiles and departs.

"Matt is forty-five, sir."

"He is your boy, yes?" A lock of yellow hair falls over Marcus' brow; he brushes it back, takes a sip, rests his elbow on the table, takes his stubbly chin in his hand and rubs it.

"Yes, sir, though not my slave. He's too—as we say in the mountains—too hard-headed and ornery for that." I want to say, *You are almost as beautiful as he,* but I suspect, powerful as Marcus is, he can read my thoughts and can already feel my desire and the way that submitting to him both shames and arouses me.

"And is he graying yet?" Marcus takes another sip. I can smell in his glass the heavy scents of sugar and lemon.

"Yes, sir. His temples are streaked with silver. His beard is as well, and the hair on his breast. He is so handsome, so ripe, a man in the fullness of his years, but...."

Marcus shakes his head. "Yes," he sighs. "*Trista.* I did that for centuries. Loved mortals. Now...not so often. Will you turn him?"

"No, sir. I don't think so. I don't know."

"Well, your other types?"

"Ah, Jesus lookalikes!" I laugh. "I like to ravish Christs. Slender boys with shaggy dark hair and beards. They make fine sacrifices. Occasionally, as understanding as Matt is of my feeding needs, they make him jealous. I do tend to dote on men such as they. Sometimes, when Matt's away on business, I kidnap one for my amusement and keep him for a few days."

"And have you had one of our Roman Christs yet?" His blue eyes flicker over me. Hunger is there in his glance, deep and fierce.

"No, sir, not yet. As you recall from our correspondence, this is my first visit to Rome. I only arrived last night, and I was told not to feed until...."

Marcus' foot nudges my boot beneath the table. "Very good. Yes. It is well that you obey. I can tell from the gray in your hair that you need to feed. Soon, I promise. Meanwhile, please sample your liqueur. That is black *liquore di sambuca*, which, according to the bottle, 'captures the spirit and allure of the Roman night,' a sweet, dark night such as this one in which we meet, Scotsman." Another faint smile flickers around his lips. With the ball of his thumb, he rubs the tip of his right incisor: quick flash, sharp, white, anticipatory. "And tell me if tall blond dominant Roman aristocrats meet your fancy."

Undead for centuries, yet I can still blush. No reason to lie. Old and experienced as he is, he could tell if I did. "Not normally, sir. I tend toward dark-haired men. But there are exceptions. You are indeed not what I expected of a Roman." I take a sip—more sugar, the odor of anise.

"Yes, most of us are much darker than I. During my human days, my friends teased me for my fairness. They said that a warrior from Germania had infiltrated my mother's bed. During my days with the army, my men called me *Aquila Aurea*, the golden eagle. Many of them loved me. My lovers called me *Splendidus*. From what I can sense, you might agree with them." The faint smile goes broad only for a second before returning to that intense gaze, that impassive expression. "You will be my lover tonight, Derek? My boy? You will pay the price we agreed upon? In return I will share my city with you whenever you please."

My face is on fire. I can only drop my eyes, sip my liqueur, and nod. The sambuca is as rich, sweet, and thick as old blood, strong blood.

"Do you like it? The liqueur?"

"Yes, sir, I do. In future, when I drink it, I will certainly think of you. And you, sir? What is your type?" I lift my glass, stare into its blackness, then put it down. *Stop fiddling, Derek. Stop being such a bashful flirt.*

"Ah, in men? Many, many kinds. Men both sleek like me and rough like you. Both young men and mature men. Both humans and vampires. Tonight, I want a man who is wild and proud and in need of discipline. I want a man accustomed to being in control to submit to me, to feed my strength. Have you ever known a man like that?" Marcus chuckles. "One whose manhood might be tempered and refined by submission?"

"Yes, sir." It's all I can do not to stammer. "I love those men too. It's just that it's been so long since I myself—"

"Relax, boy. We shall have a fine night on the Palatine Hill, there among the ruins of the Caesars. I will care for you well. I will not harm you...much. And you will be the stronger for it. I must admit, you are surprisingly handsome and well-mannered for a mountain barbarian."

I look up and laugh. His blue eyes probe me. I can feel his thoughts rummaging through my head, turning over the mental stones of memory and motivation.

"Oh yes, a barbarian," says Marcus. "You Scotsman were certainly trouble. Hadrian had to build that long wall against Caledonia."

"Yes, sir. And you all never conquered us." As subdued as my customary pride must be this night, I can't help but remind him. "We Scots were about the only folks whose asses you couldn't whip."

Anger flashes in his eyes for a split-second. Then he nods, another smile flickering over his stony features. "Not worth the trouble. Those thistle-sharp mountains? Those scruffy clans in their dirty tartans? Though you do present yourself well tonight." He leans forward, his glance roaming over my black jeans, black T-shirt, black cowboy boots, and the thorny tattoos on my left forearm. "You are a fine specimen of a...redneck? That is the expression?"

"My boots give it away, I guess. And my ink?" I can't help but grin. I must indeed look like a well-dressed hillbilly compared to him. An observer would find us an odd combination. On top of the tattoos and the informal attire, my hair is long, pulled back in a ponytail, and my goatee's like a biker's, bushy enough to braid. I most likely resemble a Hell's Angel trying to look nice but not quite pulling it off. Marcus, on the other hand, is the picture of a wealthy, pampered European, with his white silk shirt, beige linen pants, expensive watch, golden neck chain, and designer leather dress shoes. Scottish Highlander in my human years, Appalachian for most of my vampire existence, I can't hide my rough edges even when I try. Especially from a gaze as steady and searching as his.

"And your beard betrays you, *paganus*, *rusticus*. You look like a Confederate general. You remind me of Enkidu. In need of taming, I think."

"Enkidu? In the Sumerian *Epic of Gilgamesh*, right? The hairy wild man who came down from the mountains to be the comrade and lover of the great hero Gilgamesh."

"You are better educated than I expected. That is correct. Let me see your bare chest, please, my mountain redneck, my Appalachian Enkidu."

My cock hardens beneath the table. I'd forgotten how exciting it is to be told what to do by a man much stronger than I.

"Here?" I say, half-turning toward the tables of diners.

"I own Rome. I do what I please. Tonight you will do what I please. Just a glimpse."

Blushing, I pull my T-shirt up to my neck, baring my belly and chest.

Marcus takes a long, low breath, staring at my exposed torso. "Just as I imagined. Hairy as a savage. As an animal in need of a rider. Finish your drink, boy, and I will give you a tour of the Palatine. I will break you. I will make your chill skin sweat."

II.

The ruins are fluted gray in the moonlight. Under flat-topped cypresses, upon the crest of the Palatine Hill, we explore the remains of imperial palaces long abandoned, strong with the scent of pines and, this late at night, closed to tourists. Rubble now, once the homes of Augustus, Tiberius, Septimius Severus, Domitian. The fragments of columns, arcades, fountains, even a small stadium. Below us, modern Rome steams in the night, the lights of traffic pouring along its streets like phosphorescent lemmings.

"Did you know any of them? The Caesars?" I stroke a clump of oleander bloom. It is silent here, save for the distant noises of traffic and the cheeping of summer insects in the bushes and trees about us. Moonbeams slant over Marcus' white face as he moves closer to me.

"A few. Caligula raped me. He was assassinated long before I could take my revenge. I was turned in the reign of Claudius." Marcus looks down at the ruined rocks of the Forum, illuminated by searchlights for the benefit of tourists, and toward the monumental buildings atop the Capitoline Hill. "Take off your shirt."

I pull the garment over my head. Marcus takes it, laying it carefully on a jagged chunk of marble he first brushes off with the side of his hand. He turns to me now, resting his hands on my shoulders. "So you have come to Rome to pay your respects?"

I gaze up at him, trying not to tremble. "Yes, sir."

"To the Caesars or to me?"

"Both." It is hard to meet his gaze, yet impossible to look away. My victims must feel the same when I entrance them. "In all my centuries, I have never come to Rome. It is more beautiful than I ever imagined. I would like your permission to linger here, and to return when I please."

"And you are ready to pay the price? For a nest in my realm? For the freedom to feed here? This is, I sense, a price you are unaccustomed to."

"I am unaccustomed, but I am ready," I say. "Sir."

Marcus nods. Moonlight gleams off his teeth, a true smile, wide with triumph. His fingers find my chest, stroking the thick fur there. I wrap my arms around his waist, bow my head, and lean against him. He tugs at my nipples, then the rims of hair around them, then the tangled bush of my beard.

"Strip," murmurs Marcus. He gives me a gentle shove backward. "And unbind your hair."

Boots first, then jeans, then the leather cord in my ponytail, discarded one by one in dry grass. Entirely naked, vulnerable, I stand before him, in warm Roman breezes, in the scent of wildflowers, in moonlight. I stare down at my exposed body, at my inked and muscled arms, at my hairy belly and chest, my hairy legs, trying to see myself as he sees me. It has been many, many years since I have submitted to another vampire, or felt undead lust raking me with such sharp zeal. Marcus' eyes are gleaming, the blue gone a fiery red.

"Shaggy brute," he whispers, tousling the long hair framing my face, ruffling my belly fur, patting the face of the Horned God inked into my left arm, the barbed wire band inked into my right. "Tattooed like your feral ancestors, those mad Celts. The antlered god of the Gauls, I see. God of beasts and mountains, yes? A hirsute, hard-cocked Dionysus. Apropos. My deity is Mithras. You will show him homage later."

From his back pocket, Marcus fetches something gleaming. "A surprise," he says, holding it before me. I can feel it already, the shining power that can make my head swim and my muscles grow feeble. Silver. He's brandishing a pair of leather-lined silver handcuffs. Open and ready to use.

I step back, unsure. "Sir? You never mentioned this. I never agreed—"

Marcus outflanks me in a split-second, faster than I can further react. Again the difference in our powers gives me some sense of how outmatched my human victims must feel. He pulls my wrists behind me before I know he's there. But rather than subdue me further, rather than locking the cuffs, he simply stops. I stand there, trembling. A blunt hardness that must be his erection bumps my back. It seems that subduing me is exciting him as much as being subdued is exciting me.

"Trust me, barbarian. I will make this sweet. I will make you enjoy this." Marcus sniffs me and noisily licks his lips. "Ah, you are sweating now. You stink. You smell like mud and grass and woodland. You smell like the Gallic prisoners I used to take in Mamertine Prison, only yards from here. Your hair"—he takes a strand in his teeth and pulls—"and your unruly beard remind me of them." He nips the skin over my spine. I can feel his chin's scratchy stubble. "Dirty and wild...forest scum, so proud at first before they were chained and raped and broken. Warriors become slaves...they sobbed and shook beneath me. They lay in the prison's straw and dung and wrapped their mighty arms about my feet and begged me for release. Will you sob for me?"

"No," I say, teeth gritted. "I'm no slave."

"But you will submit?"

"Yes."

"You might sob yet. We shall see." The cuff snaps over my right wrist, painfully tight. The leather saves me from that terrible burn, but the poisonous silver's near enough to cause my knees to buckle. I would drop to the ground, but Marcus wraps an arm around my neck and heaves me upright. His knuckles graze my ass-cheeks before the cuffs lock just as tightly about my other wrist. He releases me; groaning despite myself, hands firmly secured behind me, I sink to my knees and fall onto my side in the grass. The silver weakness shudders through me, nauseating.

Marcus nudges my chin with his elegant shoe. Then he steps back, toes off each shoe, and strips, very slowly, laying each article of clothing in the grass with such care you'd think the fabric were fragile as glass. I roll with discomfort onto my cuffed hands to watch as his muscular body, as hard and perfectly defined as a gymnast's, is revealed. Entirely naked, he stands over me, astride my waist. His body is pale, smooth, gleaming like the face of the moon, a study in Carrara marble, with a dusting of gold. "I was quite the athlete when I died," he says, running hands over his curved pectorals, big brown nipples, and ridged stomach before taking his fur-clouded cock in hand. It lengthens rapidly in his grasp, escaping its skin-sheath. It is intimidatingly huge. The head glistens, slick and knobby, moonlit pommel of a sword. I am, I suspect, soon going to be hurting bad.

By now I'm hard as well. "I can see your appreciation, boy." Laughing, Marcus presses a bare foot against my cock. "Stiff with shame, I see. I know men like you. I know them and I love them. There is a secret slave, very frightened yet very hungry, inside that coarse Scots warrior, is there not? Something tender, submissive, shy? A boy eager to suffer, to endure, to be enveloped and devoured and rocked like a child?"

I shake my head, but my denial has no power. There's my body's unarguably honest answer, beneath Marcus' foot, hard between my thighs. He presses down, and I gasp.

"Not much fight in you with those cuffs, Highlander?" He presses harder.

"No, sir. Silver saps my strength almost entirely. How did you—?"

"Handle silver without consequence? After my first thousand years it lost its power over me. Now it barely makes me tingle." He lifts his foot from my crotch only to press his sole against my mouth. "Lick, boy. Let Caledonia at last give Rome her due."

I run my tongue over his foot. Hard as embossed steel. Smooth and taut as the skin of ripe fruit. He nudges me onto my side. I moan as he pushes his big toe into my mouth.

"Suck, barbarian."

I do. I suck, lick, nibble. More toes join the first, my mouth crammed full. He tastes like metal and wind. I stretch my jaw, taking him further in.

Abruptly he pulls his foot from my face and steps back.

"Get up here, wild one, my Enkidu. It's time to show your fealty."

With effort I rise to my knees, and, kneeling, shuffle over to him. I've hardly opened my mouth before his bulky cock's thrust inside me to the hilt, balls pressed into my beard. His hands grip my long hair, holding my head still while he rides my face. My throat expands, contracts. I choke and slobber. My gorge rises; I force it back. He pounds my mouth steadily, his pre-cum streaking my tongue with salt. Drool drips off my chin. I try to bring subtle techniques into play, try to lick the head, run my tongue up and down the shaft, but to no avail. Marcus wants nothing but a hole, a deep one. He batters the back of my throat the way Hebridean oceans batter sea cliffs, unceasing, inexhaustible.

Just when I think the savage throat-beating I'm getting will soon insure me a white mouthful of sex-foam, Marcus lifts me by the arms, spins me, and throws me onto my belly in the grass. He's on top of me a split-second after I hit the ground, one hand on the back of my neck, shoving my face against the earth, an arm wrapped around my chest. "Ah, yes. This is what you came to Rome for, is it not?" he whispers in my ear, his cock bumping my buttocks. "I enter you; you enter my kingdom? Yes? Yes?"

"Yes," I groan. Heat-dead grasses scrape my face; Roman earth dusts my lips. I grit my teeth, readying myself for the pain.

But Marcus is taking his time. His lips brush my ear. "How long, barbarian? How long since you were taken this way?" Beneath me, his fingers trap a nipple. His nails begin to dig.

"Sir, my lover Matt sometimes...we switch. We even...we have silver cuffs at home."

"Ah, so you bottom occasionally? Then this will not be as grand a trauma as I'd imagined? A pity. How long since another vampire took you then?"

"Half a century, sir. In Santorini."

"Yes? The blood is strong there. Older even than mine." Marcus' hand leaves my neck, positioning his cock against my tightness. "You want this, do you not?"

Again, I know better than to lie. "Yes, sir. I don't want to want it, but I do."

"Beg me, my hirsute captive," Marcus sighs. "Beg me to take you."

I hesitate only for a second. That long submerged part of me is rising, eager. "Please, sir. Please, Marcus. Take me...." I arch my ass, rub it against him, brush his hard belly with my bound hands. "I can't fight you. I'm too weak. I'm your captive, sir. Do what you please."

"And so I shall." He slips down my body. His fingers play over my ass, tugging on the cheek- and cleft-hair, and then his hands clutch my hips and his teeth sink into my right buttock.

"Huhhhh," I gasp into the grass. His lips clamp down, sealing the sudden wound, sucking hard. I can feel my strength receding further, the silver-weakness mingling now with blood-loss.

The suction stops. Liquid smeared between my ass-cheeks. Lubrication of my own blood. I grunt as his finger enters me. I buck back onto his hand. Another finger slides inside. "Open. Open for Rome," Marcus whispers. His muscled weight, like a great sculpture, settles atop me, his cockhead pressing against me, his arm wrapped around my torso.

"Be easy, Highlander. I will care for you well."

I nod, trying to will myself open. His cockhead replaces his fingers, easing inside. Damn, so thick. Pain spasms through me, forcing out a whimper.

"Easy, boy." To my surprise, Marcus does not simply shove it in and rape me, as the earlier mouth-pounding suggested that he might. Instead, to my relief, he moves the head in and out in short strokes. He pulls out, adds more bloody lube, and pushes the head in again. More shallow strokes, till the pain at last recedes and he can sense my readiness. Then, very slowly, with surprising gentleness, he slides entirely inside, filling me completely. More waves of pain; I give a loud, deep moan. Marcus' hand grips my jaw, palm pressed tightly over my mouth.

"Quiet now, boy. There, there. Yes." Cocking his hips, he moves slowly in and out, in and out. I moan inside his muffling grip. "Ruffian. Lovely, smelly, hairy Scot. I will use you now, mountain man, will I not? Beg me to use you. Do you not want used? Used hard?"

He pulls out, resting his cockhead against my entrance. The sudden emptiness is an ache.

"Use me, sir. Hard, please, sir. I can take it." Muttering into his palm, I flex my ass-cheeks, grinding back against him.

"So reluctant to be ridden, now so eager to be used? If you insist." Marcus thrusts, quick and hard, shoving his entire length up inside me. I wince, gasping against the tight gag of his hand. A steady pounding begins. Cuffed, silver-weak, I lie there entirely helpless, impaled by bliss, deep grunts—"Huhh, huhhhh, huhhhh, huhh!"—forced out of me by the rhythmic hammering of his hips. Marcus's growl is as steady as my grunts are staccato.

He's off me before I know it. Again I'm aching and empty. Not for long, I sense. Seizing my bushy goatee, Marcus drags me across the grass to a broken column lying on the ground. He heaves me across it, bends me over. My face and knees are sunk in dead grass, my ass cocked in the air. He fang-nips both cheeks, spreads them, roughly cock-shoves up inside me and begins pummeling me anew.

I've no sooner started a new series of rapturous, stuffed-full-to-the-brim grunts than his right hand's again clamped over my mouth. His left hand finds my left pec. He manhandles the thick flesh, tugs painfully at the chest pelt. "A better angle, is it not?" Marcus pants into my tangled hair. "And a small price for all of Rome?"

What ecstasy it is to be completely vulnerable and completely owned, thoroughly plowed. I had almost forgotten. Nodding, I close my eyes, spread my thighs, push back onto him, and grip him from inside, as if I were squeezing the handle of a sword. "Ah, yes. Very nice. You are skilled for a dirty savage," Marcus says, increasing the speed of his thrusts. "You have learned well beneath my predecessors."

Smiling beneath his palm, I squeeze and relax, squeeze and relax. He rides for a bit, sighing with delight, letting the sweat build up between us, before he says, "I will hurt you now, boy. Yes?" Marcus pants into my ear. "You are ready to suffer for me? I may mark you?"

I grunt an affirmation, nodding against his firm grip. Immediately his fingernails sink deep into my nipple. I clench my teeth as he brings blood, twists and tugs the tiny nub of flesh, cuts deeper still.

Keeping one hand over my mouth, with the other he rakes my torso, my nipples, and my back with his sharp fingernails, leaving long, deep wounds. Blood wells up, trickling into my chest hair, down my spine. "And now, I think...." He shifts the position of his loins just a fraction, pulls back, shoves forward hard. My eyes roll, my fangs gnash my tongue, my own blood tinges my mouth.

"Here, I think, is the bodily seat of your submission, yes? This spot here?" Marcus chuckles. "Am I right, forest trash? Wild one so sweetly tamed?"

Yes, deep inside me he has found what few men have ever found, the point that makes me shake with such great pleasure. I go wild, bucking and writhing in his arms, crying out against his hand, trying to pull him into me even deeper. Giving my chest one last savage clawing, he locks his arm around my head and sinks his teeth into my neck.

The sucking begins—an irresistible gravity, a riptide more and more intense—hard and steady to match the pounding below. Within a minute, I'm immobile, sprawled limply across the column that once bore the weight of empire, rocking helplessly inside his thrusts. I hear him hissing against my split skin, feel him stiffening atop me, pumping my depths. Then Marcus's bloody hands grip my shoulders, his fangs slip from my flesh. He gives a shout, a final thrust, gushes semen into me, and collapses.

Blood tickles my neck. The column's marble is cold against my belly; my master's weight is great upon my back; my hole's a throbbing circlet of fire. The grass before my eyes smears, a brittle gold. That grades to red, then unbroken black.

I wake cradled in his lap. He is rocking me, blond hair curtaining his face. Again that faint smile. Tenderly he caresses the blood-ooze claw-trails his nails cut into my chest. I try to embrace him, only to find myself still weak, still cuffed. His lips meet mine. I can smell and taste my own blood in his kiss.

"You will be scarred for a time," Marcus says. "My nails leave welts even undead bodies have difficulty healing." He runs a finger along my chest, daubs up some blood, and laps it off. "But you are even more beautiful scarred, no? And these scars will mark you as mine during your stay in Rome."

From the seat of a ruined altar, he rises, lifting me into his arms. "The temple of Cybele once," he says, wistfully. "You should have seen it as it was." Enervated, I lean against him, wrists throbbing in the tight cuffs. Birds are singing somewhere. "Almost dawn, yes," he says, carrying me through aromas of pine, crunching of needles, then beneath an arch and down a long underground tunnel. "You may use this nest in future, if you please," Marcus says. He shifts me with ease from his arms to his shoulder, then edges aside a flat rock. Here, a grave large enough for the both of us. He lowers me gently onto my side, climbs in after me, and pulls the rock in over us. "I have hidden our clothes nearby. We will spend the day together here, my bound barbarian," Marcus says, gripping my cuffed hands and pulling me against him. We kiss, lengthily and deeply, before he presses his hairless chest against my mouth and says, "I can feel your famine. Drink, boy."

"Thank you, sir," I whisper. "Gladly." My tongue finds his nipple. I tease it into hardness, then push my fangs into him. He sighs, running his fingers through my hair and along the gashes on my back. His semen oozes from my ass and trickles down my inner thigh. Dawn must be near, for sudden drowsiness washes over me. I fall asleep suckling Marcus's breast, feeling the old blood glow and shimmer inside.

III.

"We should have killed them all," Marcus grumbles. "What trouble those beasts have caused."

We are strolling through what remains of the Colosseum. He's dressed in a dove-gray suit, crimson tie, and leather loafers, I in camo pants, black work boots, and a black tank top that allows Marcus to savor the sight of both my tattoos and my fresh scars. At his request, my hair's unbound. It's approaching midnight of our second night together. The great broken bowl of the stadium is empty of tourists. We walk along the corridors, under the barrel vaults, and take seats where emperors once did. Only a few feral cats are our companions tonight, and the moon, nearly full. Before us is the cross erected by a long dead pope to commemorate the Christians who died here.

"Are they as troublesome in your land, my Highlander? The Christians?"

"Oh, fuck yes!" I snarl. "They're a plague. They run through my mountains like a virus. They befoul the air!"

Marcus wraps an arm around me. "You are passionate about this, I see."

I flush and nod. "I do hate them. The hard-core kind, at least. They've caused me and mine much grief. Still, forgive the language, sir. We 'forest trash,' as I believe you called me during that fine pounding.... I'm still a little sore, by the way. Not that I'm complaining." I rub my butt and grin. "We forest trash do tend to be dirty-mouthed. I don't mean to be vulgar. I suspect a sophisticated man like you is used to fairer-spoken friends."

Marcus pulls me against him. I lean my head against his chest. It is a great relief, to relinquish strength and control for a change. "But you *are* vulgar. And I love it. I grow weary of refinement sometimes. Yes, we should have fattened our lions more efficiently. And speaking of flashing fangs and vigorous devouring, are you ready for your gift? You took little blood from me before you slept; your hair and goatee are still silvery. It's time to remedy that."

"Yes, I'm ready. What have you been up to?" Marcus has shown me several sights tonight—the Forum, the Capitoline, the Arch of Constantine—but before that tour, he'd left me silver-cuffed for several hours in our Palatine tomb while he "attended to business."

"Come with me." Marcus rises and takes my hand. "It's five minutes from here, down Via San Giovanni de Laterano."

Leaving the ancient stadium, we make our way past well-lit cafés, noisy, fragrant restaurants. We hold hands, the sleek aristocrat and the undead mountain man. God help the homophobic human who might object. But we meet with no objections, just a few stares, and soon we are swathed in shadow again, slipping down a narrow street and then inside the colonnaded courtyard of a church.

"San Clemente," Marcus says, pulling open the broad wooden door and ushering me inside. "I worship here."

"A Christian church?"

"No, no. Come, come." Marcus takes my hand. He's moving fast through the dimness, leading me past columns, mosaics, and choir screens—Christian irrelevancies— then through a swinging door and down broad stone steps. Here is a lower floor. I can make out bare stone walls, a distant flicker of candlelight; I can smell earth and human sweat, hear a faint, very human moaning. "Here?" I say. My fangs throb and lengthen.

"Not yet, young one, eager one. First you must pay homage."

Down another flight of steps, a deeper level yet. The sound of rushing water.

"Beneath the floor. The Cloaca Maxima, ancient Rome's sewer. That is what you hear." Marcus pulls me down a corridor to a doorway in the rough wall. "Here, here is where we need to be. The Mythraeum." Behind a locked grate is a low-ceilinged cave, a white marble altar flanked by stone benches. Marcus fetches a key from his pocket; the padlock snaps open; we enter the shrine.

"The Lord Mithras. He is the god of soldiers." Marcus runs his hands along the low reliefs. "Here, see, he sacrifices the bull. He cuts its great throat. And here, here are the dog and serpent. They drink the blood." He grips my shoulder. "On your knees, *rusticus*."

I do as I'm told, kneeling beside him. Closing his eyes, Marcus mouths a few words I can't make out. Bowing my head, I give thanks to this foreign warrior god—for the splendid man by my side, for his beauty, ruthlessness, and strength, for his marble-white, marble-hard muscles, for his sharp golden desire.

Marcus tugs my beard. I jerk with surprise, then rise. His arms enwrap me, hugging me hard. "The god gives his approval. Now for your gift."

Back along the corridor and up one flight of steps. "This was a fourth-century church," says Marcus. "It also makes a fine feast-hall for my coven." There's a distant sound of sobbing. We follow it, turning several corners before coming into the low nave. I stare down the rows of double columns and flickering candelabra, to the stone canopy of the baldacchino at the far end, the high rectangular altar beneath it, and, most especially, what lies atop that altar. I growl deep in my throat. I run my tongue over my fangs.

"You are pleased? You said you doted on Christs."

"Oh, fuck. Oh, yes!" My lip curls up; I snuffle the rich air, heavy with terror and sweat.

Bound belly-down upon the altar is a young man. He's naked. His limbs are spread, wrists and ankles shackled and chained to the posts of the canopy. He stares at us with black, long-lashed eyes before breaking into soft fear-sobs again.

I cross the yards between us in a heartbeat. I wrap my fingers in his long black hair and pull his head back. Thick chain has been threaded between his teeth twice and padlocked behind his head, filling his mouth, muffling his cries. I study his handsome face, his tear-stained, half-crazed eyes. His weeping grows more violent still. He squints against his tears, then, unable to hold my gaze, clenches his eyes shut.

"His name is Francesco," Marcus says, somewhere behind me. "He's twenty-one. He speaks English fairly well. He lives with his old mother in the ghetto south of Rome; he uses his good looks to hustle tourists on the Spanish Steps. No one will miss him save her. He is yours now. To drain, enslave, keep, or kill."

The mention of murder evokes in Francesco a fresh bout of sobs, a few weak pleas his gag makes unintelligible. His white teeth grit the chain. He thrashes in his bonds. The steel links rattle and clink.

"*Aiuto. Per favore.* He's crying for help. So delicious." Marcus stands beside me now, fingering the spit-shiny chain between our prisoner's plump lips. "The boy's half-starved. But he gave us a fierce fight, like a wild animal. Rather than damage him badly, we drugged him. He's been kept bound down here for hours, watched over by some helpful minions of mine. He has little strength left. So he will do?"

"Ohhhh, yes," I hiss. "He's fucking *fine*. Thank you, Marcus!"

Francesco's face is thin, with prominent cheekbones and an aquiline nose. His shoulder-length hair is ink-black, as is his neatly trimmed goatee. He's very lean, rib-staves and hipbones ridging dirty skin. He's shiny with sweat; he smells of the street, of urine and long hot days without a bath. Other than the whiteness of his buttocks, his skin's an olive hue. Here and there are bruises, the result, I'm guessing, of the struggles he put up during his capture. I circle him now, stroking his long, thickly hairy legs, the muscles' straining definition. I caress the wet hair-nests of his armpits, the hair dusting his belly and chest. When I touch his buttocks, hard curves covered with fine black fur, he starts and shudders, shakes his head violently, cries out more chain-hampered words I can't make out. His fear's a liqueur, black and sweet. I laugh low, running a fingertip along his ass-crack. So moist, so warm, so aromatic.

"Oh, yes, he can guess what's coming next. Do what you please, barbarian. Use him as I used you." Marcus fetches two glasses and a bottle from the floor. Black sambuca again. He pours out the liqueur, hands me a glass, and clicks his glass against mine. I take a sip, lick the sugary anise off my lips, rest the glass on the corner of the altar, and strip.

I am naked now. Marcus brushes his fingers across my chest, along my arm. "White scars amid such black, black fur. Black tattoos against such white, white skin. Snow and coal. Comets streaking the darkness. The white wake of waves across the Mediterranean at midnight...." He sounds almost reverent, his eyes gone vague. "Ah, I am a bad poet. My apologies. But I am very glad you came to Rome, Derek Maclaine." He steps back, face again an ivory mask. "I may watch, may I not?"

"Yes, sir. I'd relish that." I leap up beside Francesco and stretch out. His face is pressed against the altar. I cup his bearded chin in my hand, turning his face toward me.

"Oh, you are so *fucking* beautiful," I sigh. "I am going to take you now, little Jesus. I am going to fuck you up the ass. Do you understand?" I smile, showing my fangs.

Francesco gives a sharp gasp. Francesco stares. Francesco pants with panic around his mouthful of chain. Drool wells through the links, dribbling onto my hand.

"I'm guessing you've been ass-fucked before? What with those eager clients on the Spanish Steps all salivating for your sweet favors?"

My prisoner continues to stare and pant, speechless. Customary behavior at the first sight of fangs.

"You'll answer me if you know what's good for you. I like my slaves mannerly."

"Uh huh," Francesco grunts, nodding.

"If you obey, you'll survive. If you struggle, you'll die. And if you give me enough pleasure, I might decide to own you, to keep you around. You understand? I need a slave here in Rome, to watch over me and my new home. If I own you, I will care for you. And your worries will be over. You will live long and prosper."

Francesco nods. More warm drool, clear as water, drips onto my hand.

Fetching my glass, I slip down to kneel between my captive's wide-spread thighs. Across the pale curves and fuzzy crevice of his ass, I drip sambuca. I can hear Marcus' chuckle as I spread Francesco's cheeks and begin a deep nuzzling.

IV.

Francesco limps beside me through the old neighborhood of Vecchia Roma, over bumpy cobblestones, past pink and cream stucco walls. His stride's stiff, a little less than graceful. With good reason. Last night, after entering him as gently as Marcus entered me, I rode Francesco long and hard, on and off, for hours, wanting our first time to last. As I pounded him, I drank his delicious blood till he fainted. I sipped sambuca with Marcus till my captive came to. I beat his brown back and white buttocks with my belt, leaving bruises and welts, before climbing upon him, embracing him, entering him, drinking from him again. Francesco pleasured me with his ass, with his street-taught skills, coaxing cum from me time after time. He obeyed me in everything, didn't struggle or shout, was entirely acquiescent, limp with blood loss as dawn approached. We unchained him then, carried him to a secret crypt near the Mythraeum. We bound his hands and feet with rope. We tenderly gagged him with Marcus' silk tie. Marcus stripped, and the three of us lay together. Francesco spent the day between us, paralyzed and entranced, curled against the naked dead.

Tonight he is clearly hurting. But a slave is the last to complain. By now he bears a chain I have locked around his neck. By now he bears the marks of my teeth, on his buttocks, on his shoulders and neck. By now he is entirely my thrall.

This is the address. As Marcus promised, the medieval tower is in fine shape. I unlock the door, tugging Francesco after me by his collar. Together we ascend the winding stairs. At the top is a thick wooden door, and, behind that, the snug apartment. It is furnished beautifully, a mix of both antique and modern furnishings. And its little kitchen table is heaped with steaming food.

"Oh, *Signore!*" Francesco's belly growls. "May I?"

"Wine first, slave." I nod to the sideboard. Beside a bowl of red roses, Marcus has left a bottle of red wine, another of black sambuca, and several glasses. Francesco jumps to it, opening the wine and pouring out a glass. He looks up expectantly.

"Take off your clothes."

Francesco hurriedly shucks off his dirty garments. Again the arch of an expectant black eyebrow.

"Yes," I say, running a finger down the line of hair bisecting his flat belly. "You may eat. From a plate on the floor."

Not a second's hesitation. In a flash my handsome little Jesus has fetched a plate from the cupboard and is holding it out. He's positively salivating, staring first at me, then at the heaped table. I study his nakedness for a moment, his olive skin, his midnight-black pubic bush, his limp, uncut cock. This one will prove precious, I can already tell. And sweet Matt, back home, is going to love him. Matt's going to have the boy's legs in the air so damn fast. I can't wait to show Matt around Rome.

"How long since you last ate?" I sip the wine. It's very fine: cobwebs and blackberries. Of course. Aristocrats like Marcus always have superb taste.

"Three days, *Signore.*" His mouth quivers.

"Poor boy. Let me." With utensils on the sideboard, I dole it out: *bucatini all'Amatriciana*, eggplant Parmigiana, roast pork with potatoes, spaghetti carbonara, Caprese salad, focaccia. I place the full plate on the floor, pull out a chair and take a seat. Francesco drops onto his elbows and knees, crawls over, and begins gobbling. I prop a booted foot upon his back and sip my wine, taking joy in his joy. When he's finished his first plate, I pile him up another. He hunches over it, shaggy black hair falling over his face, slurping and chewing with abandon.

Patting his prettily propped black-fuzzed ass, I leave him there to fill his belly while I indulge in a little exploration. Here are the big bed, the guest room, the study, and the secret panel where Marcus said it would be, behind which I will spend the days. And here, in the entrance hall, is an envelope I'd missed before, one addressed to me. I tear it open and read the note.

> *Enkidu, my handsome one, my wild forest trash, my musky butch bottom. Here is your new home. I hope it meets your needs. The rent is steep: your blood, your body, and your submission, whenever you are in Rome. I do not think you will mind paying such a fee. I hope your little Jesus enjoys his feast. Savor your sambuca. You said it would cause you to think of me. I hope that is so. I am leaving Roma for a week, for business meetings in Berlin. Meet me at the Pantheon two weeks from tonight. There is a vampire bar near there that serves an excellent blood orange gelato. Mithras bless you. Marcus.*

"*Signore?* I am done." It's Francesco, crawling down the hall on his hands and knees. His goatee and red lips gleam with grease. I lift him to his feet, kiss him, lick the oil from his mouth, and lead him into the kitchen. "Fetch me a glass of sambuca," I say, and he does. "Follow me," I say, hooking a finger under his chain collar and leading him out onto the balcony. I sit back in a lounge chair; my thrall sits cross-legged at my feet.

"Tomorrow we will move your mother into better housing. You'd like that?"

"Oh, *Signore*...." Francesco's eyes glitter wetly. He puts his face in his hands, then scoots over, wraps his arms around my legs, and rests his head in my lap. "*Grazie, grazie.*"

I take a sip of sambuca, looking out over the lights of Rome, the far, lit façade of Castel Sant'Angelo, the dome of Sant' Andrea della Valle. I stroke my slave's black hair. "Ain't you something fine? Hungry little savior. Furry little street-whore." I pull him up onto my lap, then push my thumb between his teeth. He licks it, then closes his mouth around it and gently begins to suck. I rock him as Marcus rocked me on the Palatine.

"Tomorrow, while I sleep, you'll take money and stock the shelves with all your favorite foods and wines. Buy yourself some handsome clothes as well. And some *limoncello* for when Marcus visits. He's fond of it, I think."

"*Sì, Signore*," Francesco murmurs around my thumb. His mouth is tight, wet, and hot.

"This is the reward of submission," I say, taking another sip of liqueur. "For both you and me." The moon's glow edges the eastern horizon. It will be full tonight, soon to shower the old quarter with pearl-white light. "When I'm done with this glass, I'm taking you inside. I'm going to knot a rag between your teeth and tie you belly down to that big bed and prop your hairy ass on pillows and fuck you till you bleed and come inside you and lap the blood from your luscious, hair-fringed hole and drink from your neck till you pass out. I'm going to keep you bound and rag-gagged till dawn; I'm going to hold you close all night. How does that sound, slave?"

Francesco nods, sucking harder, with all the intensity of the newborn. He suckles me and I rock him. Soon, just as it did in the time of the Caesars, in the time of the half-mad mercenary Renaissance popes and the fully mad Mussolini, the moon will rise, over the Colosseum, the Palatine, the Forum, over this renovated tower, older even than I. Bathed in summer moonlight, I will think of the few men I've loved. Angus McCormick, my first and thoroughly inescapable passion, who was stabbed to death, murdered by hateful Christians, on the Isle of Mull in 1730, the night I was turned. Sigurd Magnusson, the massive Viking vampire who gave me dark immortality. Mark Carden, my bushy-bearded Rebel soldier, who was shot through the head in the Battle of Chickamauga in 1863. Gerard McGraw, who bled to death in the trenches of Belgium in 1945. Matt Taylor, this century's spouse, who has many blessed years left, who waits for me in the mountains of home.

And now, I think, Marcus Colonna, who flies tonight to Berlin. Other than Sigurd, my maker, I have never loved a Top before. Perhaps Marcus will comfort me in a few decades, when my sweet Matthew dies, when I find myself alone on Mount Storm, my West Virginia retreat, face streaked with tears, sorrow the color of Zinfandel, while snow drifts outside, sculpted by the mountain winds. Perhaps Marcus and I will preside while hillfolk neighbors bring in comfort food: potato salad, fried chicken, deviled eggs, macaroni and cheese, cherry pie, banana pudding. We'll lift glasses of black sambuca to all the brief beauties we have reluctantly and irresistibly loved. Perhaps together we will tend Matt's grave. Stubborn, cussed, and handsome as Matt is, I will probably plant purple thistles atop his ashes.

Well, that will be years yet. There it is now, the full moon, the disk of bruised bone. It rises over the eastern hills, the silhouettes of buildings. Ah, shit. I wipe tears off my unshaven cheeks. Pulling my thumb from my thrall's fervent mouth, I rise, lifting him into my arms. "Time you were crucified," I snarl. Turning my back on all of history, I carry him inside.

About the Author

JEFF MANN grew up in Covington, Virginia, and Hinton, West Virginia, receiving degrees in English and forestry from West Virginia University. His poetry, fiction, and essays have appeared in many publications, including *Arts and Letters*, *Prairie Schooner*, *Shenandoah*, *Willow Springs*, *The Gay and Lesbian Review Worldwide*, *Crab Orchard Review*, and *Appalachian Heritage*. He has published three award-winning poetry chapbooks, *Bliss*, *Mountain Fireflies*, and *Flint Shards from Sussex*; three full-length books of poetry, *Bones Washed with Wine*, *On the Tongue*, and *Ash: Poems from Norse Mythology*; two collections of personal essays, *Edge: Travels of an Appalachian Leather Bear* and *Binding the God: Ursine Essays from the Mountain South*; two novellas, *Devoured*, included in *Masters of Midnight: Erotic Tales of the Vampire*, and *Camp Allegheny*, included in *History's Passion: Stories of Sex Before Stonewall*; two novels, *Fog: A Novel of Desire and Reprisal* and *Purgatory: A Novel of the Civil War*; a book of poetry and memoir, *Loving Mountains, Loving Men*; and a previous volume of short fiction, *A History of Barbed Wire*, which won a Lambda Literary Award. He teaches creative writing at Virginia Tech in Blacksburg, Virginia.

Bear Bones Books

Homomasculine fiction & nonfiction by and for
the adult men's Bear community

Fiction

A History of Barbed Wire, by JEFF MANN
    (Lambda Literary Award Winner)
The Limits of Pleasure, a novel by DANIEL M. JAFFE
Spring of the Stag God, by J.C. HERNESON
Bear Like Me, a novel by JONATHAN COHEN
Fog, a novel by JEFF MANN
The House of Wolves, a novel by ROBERT B. MCDIARMID
Purgatory, a novel by JEFF MANN
Waking Up Bear and Other Stories by JAY NEAL
Desire and Devour: Tales of Blood and Sweat, by JEFF MANN

Bear Lust • *Bearotica* • *Bears in the Wild* • *Tales from the Den*
    Hot & Hairy Fiction Series edited by R. JACKSON

Nonfiction

Edge: Travels of an Appalachian Leather Bear, by JEFF MANN
Bears on Bears: Interviews & Discussions, revised edition,
    by RON J. SURESHA
Binding the God: Ursine Essays from the Mountain South, by Jeff Mann

An imprint of Lethe Press
Discover more at
www.bearbonesbooks.com
& www.lethepressbooks.com.